DEEP STRUCTURE
THE STONEHENGE QUANTUM

A GATSBY DONOVAN *PARADIGMS LOST* MYSTERY

ELLERY STONE

Verbatim
Publishing

Verbatim Publishing
Portland, OR USA

Editors: Paul Wotipka, Charles King (Cox-King Media)
Cover Photo: David Charvet

Ordering Information:
Quantity sales. Special discounts are available on quantity purchases by corporations, associations, and others. Orders by U.S. trade bookstores and wholesalers.

Main category—Fiction
Other category—Action & Adventure
Other category—Mystery, Thriller
Other category—Psychological Suspense

First edition: Published 2004 by Unlimited Publishing LLC
Copyright © 2004 by Lori Stephens
ISBN13: 978-1-5883210-3-9 (pbk.)

Second edition: Published 2018 by Verbatim Publishing
Copyright © 2018 by Lori Stephens
ISBN13: 978-0-9658835-5-9 (pbk.)

Manufactured in the United States of America

ALSO BY ELLERY STONE

ALPHA OMEGA
The Holy Drug
In a London suburb, a cult disciple
gasps, dying in a pool of his own blood.
The only clue is the holy scripture that
he clutches.

Who would kill for the Librah Vaeta? What secrets are hidden within its
pages? Do the leaders of the Omega
cult know of the terrible violence it can
spawn, or was that the intention?

Dr. Gatsby Donovan's abilities to
decipher ancient writings pull her into the vortex of a
treacherous mystery. Revealing Omega's most powerful
secrets will be deadly—the question is not the salvation of
her soul but whether she will survive the night.

VIRAL GLYPH
The Rosette Rebellion
When Dr. Gatsby Donovan meets a
cocky stage magician, Maceo Affiato,
he claims that the most mysterious
artifact of all human history—the
Phaistos Disk—has been stolen, and he
needs her expertise in order to find it.

If the disk on display in the
Heraklion Museum isn't genuine, where
is the real one? And how is it connected
to a terrible massacre? Finding the answers means outwitting
the female-only syndicate called The Circle. Its global
network of agents will do whatever it takes to protect the
disk and conceal its true purpose and power, no matter the
price. Can Gatsby connect the dots—and overcome her
darkest fears—before time runs out?

www.ellerystone.com

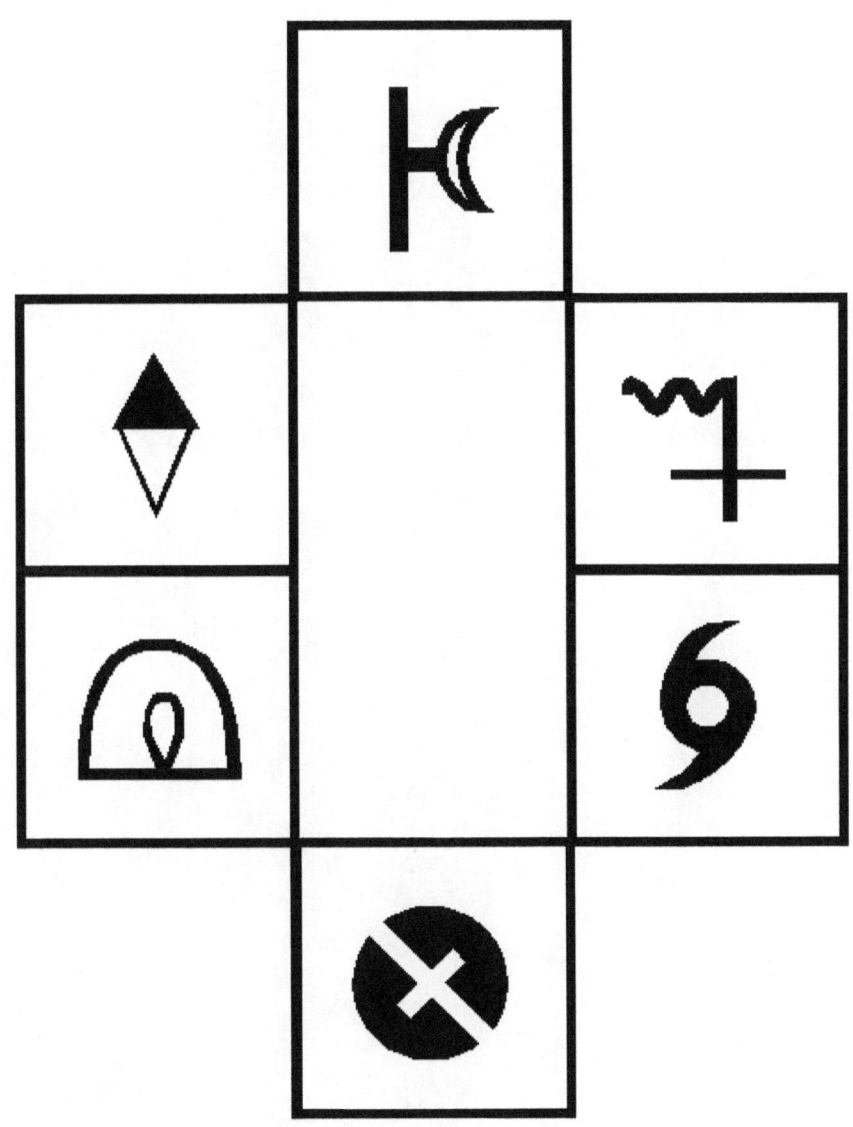

PROLOGUE

The Director tugged off his pith helmet, releasing a river of foul sweat that etched a streak on his dusty neck. He tore off his wire-rimmed glasses with a jerk.

This isn't possible!

The group of archeological conservators—four students under Quinn's directorship—stared in silent agony at the strange symbol on the wall. Their rapid, heavy breathing dampened the already dangerously humid enclosure of Queen Nefertari's tomb. Within the stone chamber that was barely large enough for five people to huddle elbow to elbow, the air temperature was rising from the fluorescent lamps at the doorway of the chamber and the morning sun burning over the Egyptian desert.

The French woman tugged a bandanna from her neck and rubbed it across her glistening forehead. "Dr. Quinn, look at the texture, the edges..." Her voice trembled. "It's not drawn on the existing hieroglyphs...it's incorporated into them as if...the—" She broke off, her eyes blazing, arms crossed tightly over her chest.

The young Chinese artist opened his mouth several times before whispering, "Could someone have broken through the security systems last night and painted it?"

Quinn moved toward the wall. His eyes squinted to slits as he examined the symbol on the wall of reliefs that his students had been painstakingly restoring with limestone dust and laboratory watercolors.

He slowly raised his hand toward the wall, inching it higher until one fingertip touched the glyph as gently as if it possessed the power to destroy the world. The leathery creases in his face deepened as he frowned and shook his head stiffly.

He turned and looked the young man in the eye. In a hoarse voice, he said, "Only if one night can last three thousand years."

CHAPTER 1

I'm so damn close! What's the bloody code breaker?

Gatsby Donovan stared into the humming computer monitor, frowning, entranced by the glyphs on the screen. A diskette containing image files of stone burial vessels, recently excavated and donated to the British Museum, had arrived on her desk two days ago. Clevis's memo noted that it was up to her to decipher the Mayan inscriptions before the artifacts arrived from Guatemala.

What a shame that my vacation starts in two hours, she thought, smirking, in the hush of her small office. Actually, it was unfortunate—she was eager to get the burial ritual legends on the vessels deciphered and had made it through most of them. One contained astronumerical references that she couldn't quite place. Had she seen them in some dusty reference book in the museum library? Were they alphabetic or syllabic?

She closed her eyes, leaning back in her padded chair, and ran her hands through her long, chestnut brown hair. Too many hours at the computer; her retinas were jitterbugging behind the dark canvas of her eyelids.

I need a break...too much epigraphy makes Gatsby a dull...

The computer screen popped to black—instead of Mesoamerican symbols, tiny stars now floated toward her like falling snowflakes, as if she'd just materialized on the bridge of a starship. A nice screensaver.

It was a few minutes past four o'clock—some of the museum staff had already gone home, some remained to work late, and in just two hours, she would savor the act of closing up her office for her ten-week sabbatical. It was a well-earned vacation, and the Mayan vessels would have to wait for her until September.

She flashed on the fact that the museum director, Nelson Clevis, had mentioned that morning he would stop by before she left—if there were benevolent gods, his visit would be short. Gatsby genuinely respected Clevis's commitment to the institution that kept her in linguistic magazines and thrift-store jeans. On the surface, however, he was to all who knew him an anal-retentive and officious prick.

The mental image made Gatsby laugh out loud, eyes still closed.

She'd made a stab at organizing but had only succeeded at rearranging the piles of books, notes, computer disks, catalogs, and files that constituted her office. It wasn't the most aesthetically pleasing office at the museum, but it truly afforded the best view, overlooking a lush courtyard of exotic plants and gurgling Grecian fountains.

A thousand years from now, who's going to care how tidy I kept my office? she thought, relaxing back in her chair and letting her mind wander as it did on the rare day like this when she felt mentally lazy, at long last detached from the intense focus of her work.

Her education at Blake University, Seattle, and then SUNY had given her a thorough background in linguistic systems. She considered herself very lucky that the British Museum's internship program had accepted her and eventually offered her an associate position. And in the last six years, she'd received a fantastic education in translating the writings on ancient manuscripts and artifacts—coming to love the challenges of the job and to endure the stress.

Moving her wheeled chair so that the late spring sunlight drifting through her window bathed over her body, she listened to the quiet. The occasional whoosh of the air conditioning system. Muted footsteps in the hallway. The hum of her computer.

All these words, thoughts. So long ago. Did the people of Palenque ever imagine that thousands of years in the future, someone like me would pour over their scribblings? And be fascinated by what was there? Be driven to know how cultures of the ancient past lived, thought, spoke, perceived?...how much we know of ourselves by studying the writings of those who come before us...the process itself of comparing the words—the symbols of thought—of cultures millennia before your own makes you acutely aware of the mutable nature of perception. What I do here, translating these scribbles and fragments from the past—will any of this prove enlightening to some culture millennia from now? Who knows how future cultures will think and write?...maybe they'll be beyond writing their thoughts. She smiled a little, lost in the daydream. Maybe they'll be beyond thought...

A jolt raced down her spine—a tingling, electric spasm that shot from her neck down her left arm to her hand. The daydream shattered and she bolted, eyes wide at the shock of the sensation. She stared down at her left hand, resting on the cool surface of her desktop.

The finger muscles quivered—her hand jittered on the laminate surface, as if something under it were about to erupt. Her heart moved into high gear and her lungs locked as she watched, terrified and helpless.

As if sentient, her hand jerked to eye level, palm away from her. The thumb dipped forward, then pulled back as the third and fourth fingers tipped down. The action repeated and repeated again, faster and faster, as if her arm were trying to flap invisible wings and fly away.

"Son of a bitch," Gatsby hissed. Her heart thudded in her ears and with each thud, the movements repeated and it wouldn't stop—there was nothing she could do to make it stop...

She swung her right hand and slapped the left down hard on the desktop.

Panting, Gatsby stared down at her hands, the right one smashing the left like the stronger of two wrestlers. A sick feeling cramped her stomach; nothing like this had ever happened to her

except

before...

What the fucking hell! Good god, some kind of stroke? Embolism? Tumor? Epilepsy? Oh christ... Other bad-to-worst-case suggestions tried to rise into her mind; she brutally shoved them out. If there were congenital illnesses in her family, they were unknown to her.

She opened her mouth to suck in a lungful of air, feeling her tongue rake over dry lips. She sat paralyzed in the chair, terrified that if she moved or breathed, it might happen again.

Waiting, watching. Barely breathing. Cautiously observing.

After two minutes—nothing. A long, shuddering sigh helped her lungs to unlock.

Jesus H...

A knock at the door made her jerk and painfully nip the inside of her cheek. Whoever it was, their timing was terrible. She rolled her neck to pop out the kinks and pressed her hands against her Levi's, trying to quickly think of an excuse scenario. A sudden phone call? An emergency sprint for the bathroom? Her body was still trembling; the cold stone in her stomach seemed to grind against her ribs.

The door opened. Nelson Clevis, short, bald, with tiny glasses and creases that screamed, appeared in his usual humor: constrained. A grey suit and burgundy tie had been his uniform since the day Gatsby had interviewed with him six years ago. He took one step into Gatsby's office and stood rooted like a Paleolithic fossil embedded in the earth's crust. She never knew exactly how it happened, but his grand efforts at reserve usually made Gatsby feel positively impish around him.

At the moment, all she wanted was to get rid of him.

"Nelson," Gatsby said, knowing full well how he hated the informality of first names. She wondered when her shoulder muscles would loosen their death-grip on her spine.

Clevis merely raised his thin grey eyebrows and parted a set of lips as starched as his shirt. "Ms. Donovan. I dropped by to bid you well for your sabbatical. You generally holiday in the warmer climes, do you not? South of France this year? Italy?" His tiny eyes, behind the lenses, reflected only the smallest glint of warmth.

"Anywhere but London, I know that. Perhaps Tenerife. Whatever I end up doing, I know I'm going to be fretting over these vessels." She managed, somehow, to keep her voice level.

Clevis blinked, one of his more subtle signals of understanding. "Yes, the Maya. One can only imagine what they did for their holidays." His hands stole into the depths of his pants pockets and Gatsby recognized Clevis's gruel-bland form of humor.

Before she could reply, her hand trembled. An involuntary gasp broke from her; she swept both arms up over her head, feigning a lazy stretch, and then clasped her hands behind her neck. "Hard to say," she murmured, trying desperately to sound casual while adrenaline raced through her bloodstream.

Clevis's reputation for wordiness was askew that day. He stared briefly and then said, monotone, "Well. Enjoy the time off. We shall see you in the fall."

"You will. Thanks for dropping by, Nelson."

An almost imperceptible stiffness drew the man up to his full height of five foot seven and a half inches. He nodded curtly and left the door ajar as he walked out.

Gatsby exhaled loud and long and pressed her hands to her cheeks, noting how hot they felt. What if Clevis had noticed? What if he had gotten the notion that she had contracted some appalling handicap and was unfit to work anymore?

Moving her hands out in front of her, as if resting them on an imaginary keyboard, she stared hard at them. Just two hands, firmly attached and seemingly once again in synch with the rest of her fit, thirty-five-year-old body. Two simple, unadorned hands; short, smooth nails, a small birthstone ring on the middle finger of the right.

She breathed in deeply, thinking, *Okay, best-case scenario is simple stress. Overwork. Nothing that some warm salt water and a few friendly White Russians won't fix in a hurry. But I'm calling Dr. Berger in the morning, just in c...* The thought dissipated, dissolving into the darker alleys of her subconscious. She sniffed, rose, and gathered up the books and files that would necessarily accompany her for the summer.

A beep signaled a transmission on her fax machine. Gatsby glanced toward the machine, stared warily as a piece of paper began chugging out of it, almost convinced herself that she hadn't seen it, and reluctantly walked to the filing cabinet on which it sat. The transmission completed and a single sheet of paper dropped.

Gatsby picked it up with a sigh and read: *Ms. Donovan, imperative that we speak immediately. An unknown glyph discovered in Egyptian tomb. Your urgent attention requested.*

The sender's identifying line at the top was blurred. At the bottom, there was a name and an address: University of Cambridge. Martin Traussbery? Where had she heard that name before?

"Martin, you're just one minute too late," she said, and stuffed the fax into the side pocket of her leather briefcase. She took one last look around at her office—not to memorize it, god knew she spent enough time there to know every inch of it intimately, but with a kind of reverence. The work that went on inside her four walls gave her a great feeling of immensity. Timelessness. Synthesis with all human endeavor.

The conquests, the glories, the discoveries—and the tragedies.

Standing beside her desk, she raised her hands, holding them at eye level. The sunlight and flora of the courtyard outside her window seemed to create a square picture frame around her outspread hands. A Still Life in Manualism, so to speak. Turning them over, then over again, she frowned and leaned to reach for her briefcase.

She flipped her PC's switch to OFF, slung her overcoat over one arm, walked to the door, and turned out the overhead light. The monitor of her computer glowed eerily, like the eye of the monster that rose from her work—the CyberBeast of Information. She stepped out into the hallway, ready to venture into a new world.

CHAPTER 2

Who the hell is calling at this hour?

Gatsby fumed as she watched steam phantoms rise from the scented water that filled her tub and rippled luxuriously around her kneecaps. The phone trilled, grating on her eardrums. *Clevis? God, we just spoke earlier!* He wouldn't call me at home unless the Tibetan mummies were dancing the bloody hula...

She groaned, swearing vehemently as she splashed out of the tub, grabbed a towel, and dashed naked to the living room, dripping lavender-scented bubbles down the hallway behind her.

Nestled on the table beside her couch, the touch-tone phone shrilled again. She snatched it up with soapy fingers. "Hello!?"

"Ms. Donovan?"

She didn't recognize the scratchy male voice. *Who the buggering?* "Yes, what? This had better be good."

There was a pause and a light cough. "Martin Traussbery, University of Cambridge, Department of Archaeology. Sorry to ring so late, but I've been trying to reach you for days. Did you receive the fax that I sent this afternoon?" The rasp of the voice suggested an elderly gentleman who ought to be in the care of a good respiratory doctor and wasn't.

Balls! What now! Gatsby thought, not surprised that she couldn't recall the message of the fax she had stuffed into her briefcase. She hadn't wanted to see it in the first place. *Traussbery...wait, was he the character who had been tossed out of a World Heritage Foundation conference for causing some kind of riot?* She tried to resurrect a hazy memory of the *News of the World* headlines from about ten years back while rubbing soap out of her eyes.

"Professor, I did get the fax but I'm in, or was in, the tub. Can't this wait until morning?"

"My apologies, but I'm afraid it can't. It is imperative that I—"

Fatigue snipped her last threads of patience. "And just how did you get my home number?"

"I spoke with Mr. Clevis at the British Museum and asked him to steer me toward an expert in decipherment of ancient text. An epigrapher. He offered your name and said that you were his top recommendation."

"Well, that's—" She stretched on tiptoe across her dining room table to reach for the curtain draw, but the phone cord pulled to its limit and kept her in full glorious view of the pedestrians on King's Road. She made a mental note of Traussbery's praise. "That's very flattering, Professor, but if you could get to the—"

"I have uncovered something that you will find extremely exciting, and I need your help."

"With what?" she muttered, warily and sick-tired.

"I have information about an undeciphered glyph in Thebes."

"And what makes a bloody glyph so astounding that you have to ring me at home at this hour? And on my sabbatical?" she shouted. Her goosebumps were trying to scramble back into the bathtub.

"Ms. Donovan, this will sound quite unbelievable, but I assure you that I am no hoaxer and far from lunatic. The symbol appears within a section of hieroglyphs that a group headed by a colleague of mine, Richard Quinn, is now restoring. The Pyramid of Nefertari in the Valley of the Queens—he's been there for several months with a group of restoration experts. One of the artists was working on a section of wall relief, re-adhering plaster and repainting the artwork and hieroglyphs. All quite routine. But as she approached the workspace she had been at only hours before, she was confronted with an unknown glyph, staring at her from the middle of the relief. It simply hadn't been there the day before."

Gatsby snorted, laughing. "What?!"

"You can imagine the reactions of Quinn and the rest of the team, especially when they had an ink sample taken from it and analyzed at Cairo University."

Gatsby lugged the phone with her as she dropped onto her couch and mopped soap off her neck with the towel. "And?"

A cough rattled over the line. "The chemical composition of the ink was consistent with that used by the ancient Egyptians. In other words, as ancient as the tomb itself."

Gatsby pulled a wool throw over her and switched the phone to her other ear. She was aching to sleep for about three days, and furious at being rung late at night by a complete stranger, yet the wild story had stirred her curiosity. "I don't understand," she sighed.

"Naturally. But I think you will, if you meet with me tomorrow at one o'clock. I'll show you the notes and photos I have received from Quinn and you'll see for yourself. Ms. Donovan, I promised Quinn that I would do whatever I could to translate this glyph, and I need your expertise to figure out how it got there and what it means."

Gatsby felt synapse-size weights seesawing in her brain. Since the strange episode in her office, the rest of the day had been free of surprise attacks from deranged body parts. A warm beach and regular massages were calling her name, seductively stretching their long, white arms toward her.

When academics say "two minutes of your time," it means two months or until they drive you insane, whichever comes first, she thought, *but even if I spend this sabbatical crocheting doilies, I'm not getting tangled up with some weird Cambridge professor and a phantom glyph! But if it's something worthwhile, something truly unique? Aww god...*

She heard the irresistible clarion call that always sounded when she was presented with a linguistic puzzle, a mysterious code to decipher. Momentarily, she sighed in resignation.

"Oh all right, I'll look at the information. One o'clock?"

Traussbery gave confirmation and instructions to his office at Cambridge. "Excellent. I look forward to seeing you tomorrow. Goodnight, Ms. Donovan."

She replaced the phone and stared out her living room window at the black sky shimmering with stars. The Pleiades shone brilliantly, as if laughing at the idea of a glyph appearing in an Egyptian queen's burial chamber or anywhere else for that matter. Gatsby would have laughed herself if it weren't so elementally ridiculous. She briefly thought of calling Clevis but brushed away the thought. He'd think she'd gone completely mad.

This is no way to start a vacation, she thought. *God. Unbelievable how this work can suck me into it...codependent on cuneiform...Sheesh, next thing you know, I'll be standing in front of the group at Archaeologists Anonymous. Well, I'll talk to this Traussbery, get a clean bill of health from Berger, and then I'm on a plane, baby.*

There was nothing to do but to mull over or forget the day's craziness, and a steaming tub was the place for both.

After an hour of soaking and almost irreparable wrinkling, Gatsby crawled into her bed with the latest issue of Verbatim and a strong cup of peppermint tea. When her eyelids began to droop, she pulled the blankets up to her chin, drifting into dreams.

In her sleep, her left hand twitched.

CHAPTER 3

With a hot shower and her usual breakfast in her—pain au chocolate and espresso strong enough to wake Tibetan mummies—Gatsby was behind the wheel of her battered forest-green Volvo and speeding down the A56 motorway.

She hummed as the English countryside rolled by her, her straight brown hair whipping out the open window and lightly over her face, her hands curled easily around the wheel or tapping to her favorite rock and roll: Beatles, Stones, Joplin, Blues Brothers. The eighty-five-minute drive seemed to take half that and, while belting out "I Am the Walrus," she amused herself by constructing a mental picture of Traussbery.

He eyed Gatsby with a crooked smile, two hairy moles, and newt-like eyes. His plump body jiggled as he approached her at the door of his office and offered her his hand.

"Ms. Donovan! A pleasure to meet you, please come in." It was the same scratchy voice she'd heard over her line the night before.

*So that's what you get when the Hunchback of Notre Dame plays pillow polo with the Queen Mother...yyhhk...*Gatsby thought, snorting under her breath.

With some disdain, she shook the hand, finding it both immaculate and spongy, quickly stuffed her hands in the pockets of her Levi's, and stepped inside Traussbery's office.

The aroma of whiskey pipe tobacco permeated the room. Gazing around and still bleary from the drive, Gatsby saw that every inch of wall space was given to bookshelves. Tucked into the crevasses of his exhaustive library were pieces of ancient artwork and culture—Gatsby recognized artifacts from Nepal, Kenya, Ecuador, China, Greenland, and Bali.

In the corner behind her, two overstuffed armchairs were fitted with extra-frilly chintz pillows and two longhaired

Shih Tzus. Their snoring sounded like miniature drilling machines.

Traussbery ambled to his chair behind an oak desk that filled the space before the room's ceiling-high windows. He motioned, smiling. "Have a seat, my dear."

She dropped into an armchair opposite Traussbery, bemused by the rattling squeak-toys. Companionship or security?

Traussbery reached toward the corner of his desk where a porcelain tray held a weathered pipe. He settled comfortably into his leather-padded executive chair as he lit the pipe and gazed at her with a placid expression. Scrutinizing his wrinkled white shirt, loose cardigan and grey slacks, Gatsby wondered if he was one of those reclusives who lived with their mothers for life. She saw big ears and bad skin and considered whether the gleam behind his thick, black-rimmed glasses spoke of genius or madness.

"Thank you," she murmured.

Traussbery coughed, a bronchial rattle that made Gatsby wince. He pulled a white handkerchief from his pocket, wiped his lips, and said, "Yes, so glad you came. I have heard nothing but kudos for your, ahm, your efforts at the museum. I was particularly impressed by the recent articles on ritual engravings of the Anasazi. Your work?"

She nodded. His reptilian stare was making her fidget.

"Tell me, Ms. Donovan, at your young age, how did you become so expert in ancient languages?"

Gatsby surveyed the room as she settled deep in the armchair and let her shoulderbag slide to the hardwood floor. "I'm not that young...thirty-six in a month. I studied philosophy and linguistics at Blake, Seattle, and did my graduate work in linguistic anthropology at SUNY. I lucked into an internship with the American Archeological Society for a year. That was when I realized that it wasn't just archaeology or anthropology or linguistics that intrigued me, it was the combination of all of them." She cocked her head. "I became fascinated with how a civilization is represented in its language systems. The importance of ancient inscriptions, some so important that they take precedence over basic survival—that meaning, that need to make contact and establish understanding—was what compelled me into this field. I wanted to know everything." She leaned back. "I applied for an internship with the British Museum, six years ago, and ended up as an epigrapher."

She glanced out Traussbery's window at a group of students scrimmaging on a nearby soccer field. Football, she thought, reminding herself of how American/British translations could be more troublesome than ancient cuneiform.

Traussbery coughed lightly and daubed his lips again. "I see. Well, your expertise is becoming quite renowned, and Clevis has only the highest praise for you."

She shrugged but inwardly warmed at the acknowledgment.

"At any rate, to the matter of the mysterious glyph. I received these a week ago via e-mail from Quinn. They are almost as clear as photographs and much easier to send." Traussbery picked up a handful of high-resolution color prints and spread them across his desk before Gatsby.

In the close-up images of the inner walls of the ancient queen's tomb, the conservators' work was evident— partially replastered sections, fans, lights and dehumidifiers, pencil lines drawn where images were to be repainted with watercolors. There, within a section of beautifully restored hieroglyphs, was a dark shape: an inverted cross, and extending to the left from the top of the vertical bar was a curved line, waving like a flag.

She stared while Traussbery commented.

"Obviously not Egyptian, but I needn't tell you that. More South American in style, would you say?"

Gatsby shook her head. "The Phoenician system contains some kind of symbol with a waving line like this but it isn't crossed. I haven't seen anything quite like this."

As she focused on the image and studied it, she became absorbed it in, blissfully unaware of movement, like the shifting of atoms, stirring in her subconscious. Unaware of a dark cast moving in the recesses of her mind, of a surge deep in an abyss into which she had not dared to look for decades.

A quiver shook her left hand.

Although she was too lost in concentration to notice, it did pull her focus sharply back to the present, like biting on tinfoil.

Drawing a breath, she looked up into Traussbery's expectant gaze. "All I can say is that I'll do some research and see if I can come up with some educated guesses. I honestly haven't seen anything like it." *Just tattoo "sucker" on my forehead, okay? she* thought, frowning furiously. "And to tell you the truth, Professor, its supposed *appearance* is a bit much." She gestured toward the prints. "I mean, who's to say that this isn't just a prank? That one of the conservators thought it would make a bloody fantastic joke?" She pinned him with a stare. "And I'm curious as to why you're so adamant about it. You said that Quinn is an old friend, correct? Why is it so urgent that you find out its meaning?"

Traussbery coughed and looked into his lap. He spoke with obvious caution. "Since you ask. Ahm, I...I feel that I should tell you something that I have told no one else, as assuredly no one would believe me. You won't either." His gaze met hers tentatively. "You see, many years ago, I saw a glyph that appeared in a similar manner."

Oh, now what? Gatsby thought in exasperation. She pulled in a deep breath and waited for him to continue, which he did.

"The Temple of Mazilaq." Traussbery puffed on the pipe and looked across the room toward a stone figurine of the Egyptian goddess Isis. "The ruined temple near Cuzco, Peru. Inside the Throne Room known as the Coricancha, there are Incan paintings on the walls, as brilliant today as they were eight hundred years ago. The site is remote and quite difficult to get to; only a handful of researchers have braved the two-day journey on horseback, three thousand meters up in the Cordillera Blanca. Most of them have found Mazilaq scenic but unremarkable as an archaeological site. But on those ruined walls, on my visit eleven years ago, I saw a symbol similar to the one we examine now."

Peru. Images of the Amazon rainforest, anacondas, and thumb-size mosquitoes slithered their way into Gatsby's imagination.

The dogs sniffled on their pillows; Traussbery continued. "The glyph there is also inexplicable and, to date, undecipherable. Do you know why?"

Propping the heel of one leather boot atop the opposite knee, Gatsby gazed at him dubiously. "I imagine you are about to tell me."

"Quite. You see, I could procure no photographs or drawings of the glyph, no records of any kind."

"Prohibited by the government?" She shrugged, well aware that governmental protection of ancient sites against tampering was always strict—in some countries, tight enough to prevent legitimate scientific studies.

Traussbery's eyes narrowed to slits behind the thick spectacles. "I wish it were that simple." He leaned forward. "It only *appeared* for a few moments."

Gatsby stifled the impulse to sputter. "What do you mean, *appeared*?"

Traussbery's eyes gleamed. "When I climbed the steps into the Throne Room, the enclosure was flooded with sunlight. It was fantastically hot and, as I walked toward the wall behind the Great Monarch's Throne, where the most colorful paintings are located, I noticed something on the wall. A spot that shimmered, wavering, like heat rising from dunes. I imagined it to be some kind of sunspot. But when I approached, close enough to touch it, I saw that the stone itself seemed to be glowing. I was perspiring madly from the heat and, at that moment, my glasses slipped off and tumbled to the ground! I groped, found them, and looked back at the wall. There, before my eyes, was a glyph, like none I had seen before. Seconds earlier, it had not been there. I reached for my camera and took six photographs in a row, and in each shot? The walls, the carvings, the colored paintings, even the lichen on the stones all appeared, but *no glyph*. I called to my companions; they came running, thinking I was being attacked by an animal or some such thing. You can imagine my shock when they arrived at the Throne Room and there was nothing to see but stones and lichen."

Traussbery stared unwaveringly until Gatsby felt compelled to look down at the Persian rug. She shrugged. "Well. That is a wild story, Professor, but as a scientist I am sure you asked yourself what, reasonably, made the glyph appear? Was it perhaps projected? Or did the natives figure out a way to play a trick on the obnoxious gringos who were foraging around in their sacred ruins?" Gatsby sighed. "Are you going to tell me you hadn't considered that possibility?"

Traussbery waved his hand placatingly. "Yes yes, who wouldn't? But I tell you, Ms. Donovan, I was alone. There was no one else within half a kilometer, native or otherwise. No machines, equipment, projectors, nothing. And since then, I have neither seen nor heard mention of this glyph in any published research, even through hearsay." He leaned over his Buddhaesque belly toward her, fixing her with a bug-eyed stare.

Gatsby laughed abruptly. "You do realize, don't you, Professor Traussbery, how far this is veering off the beaten track of science and into the land of woo-woo?"

He burst into deep laughter as well and held his belly as it shook.

Gatsby continued, "I mean, good god, you're into realms of vampires casting no reflection in mirrors and so on. Do you expect me to believe that a glyph simply eluded being captured on film?"

"That's not all, Ms. Donovan. I tried to draw it. I tried to do rubbings. I used every medium imaginable at the site— ink, chalk, even tracings in the sand. And the instant that the image was drawn, it vanished in front of my eyes, as if rubbed out with some unseen eraser. Unbelievable, entirely! It was, Ms. Donovan, inexplicable—an inexplicable physical phenomenon."

He refilled his pipe and inhaled the aromatic smoke deeply. "Any reasonable person—any scientist worth his salt—would of course be skeptical."

"No argument there," Gatsby said, leaning back in the chair, tapping on the armrest.

He took a long draw on the pipe and absentmindedly flicked at the potted fern beside the desk. "Ms. Donovan, I assume that you will be taking a summer sabbatical?"

"I'm supposed to be on sabbatical right now," she muttered.

Traussbery spoke in an intense hiss, waving his pipe as if conjuring with it. "These symbols must be investigated, Ms. Donovan—they *must*. They present an extraordinary scientific challenge, perhaps even a quantum challenge. You are a fellow traveler in the inquest of symbolism and antiquity—you must understand!" A fervent look wrestled across his pocked face and he wriggled his glasses up on his nose by squinting. "I want to take you on as my assistant and send you to Mazilaq so that you can see this glyph for yourself."

"What!? Are you out of your mind?"

"Perhaps, but imagine the puzzle to be unraveled! I'll incorporate a fellowship for you as my research assistant. It won't be difficult. Yes, go to Mazilaq and learn as much as possible about the glyph there, and see how or if it compares to Quinn's glyph in Thebes."

She drew in a deep breath, coughing lightly from the pipe smoke that was filling the room, and glanced around in case she needed to make a fast exit.

What kind of lunatic enterprise was this becoming?

Gatsby's eyebrows knitted again. "If this work is so important, why don't you do it yourself? Why do you need me? And what makes you think I'm going to just jump on a plane and fly off to bloody Brazil?"

"Peru," Traussbery corrected. A plume of smoke rose around him like a weary dragon; it crept, swirling, toward the upper panes of the windows, highlighted by soft shafts of sunlight. "My dear, if I were a younger man, I would proceed on my own. But age and infirmity are upon me. I am not up to the strains of distant travel anymore, and I have a full curriculum here at the university. There are increasingly more and more efforts I must—" He coughed, and the wrinkles on his face made him look like a forlorn hound. "I must delegate. As well, I am no epigrapher. A competent archeologist, yes, but nowhere near your level of expertise in decipherment."

Gatsby ruminated while the muted shouts of the football players rose from the cropped, quintessentially British lawns outside the window.

Flying off to Peru, for godssake? To search out a glyph that only Traussbery has seen? Once? That appeared out of nowhere? That can't be photographed? That probably has nothing to do with some glyph in Egypt? That he says he can't go back to study?

Nestled in the gods of her mind's theater, there was that weird, inexplicable business with her hand, out of control the day before in her office. Although it hadn't recurred since the single incident, the fact of it still posed dark questions. She'd been diagnosed in perfect health by Dr. Berger just two months before; how could some sort of horrible affliction come upon her that fast? And just how much sense did it make to skip off on a trip into the Andes that would push her physical limits?

Rather than share her darker thoughts with Traussbery, she switched to a question about the Peruvian glyph.

"If I go to check out this mysterious glyph, what guarantee is there that it will appear?"

"Ha! Oh, Ms. Donovan, you surprise me. There's no guarantee. I saw the thing once, eleven years ago, three thousand meters up an Andean cliff where I could have been suffering from oxygen deprivation. But I wasn't. I know my own senses, and I am—then as now—as lucid as you. Its appearance is as mysterious as the appearance of the glyph that you have seen yourself today. Do you doubt that it is there, on the wall of Nefertari's chamber, in plain view of Quinn and his restoration team? No, you do not, I can see by your expression. So go to Peru! Find out the glyph and what it means!"

Buggering jesus, Gatsby groaned inwardly. That clarion was back, calling her to hunt, to solve the mystery of symbols, to decipher the riddle of language, just as the ancients struggled to understand the riddles of the Sibyl. It came upon her all at once, undeniable—with all the forces of the cosmos, she couldn't have stopped it. Even if her hand flipped around until it popped off and was eaten by anacondas, she couldn't have rejected the challenge. Even if she had wanted to. And most of her wanted to.

She dropped forward, her forehead pressed to her hands, groaning. "Oh god. I can't believe I'm saying this. All right. Give me the details and I'll make some arrangements. All expenses paid?"

"Naturally."

"Let me see if I've got this right. I go to check out this hide-and-seek hieroglyph at Moz...Mazilaq...and determine if there is any correlation with the glyph Quinn has found in Egypt?"

"Correct."

She sat up straight. "And if there is a correlation, Professor Traussbery, who will we share this knowledge with, the World Heritage Foundation?" There was no hiding the smirk in her tone. "And would they come to any conclusion other than the obvious—that two otherwise respectable scientists have spontaneously lost their marbles?"

Traussbery laughed so hard that his spectacles flew off into the papers on the desk. "Ms. Donovan, I suspect that the WHF already believes that of me. Your reputation and dignity are, of course, in your own hands."

Gatsby couldn't help but smile as she gathered her leather bag from the floor and slung it over her shoulder. "Well, my dignity has been injured before but never fatally." She stood and held out her hand to shake Traussbery's, and this time the experience wasn't quite so distasteful. Beneath his magnificently abominable exterior, she imagined that she might be able to think of him as pleasant, if quite eccentric. She pumped his arm.

Traussbery showed her to the door, accompanied by his sputtering dogs. They appeared to be as failing as he was, from the way they toddled next to his faded shoes. Gatsby decided that no matter how friendly she felt about Traussbery, he'd better keep his dust mops away from her.

"Good day, my dear. I'll be in touch."

With a trail of smoke following her like a fragrant shadow, Gatsby made her way down the empty corridor. The Gothic building, made of the same eternal materials as the lessons that took place within it, was silent as a corpse. She tried to walk as quietly as possible but kept tripping over visualizations of Incan ruins, water snakes, Egyptian mummies, and skewered Shih Tzus.

CHAPTER 4

She slammed the book shut. Eiffert's *Tombs of the Ancients* had nothing that even remotely resembled the glyph in Thebes.

She shook her head, nestled the book back into its place on the top shelf of her bookcase, and leaned back in her chair—the skittering squeak of its hinges giving voice to how her neck tendons felt. She sipped from her coffee mug, breathing in the rich aroma and gazing around at the massive collection of texts on language, anthropology, archeology, literature, and philosophy that made their home with her. A gooseneck lamp lit the stacks of books piled on her only treasured possession, an antique mahogany desk. It had been a gift from her parents, just after her graduation from Blake, the entire thing wrapped in bright ribbon, with a note: *"We're so proud of you! May this give you a good place to make your goals a reality. All our love, Mom & Dad."*

Outside in the night, a horn tooted and cars rushed down King's Road, five thousand miles away from where those parents lived in Seattle a few miles from her sister, Penelope.

Gatsby sat the mug on her desk with a sigh, fixated on the image of Traussbery's hairy moles and the lunatic bulging of his eyes as he had described his adventure in Peru. An eccentric kook and his mutts. And a vacation, once scheduled for flagrant hedonism, now to be potentially spent trekking across continents to learn the etymology of a glyph whose very existence defied rational explanation.

"Good gods," she muttered—and pulled down another book. *The Great Pyramid: Observatory, Tomb and Temple* by Richard Proctor opened itself to page ninety. She let her eyes roam over the color images of the chamber walls of the Pyramid of Cheops and the descriptions of ancient Egyptian culture.

She saw pages of garden-variety hieroglyphs, ones that first-year linguistics students learned to translate. But Gatsby found nothing that resembled the glyph she had seen the day before in Traussbery's smoke-filled office.

She thought of the engravings on the monoliths at Stonehenge—a two-hour's drive from where she sat sipping lukewarm French espresso. There were cross-like markings on some of the stones there, which were thought to mark alignment with the sun at solstices and equinoxes. There were also engravings that resembled daggers. Etched communiqués from ancient worlds that no living person could interpret.

Yet.

If there were only a way to *know.*

Gatsby reflected, once again, on how she would spend her life attempting to decipher history's hidden messages and secrets, and that, at best, it would amount to a lifetime of guesswork.

She went back to studying. Brennan's text on archeological sites in Ireland showed the massive stones at Knowth, a prehistoric passage grave. They were covered with circles and spirals that were speculated to represent phases of the moon.

She tipped her head back, ran her hands through her hair, sipped more coffee, and plowed through the books, one after the other. The digital clock on her well-used microwave silently conducted her, minute by solitary minute, into the future.

Texts on Mesoamerican ruins. Mayan calendar stones with fantastically elaborate mythological symbols. Aztec sculptures showing the emblems of the Four Cosmic Ages.

The Neolithic shrine at Çatal Hüyük in Turkey, covered with honeycomb patterns that probably referred to the swarming of bees at the vernal equinox.

The Egyptian glyph for *horizon*: a sun disk cradled by the rounded peaks of two mountains.

Spiral petroglyphs on the rock slabs at Fajada Butte, New Mexico, where Anasazi Indians inhabited the canyon over a thousand years ago.

When her vision blurred the paragraphs into bizarre spider webs, and the effects of the espresso had long since posted a "closed for the season" sign, Gatsby switched off the lamp and wandered to the living room to sprawl out on her couch.

All these people, cultures, she thought, sighing as the cushions sank under the weight of her body. *Literally making their mark on the planet, to show that they were here for a while, to say something—something meaningful. What in hell is going to come out of this mysterious inverted cross with a horizontal wave on the wall of a tomb? Or some allegedly appearing glyph in an Incan ruin?*

She sighed, looking over at the coffee table and the pile of books recently checked out from the library. *The Real Guide to Peru. Adventuring in the Andes. Exploring Cuzco. Lost City of the Incas.* Impulsively, she picked up the top one.

Browsing the guidebooks earlier that day, she'd realized that a jaunt to Peru would be more risky than she'd initially imagined. Her passport was current but her immunizations were not—there were hepatitis, malaria, dysentery and rabies to worry about. She would have to arrange for a reputable guide to get her from Cuzco to Mazilaq, and camping out in the Andes, three thousand meters above sea level, offered such pleasantries as altitude sickness, hypothermia, and giardia.

She thought back to digs she'd been on in the Caribbean and southern Africa, where some of the hazards were similar to those of Peru. She'd always been able to stay with a local family or at a decent hostel. Mazilaq promised hot days on a sweaty horse and cold nights on a rock mattress.

Soon, the guidebook dropped as she lay back in the cushions, feet propped up, eyelids heavy enough to sink a continent.

The digital clock on the microwave blinked 3:14 when she woke, rubbing her eyes.

She glanced up at her framed print of Einstein, hanging on the living room wall. The quote next to the image of the white-haired man with gentle eyes read, *Great spirits have always encountered violent opposition from mediocre minds.*

"What's your opinion on this weird shit, Al? Wait, make that mierda loco," Gatsby said aloud in the quiet of the flat she shared with no one but a cranky espresso machine, and went to brush her teeth, wondering what brand of mental dentifrice would scrub away the thickening plaque of weirdness.

CHAPTER 5

The terminal was full of white-robed Arabs. *What would they do in Peru?* Gatsby wondered. Their robes and beards swished around her as they chattered in a dialect she didn't recognize.

Heathrow Airport, Gate 36, AeroPeru. Gatsby flopped down on top of her suitcase with a sigh and dug a Cadbury chocolate bar out of her pack, feeling the dread of a twelve-hour flight huddle up next to her and try to bum a bite.

When she was finally called to board, she wound her way down the ramp and found her seat. She stowed her suitcase overhead, dropped into seat 11A, and closed her eyes.

How on earth have I gotten here? One week ago, I was lounging in the Chelsea Club sauna with Celia Devereaux, discussing where to buy condoms in Tenerife. Then a phone call in the middle of the night, and why go to a five-star resort when you can see the Peruvian Andes for godssake, contract dysentery or malaria, and end up sharing your sleeping bag with a scorpion and all his closest friends? Just to track down some ghost glyph? Nuts! The only thing more amazing is the fact that I bloody agreed to do it...

She opened a bag of peanuts and munched absentmindedly; she'd spoken with Traussbery before leaving, getting instructions for finding her guide, the layout of the site, and where to look for the glyph. The immunizations hadn't been as horrible as her new passport photo; the young man who had posed her against the wall of the photo shop must have wondered if the agitated look on her face spoke of rectal itch.

Images of London flitted through her mind. The colorful tin canisters that her parents sent her last Christmas, filled with cooking utensils that had never seen the light of day. The look on Clevis's face when she'd caught him in his office leafing through a magazine called Unzipped! The last luncheon engagement she'd had with Celia, discussing Ms. Devereaux's field of expertise: tantra for fun and pleasure. Out of the blue, she thought of sucking on hard candies—

cinnamon and peppermint—as a child, bought from the corner mom-and-pop grocery. Gatsby smiled and then felt the corners of her mouth slip. Something was coaxing up peak experiences from her past, and she didn't know why, or how to make it stop.

Twelve hours, two fantastically inane movies, and seven ginger ales later, she disembarked.

May in Lima was not only something she had never imagined she would experience—at the moment, she wondered if she would simply survive it. Hovering at about eighty-five stagnant degrees and one million percent humidity, the air teemed with whizzing bugs, screeching birds, and levels of air and noise pollution that she would have expected in a much larger city. In the distance, over the skyline that combined modern and colonial structures, she saw her destination: snow-capped mountains.

She looked around for the man who was supposed to meet her, a friend of Traussbery's named Eric Hardy. Traussbery had described him as middle-aged, husky, blonde, and boisterous, and had also said that he had been in Peru for several years, studying Quechuan and Aymaran cultures.

A stout man in a Fedora was ambling toward her, shouting her name. Gatsby started toward him.

"Ms. Donovan?"

"Yes. You're Hardy?"

He tipped his hat and spoke with a bright semi-Cockney accent. "Pleasure to meet you. Traussbery spoke 'ighly of you. Won't you please come with me?"

Gatsby shook his hand and followed at a brisk pace as Hardy herded her through the terminal and out into the blazing sunshine and the bleeps of tinny horns. They found his rusted Jeep, climbed in, and made their way out of the cement parking structure.

"I understand y'want to see the Temple of the Sun at Mazilaq," Hardy shouted over the intense, teeth-shaking clatter of the Jeep and the whistle of the wind. He sped out onto a two-lane highway lined with swaying palm trees.

"That's right...what else did Traussbery tell you?"

Hardy looked her over with an affable leer. "That you were pretty and available! Ha!"

She rolled her eyes. Hardy swerved abruptly to pass a van full of camera-wielding tourists.

"How long until w—ooof!—until we get to Cuzco?" Gatsby yelled, as she was thrown against the wall of the cab.

Hardy swung hard again as he careened into the right lane. "Put your feet up!" he shouted back. "It's six 'undred kilometers, even if we take the central highway through Huancayo. We'll have to go through a dangerous stretch, but it's faster than going south through Pisco, and you'd do well to get settled in before dark."

"What do you mean, dangerous?"

Hardy's smile disappeared. "Sendero Luminoso."

Gatsby thought back to the police and security guards she had noticed at the airport in Lima, the tightness around their dark eyes.

"What else can you tell me about Cuzco?"

"Dates back to the twelfth century. The metropolis of the ancient Incan civilization. Thirty-three 'undred meters above sea level, so it will take you a day or two to adjust to the altitude. About two 'undred thousand people. Plenty of shops, open air markets, cafes, churches, taverns, museums. Lots of self-described tour guides and pickpockets of course, especially kids. Stick to bottled water, cooked food, peeled fruit. Don't 'ang in the streets after dark—cocaine dealers. You'll probably be coming back to the city smack in the middle of the Inti Raymi festival. It's a great party, but watch yourself."

Gatsby nodded, dust gritting between her teeth, taking it all in and already feeling twinges of what was either hunger or nausea. His driving would give a Zen master an ulcer. Hardy continued shouting.

"I'll take you to the central plaza, Plaza de Armas. Most of the tourists you'll see in Cuzco are there to take the ten-hour train trip up to Machu Picchu. My friend, Louis, is one of the few guides who can get you up the mountains to Mazilaq. The trip is ninety-five kilometers—two days on 'orseback. It's not as well known as Machu Picchu but just as worthwhile. It will get cold at night, and campesinos—peasants—you'll meet along the way may give you coca leaves to chew. It's legal and staves off cold, fatigue, and other discomforts of the altitude. Take some Diamox if you need to."

Hardy laughed loudly as he careened and honked at a dilapidated Pinto. "You are certain to be amazed, Ms. Donovan! Some say that Mazilaq is one of the undiscovered wonders of the world. The Inca call it 'the seat of heaven.' "

She gazed out the window as they bumped along, taking in the occasional crossing of a pack of llama and, as they reached the outskirts of the city, the ramshackle signs of extreme poverty.

"Can I use standard Spanish?" she yelled, pushing her hair off her face.

"Mountain people speak Quechuan. Louis speaks Quechuan, Spanish, and passable English. In Cuzco, don't call anyone Indian—it's very insulting—and use formal pronouns or you will find yourself in hot water."

Super, Gatsby thought, imagining herself in a boiling vat of seasoned water, surrounded by hooting Incan descendants preparing a tasty human sacrifice to go with their huevos and patata. *And I'll have a wicked tan when I go.* She swiped beads of sweat and dust from her forehead. She settled back in her seat and closed her eyes, knowing that with Hardy at the wheel, sleeping would be like trying to do needlepoint while roped to the nuts of a rutting bull.

Hardy brought the Jeep to a thumping halt, jerked the brake up hard, and sat back in his seat, mopping his forehead with a red bandanna.

"'ere we are! Beautiful, isn't it!"

Gatsby roused herself from the fetal position she'd held for the last seven scenic but bumpy hours, squinted and rubbed her eyes, looking around at the city that the Incans had named The Navel of the Cosmos. Cuzco. The Plaza de Armas was surrounded by colonial arcades and churches where Quechuan women squatted on the steps holding onto the reins of their llamas. Brown-skinned children in colorful, woven shorts and sandals skipped and shouted, and musicians strolled, playing lilting melodies on pipes and guitars. On all four sides, the red and white Peruvian flag fluttered in the breeze.

"Yes, it is," Gatsby said, running her hands through her hair, breathing heavily and blinking against the bright sun. Sweat had already pasted her cotton T-shirt to her back, and she swatted flies from her shins.

"Now to find Louis. The only person I've met 'ere who understands a meeting time like you and I do."

As Hardy scanned the plaza, shielding his eyes with one hand, a wiry man with a grin on his leathery face and few teeth hopped from the doorway of a tavern and strolled up to the Jeep. His open T-shirt flapped in the breeze and his sandals clapped against the bricks as he approached. "Señor Hardy, I am with joy to see you! Ah, Señorita, my friend, he has tell me about you. I take you to the temple, sí?"

"Sí," Gatsby murmured, taking the man's claw of a hand as he helped her from the Jeep. She got her pack from the cab, slung it over one shoulder, and turned to Hardy.

"You say it will take two days on horseback to reach Mazilaq? There's no other way? No buses or trains?"

"That's right. The trail is accessible only by 'orse or by foot."

She wiped sweat off her forehead with the back of her arm. "All right, I'm going to need a day to see the temple. So five days from now...that's next Friday...I'll meet you right here in the plaza at nine o'clock in the morning. I need to be at the airport in Lima by six—my plane boards at seven. Friday, nine o'clock. Agreed?"

Deep creases furrowed Hardy's tanned face as he smiled and a breeze blew a shock of sun-streaked hair over his forehead. "Friday morning it is. If we both arrive early, I'll buy you a drink in Louis's taverna. You'll need one!" He laughed heartily.

Gatsby shook his hand. "I'll look forward to it. Thank you for your help. I appreciate it."

Hardy tipped his Fedora, winked at her, and hopped back in his Jeep. He gunned the engine, blowing a fat black cloud of exhaust, and careened away, singing in Spanish at the top of his lungs.

Gatsby coughed on the smoke and turned to face her guide. "And you're Louis?"

"Louis Garacilaso."

"So, Louis, I understand that you provide the food and equipment for the trip, correct?"

"Sí."

"And you charge forty dollars?"

He smiled and nodded.

She did the math in her head and figured that in the Peruvian currency, forty dollars came to something like six million Intis. She also realized that Louis was probably one of the higher-paid citizens in Cuzco; most nongovernment workers made only two or three dollars a day. It was indeed, as she had read, a city where barter was prevalent and dollars scarce.

She clipped the canvas straps of her pack around her waist. "Okay, let's go."

He gave her a toothless grin, turned, and started across the square. Gatsby followed, elbowing her way through packs of children, beggars, llamas and vicunas, jabbering merchants and other open-air vendors and hawkers, dogs, tourists, and a few armed soldiers.

As she trudged along behind Louis, sweating furiously in the midday heat, still reeling and bruised from Hardy's driving, she thought that, without a doubt, the first two words she would to learn in Quechuan were *bathroom* and *water*.

Then she would learn the Quechuan phrase for *how the hell do I get out of the Heart of Darkness and back to the Chelsea Club sauna?*

CHAPTER 6

Louis called Gatsby's horse Tacmas, but by ten o'clock the next morning, she was calling it, among other things, The Antichrist.

She'd slept fitfully the night before in the back room of Louis's taverna, tossing on a hard cot next to an open window. A rampant mix of dread and adrenaline had kept her wide-eyed for most of the night. Louis had barged in at daybreak, offering techniques on how to convince the horse she would ride that she was the boss.

Now the animal had waded into the middle of a rushing stream and parked, and Gatsby couldn't find the release catch. She kicked, shouted, pulled its mane, poked its sides—and the beast wouldn't move. She hadn't been astride a horse since she was thirteen years old and chin-deep in horsy love.

She was filled with none of that love at the moment and, in fact, was hurling vehement curses at the beast and all its descendants.

On the other side of the stream, his horse's reins in hand, Louis leaped about like a frantic gibbon. "Señorita! Patear los pelotas!" He pointed toward some indefinable part of the horse's back end and doubled over with laughter.

"Move, you hijo de puta," Gatsby growled between clenched teeth, digging her heels deeper into the horse's ribs. It cast its brown eyes in her direction and snorted with obvious belligerence. The water was already splashing her boots and the stream seemed to be rising—if she didn't get the bloody animal out of there soon, she'd be swimming to Mazilaq and perhaps back to London.

"Los bolas! Cajones!" Louis shouted again and smacked his bare thighs with his palms, close to the groin.

Ah, those *bolas,* Gatsby thought and jabbed her heels deep into the horse's flanks.

The Antichrist reared and bolted toward the shore, splashing greenish water onto Gatsby's legs as it plodded up the muddy embankment. As Gatsby sidled up beside Louis, now atop his mare and snickering under his breath, she shot him an imploring look. "Look, Louis, in a crisis, English. Speak English. Entiende?"

Louis's eyes glittered and he gave her his dentist's-nightmare grin. "Inglés, sí, claro." With a chuckle, he reined his horse to the right and started up a trail that zigzagged up the hill before them.

Three hours into this madness, four days to go, she thought. Gatsby trotted along behind him, watching the bobbing rump of his mare, in a hot wake of dust and horse sweat.

That night, they set up tents, spread their sleeping bags, built a small fire, and cooked dinner—canned chicken stew for Gatsby, a furry animal for Louis that he called *cuy* and Gatsby was surprised to learn was guinea pig.

Three thousand meters above sea level, the air was as uncomfortably thin as Hardy had predicted. For most of the day, Gatsby had forced herself to take slow breaths and aspirin for an insistent headache. They were well into the Cordillera Blanca and surrounded by towering mountains with cliffs that were sparsely covered with dry scrub and capped with snow. She'd spotted condors, goats, and a few scampering viscachas. On their way up the rocky, winding path, Gatsby had been able to peer down into some of the deep canyons and view vistas of tended farms that looked like patchwork quilts. She had been amazed at how the virtually sheer cliffs were terraced by the campesinos to provide farmable ground for potatoes, corn, cocoa, and cotton.

Gatsby hunkered down on a flat rock, gazed into the fire, stirred the contents of her aluminum pot, and listened to the sounds of the mountains: the occasional bleat of a wild llama or burro, the scurries of lizards on night patrol. Above, the velvet black sky blazed with stars.

As Louis turned his cuy on a makeshift spit, he asked, "You have not been in mountains before?"

"No. Many places in the world but never this high up. Is it dangerous?"

The fire crackled as fat dribbled into the coals. "No big animals, no tigre. But víboras." His forehead wrinkled as he shook a bony finger at her. "They try to share your bed sometimes."

"Víboras?"

"Sí. Snakes."

Gatsby swallowed her mouthful of chicken and freeze-dried celery with some difficulty and no desire to put anything else in her stomach. She sat her pot beside her on the rock. "Snakes, uh?" Turning, she dug into her backpack and pulled out a bottle opener and a warm bottle of Beck's—the single luxury she had brought on this adventure into the wonderland of South America. "This should help me sleep through any night visitations," she said, lifting the bottle toward Louis and drinking down a long, satisfying swallow of beer. Louis nodded, still turning his dinner with slow deliberation. They both stared into the dancing flames as the night cries of the sierra moved around them.

She sipped again and looked up at him. "You've been to Mazilaq many times?"

He nodded without looking up.

"And you know that I want to go inside the temple?"

"Sí, many come from other countries to see the temple and I take them."

She peered at him inquisitively. "Do you know anything about drawings on the walls there? Drawings that...that only certain people can see?"

"I do not know. But maybe you will see charosas and they will tell you."

"Charosas? What are they?"

Louis finally looked at her, with large eyes as dark as the night. "People say there are spirits of the ancient Inca—charosas—who live in Mazilaq. Maybe you will see one. If you do, you can ask him."

She took another long swallow. A shiver rippled through her body; their isolation was palpable, sitting right there next to her, its cold finger caressing her skin. She stood wearily, beer in hand. "Charosas. I see. Well, I...I think I'll go to bed now."

"Mañana." Louis went back to slowly turning his dinner and poking at the fire. Soon, she heard chewing sounds as he began to eat the roasted cuy.

Inside her tent, Gatsby undressed to her thermal T-shirt and long underwear, pulled out a wirebound journal, and crawled into her sleeping bag. By the light of a kerosene lantern, she wrote a few notes about the day and what awaited her at the temple. About Louis's charosas. She finished off the beer and zipped herself in tight—tight enough to keep out any friendly, or even not so friendly, víboras.

Eyes closed, she shivered, realizing that it wasn't from the night chill. A line from an old song ran through her mind: *though it's cold and lonely in the deep dark night...*

The fear was the coldness; the aloneness was even colder.

CHAPTER 7

"There," Louis said, pointing ahead. "The Temple of the Sun."

Gatsby reined her horse to a halt, her heart pounding as she gazed up the dirt path and felt her eyes widen to take in the enormity of Mazilaq.

The site was essentially rectangular—close to two hundred meters long and forty meters wide, the square footage of two football fields. The ground on which it sat had been carved flat from the cliff side—sparse groves of trees and shrubs grew at both ends. To the right, Gatsby noted a white, one-level stone structure with three entrances; to the left, a tall, pyramid-shaped building—The Temple of the Sun. The central grassy area between the main structures was bare, probably at one time a court for games or rituals. And lining the sides of the rectangle were toppled remains of arched doorways and footpaths, possibly the walls of smaller worship houses, now in crumbling ruins and carpeted with moss.

Behind the site, the Cordillera Blanca rose to white peaks, giving the place a sense of haute grandeur. A cool breeze whistled like the spirit of an ancient singer—or a charosa—and whether its song beckoned or forebode, Gatsby couldn't tell.

"Good gods," she whispered. She checked her watch. Quarter past eleven. Adrenaline practically ran out her ears. "Let's go, Louis, vamanos!" she urged. Louis nodded; they prodded their horses.

The trail dissipated as they entered the enclosure that was marked off by rows of flat stones. Gatsby dismounted, adjusted her backpack, and tied her horse to a balsa tree at the base of the temple steps. She stood before the monument, remembering the passages from all the books and photos that she thought had prepared her for this moment. They hadn't. The feeling of awe almost literally took her breath away.

A pillar of stone stairs rose twenty meters or more from the base of the temple. Seven septagonal columns, holding what was left of the structure's roof, were covered with elaborate carvings of animals and deities. At the entrance, the temple's main doorway was a monstrous curved arch, flanked on both sides by life-size stone jaguars, snarling, crouched to pounce.

She stopped to check her equipment—camera, journal, pencils, film, a copy of Peru's Ancient Sites—and glanced back toward Louis. He too had tied his horse and was now quietly smoking one of his leaf-wrapped cigarillos in the shade of a nearby grove of wild marijuana.

She suddenly realized that they had seen no other people since leaving Cuzco—campesinos, tourists, guide groups, nothing. She let the thought move to the back of her mind so that she could worry about it later, took a deep breath, and started up the stairs.

The last twenty steps were murder. She sucked in air that was fantastically lacking in oxygen and made her head throb. A faint fruity smell wafted from inside the ruins and she hoped to god that she wasn't about to stumble over the rotting carcass of some puma's lunch. Or perhaps a charosa, its empty eye sockets, picked clean by vultures, staring at her from a sun-bleached skull.

At last, panting and slightly nauseous, she leaned against the cold stone of the snarling jaguar statues. She glanced around and noticed tiny yellow flowers like buttercups, pushing up between the stones under her feet. With one more deep breath, she crossed the mantle and stepped inside the temple.

A ghoulish face, three meters high, jutted from the inner wall before her, its thick lips turned down in a menacing snarl. *Probably a guardian deity that loves to scare the crap out of nosey gringas like me,* Gatsby thought, slowly recovering her breath. She pulled out her Nikon 680 and began snapping shots.

The ancient, crumbling walls around her were covered with Incan designs. Most looked like astrological icons, and the geometry of the designs was unbelievable; they were perfect squares from which spokes of elaborate triangular pictograms emanated.

Gatsby gazed in awe for a few moments and then thought—where had Traussbery told her to look for the glyph? A "throne room" called the Coricancha. When she had asked Louis about it the day before, he had told her that it was in the smaller temple, the one carved directly from the base of a cliff wall at the south end of the site.

She turned back and crossed over the stone threshold to where she had stood a few minutes earlier, at the top of the stairs with the jaguars. Swatting at mosquitoes, she scanned the topography of the ruins. The building directly ahead, at the end farthest from her, protruded from a steep cliff wall.

That's it, the Coricancha! It must be!

She scampered down the stairs. Louis, working on either his first or his fifth cigarillo, watched with a wan expression as she dashed past him, her pack thumping against her back.

Soft mist rose around her as she ran across the play field, her hiking boots squishing in the muddy grass. Before her, the crumbling stone building rose from the scrub and white rocks; it was broad at the bottom and narrowed as it rose to about eight meters in height. There were three doorways in front and one on each side. She held her breath and stepped through the central arch.

A rush of air, cold as the aged stones themselves, slid over her.

She found herself inside a courtroom-size chamber that held toppled remnants of benches and columns. Sunlight streamed through gaping holes in what was left of the ceiling. Gatsby reached for her camera and began systematically taking shots. She noted that low-ceilinged hallways led away on both the right and left sides of the chamber and, directly ahead, rising from the floor on which she stood, a flight of stairs rose two meters to a smaller room on an upper level. She bounded up the stairway into the room Traussbery had spoken of. The Throne Room.

A chamber five meters square opened around her, and she gazed at an enormous throne in the middle of the room, carved from white rock and roomy enough for two kings and several favored concubines. The Monarch's Throne. Carvings on the chair depicted Incan symbols for life, death, resurrection, the seasons, the sun, and royalty. She let her gaze wander over the throne and then noticed the walls.

A mosaic of twisting, intertwined glyphs and intricate artwork covered a one-meter-high section, at eye level, on all four walls. As Traussbery had said, the inks were amazingly vibrant, given that they had been exposed to the elements for eight hundred years. They illustrated scenes of royalty, children, animals, plants, stars. It took Gatsby a few minutes to take it all in, pulling the crisp mountain air deep into her lungs and reminding herself that while certain parts of the more famous site, Machu Picchu, had undergone limited restoration work, there wasn't a shred of evidence that a conservationist had ever set foot at Mazilaq. The paintings were absolutely virgin.

She rummaged in her pack and retrieved the printout of Quinn's glyph in the Egyptian tomb—the inverted cross with its waving line. *I came thousands of miles and battled many reptilian oddities to get here, Traussbery, so your goddamn glyph had better show.*

She let her gaze wander over the art until an image on the north wall caught her attention: a globe-like sphere of intertwined snakes and, within the circle, celestial shapes— moons, stars, crescents. She raised her Nikon, peered through the viewfinder, and heard a hiss, a soft noise from behind the throne that might have been a foot whispering over stone.

She jumped. "Who's there?"

there...ere...ere... Her voice echoed in ghostly parody.

Gatsby shook her head. Were Louis's charosas playing hide and seek with her? *Okay*, she thought, swaying a little on her feet, sweating profusely. *The acid test. Let's conjure this Peruvian genie. What do I have to do, whistle dixie? Sacrifice a goat? Say abraca...*

Something shimmered—a bright flash struck her eyes, like sunlight reflected in a mirror. Gatsby felt the hairs rise on the back of her neck. Energy careened crazily through her body while a fantasy of tapping her ruby slippers together and popping back to Kansas rolled through her mind. A centimeter at a time, her gaze rose up to the spot, just even with her nose, where a sunspot was beginning to glow.

Motionless, she peered. Her vision went out of focus for an instant and the image seemed to burn eerily. She blinked and it came into focus: an upward-pointed triangle, darkened as if filled in with Indian ink. Supporting it below, a notch, like a letter V. The glyph was about as tall as the space between the tips of her thumb and first finger.

It glowed spectrally, like sulfurous ectoplasm.

She swallowed so hard it hurt.

Now for the moment of truth.

She pulled out the Polaroid Land Camera that she had bought just before leaving London. She centered the glyph within the viewfinder and pushed the shutter release. The camera's guts whirred and spat out a black square of laminate.

Gatsby reminded herself that she had double-checked all her equipment—including the Land Camera—that morning and found all of it working perfectly.

Grey and brown tones slowly began to appear in the instant photo, cracks and chips in the wall, the artwork of the royal family, the sphere of snakes, flecks of sunlight, smudges of dirt.

And any second now, the glyph would fade into view.

"Any minute now," Gatsby whispered, feeling a knot tightening in her stomach. "Aaaaany second now..."

A full minute went by. The sweat from her hands glistened on the edges of the laminate.

"Not possible," she whispered, hearing the tremor in her voice. With shaking hands, she took another shot and waited while it developed.

She took another.

Twenty minutes later, she had eleven sweat-smeared Polaroid photos—all close-up shots of a crumbling, Incan stone wall.

And all devoid of the double-triangle glyph that glowed before her eyes.

"Bloody hell!" A coppery taste had coated her mouth; her tongue slid over parched lips. She stretched her hand out toward the glyph. The tip of her finger touched stone—as she moved it to the edge of the glyph, she was surprised to find that rather than feeling raised, as most wall paintings felt to the touch, it felt indented in the stone.

I can feel it with my hands, see it with my own eyes! It's not hallucination, not a dream—it's real! A bead of sweat ran into her eyes, stinging fiercely.

Okay, plan B...

Digging in her backpack, she pulled out a pad of paper and a ballpoint pen. At the top of the pad, Gatsby wrote the date: May 23. She moved the pen to the middle of the pad and, directing her eyes to the glyph in front of her, began to draw.

Ink ran out in a steady black line as she began to draw the notch of the upper triangle. Then, like the death trickle of a creek seeping into the soil, the ink thinned and then disappeared altogether.

Bastard, Gatsby thought, not sure toward whom the curse was directed. She shifted to the lower half of the paper and started again. The results were the same. Tossing the pen into her pack, she pulled out a pencil, thinking, *Okay, can you keep lead from marking on paper?*

As she drew the pencil's tip across the pad, a dark grey line emerged. Exultant, as if she had outwitted the Loki of Mazilaq, Gatsby continued drawing, generating the upper triangle and beginning to sketch the downward lines of the lower V shape.

Abruptly, the grey carbon line became nothing but an indentation in the paper fiber. Gatsby found herself drawing with a pencil that left no mark. She threw the pencil across the room where it clattered against the foot of the throne. Digging feverishly, she pulled out two more pencils and tested both.

The same results, each time.

Gatsby slumped cross-legged to the cold floor and heaved a sigh. *Gods! What is the bloody explanation? There has to be one!*

"And I'm going to find the fucker," she whispered between clenched teeth.

Desperation wriggled through her like a malevolent virus, driving her to take a half-dozen more Polaroid shots and to attempt the drawing again. All efforts had the same negative results. Finally, with sweat running between her collarbones and shaking from the need for food and oxygen, she gave up.

If you're so damned intent on keeping this glyph to yourself, keep it! You win.

She rose with difficulty, her knees popping from holding a half-kneeling position for almost an hour, and stumbled down the steps, out of the building and into the glare of the sun at the navel of the world.

The Andean heat burned across her face and the back of her neck as if the sun were angry with her. For what? For trespassing into the Coricancha? For trying to draw the glyph?

Or for not really believing that she'd seen it?

CHAPTER 8

Louis was waiting for her at the base of the temple, a cigarillo between his brown fingers—not that Gatsby thought he would have gone anywhere. But she was more than a little glad to see his amiable face. He flashed his mostly-toothless smile as she approached.

"Señorita, I am with joy to see you. You found what you were looking for, sí?"

Did I? she wondered.

"Well, part of what I was looking for. New questions but no new answers."

"No charosas?" Louis asked, smirking.

"Not today." She sighed. "I'm ready to go."

"We go," was all the Louis had to say. Gatsby hauled herself back on her horse and a light tap of her heels nudged The Antichrist forward toward the trail that had led them to Mazilaq. Over the caps of the Cordillera Blanca, the afternoon sun blazed, warming the tops of their hats.

The horse's trotting movements made Gatsby's pack bounce lightly against her back. One of the pencils inside it was poking into her ribs like a dull knife. She reached back with one hand and moved it around until it lay flat against the small of her back.

Pencils that don't write, glyphs that won't photograph... She began to mentally catalog her experiences on this adventure—and how she was going to relay them to Traussbery, who would no doubt encourage her in this lunatic goose chase, and to Clevis, who would no doubt advise her to seek a competent mental health professional.

As their horses clattered onto the paved road that dipped and dropped back into Cuzco, Gatsby heard music and shouting.

"What's going on, Louis?"

"Inti Raymi. There is much dancing, singing. Drink beer, make love. Four days."

A Peruvian Saturnalia, she thought.

In ten minutes, they were at the outskirts of the city. The Plaza de Armas was a cacophony of guitars, drums, whistles, and flutes, along with lively singing and a bustling crowd. Wearing masks and bright costumes of feathers and beads, the celebrants yelped as they drank corn beer out of gourds and jugs, danced, and played out various other forms of mating behavior. Gatsby and Louis dismounted and walked their horses into the plaza.

"It's like Mardi Gras!" Gatsby shouted over the noise.

"Que?" Louis shouted back.

She shook her head, laughed, and pointed to her horse, gesturing as if tying rope. Louis nodded and started forward.

They made their way around the perimeter of the plaza and finally approached the entrance of Louis's taverna, where his ample wife, Catalina, kissed him and hugged them both. Louis motioned to Gatsby to follow him to the back of the taverna, where they tied the horses next to a steel watering trough. As the sweat-slicked animals drank noisily, Gatsby turned to Louis and said, "That's what I need. Let's go inside and I'll buy you a drink, to show you how grateful I am for your services."

The familiar cheery, toothless grin appeared on the Quechuan man's face, and he nodded enthusiastically as they walked into the taverna and dropped their bags. Moving behind the wooden bar, Louis took on his role as owner and host. He drew a dark beer for her and handed her the glass, then poured one for himself. Gatsby sniffed it, grinned, and drank it down in three huge gulps.

An hour later, when Louis tried to fill Gatsby's glass for the third time, she murmured, "Oh no, no, uh vreally han-enough." The fuzziness from the beer had blended with the post-traumatic shock syndrome-like effects of the trip. The adventure was a reminder of how cushy her desk job at the British Museum really was and how only a part of her missed the intensity of globetrotting.

"Yep, nothing like a trek unto thuh Andes to wake you up." She heard herself slurring and giggled wearily. "I, uh, I've been meaning to ask you, Louis, how often do you go to Mazilaq?"

Louis stared out the window into the noisy plaza as he rolled a glass in his hand. "One, two a month. Most touristas go to Machu Picchu. There are not that many who know of Mazilaq." A pensive expression moved over his brown face. "Maybe that is good."

"What makes you say that?"

Louis replied slowly. "The spirits of Inca ancestors, they are there. For us, it is a sacred place—it must be respected. People from other countries, when they come, they do not respect Mazilaq."

Typical. Arrogant, brainless tourists who want to see some ruins and run amuck as if they were at Disneyland, Gatsby thought. "Yeah, I know what you mean."

Louis sipped his beer with a faraway look in his eyes. "I do not like to go there too much. Sometimes, I have seen people go there but when they come back, they are different."

"How?"

Louis's eyes narrowed. "They bring visions back with them."

"Visions?" She sat up. "Visions that have anything to do with the drawings in the Coricancha?" Gatsby leaned forward, suddenly alert.

Louis's eyes widened. He drew in a breath. "They—"

BAM! The door of the taverna flew open and banged against the wall. A horde of festival-soaked musicians staggered inside, singing and spilling beer from their gourds. They greeted Louis with sloppy hugs and a verbal sludge of Spanish and Quechuan. In a moment, Louis was swarmed at the bar where they demanded alcohol, tipped over chairs, and knocked each other around while trying to stay vertical and fermented at the same time.

Damn it! Gatsby thought, seeing that Louis was unable to finish his story. She laid a fistful of Intis on the counter for the beer and what she owed Louis for the trip. She caught his eye and pointed to indicate that she was headed toward the back room where he'd let her sleep the night she'd arrived. He nodded quickly and smiled, then turned his attention to the rowdy musicians.

Shuffling into the small room that held only a cot, a nightstand, and a tin bucket, Gatsby felt her eyes slowly adjust to the dark. She made her way to the cot and, stretching out, lay back and sighed contentedly, eyes closed, too tired to notice the raw wool blanket scratching against the backs of her legs.

A hundred questions poured through her mind, demanding audience all at once. Relief and frustration battled inside her; she could almost see them decked out in Andean regalia of warfare. As she felt herself drifting off, listening to her heartbeat murmuring in her ears, reconstructing the sequence of events on the strangest day in memory, she thought back to Traussbery's excited expression as he had told her his story: *I saw the thing once, eleven years ago, three thousand meters up an Andean cliff where I could have been suffering from oxygen deprivation. But I wasn't.*

But had he? Had she? What could explain the glowing, ethereal image? Was it possible that it had been hallucination? That she'd wanted so badly to see it that she'd merely...

She stopped in midthought. From outside, the festival carried hoots and whistles in through the room's curtainless window. But she felt something else, something close. A ticklish sensation, like the breathless eternity just before a sneeze. Then she knew what it was.

Someone watching her.

She sat up, her gaze riveting to the window on the opposite side of the room. Gatsby stared in wonderment; the face—or rather, the girl—stared back. They studied each other silently.

It was the face of any Quechuan child of about ten years—large dark eyes, clay-brown skin, black hair, a somewhat flattened nose, a serious, inquisitive expression. But there was something in the expression—in the girl's eyes—that opened a strange sensation deep in Gatsby's psyche. The child's eyes didn't move, didn't even twitch, but they seemed to offer something...an image, a word? A signal that neither used nor needed language; it was a language of its own. A language that, in a place inside her, in a deep cave long boarded up, Gatsby could have understood but would never hear again unless...

Transfixed, Gatsby breathed, "You—"

The child bolted.

She pulled in a deep breath to yell and then blew it out; fatigue pulled her back. Shaking her head, she blinked a few times and lay back on the cot. As her breathing returned to normal, she draped one arm over her eyes and thought, *With everything else, visitations from Peruvian kids? Now I know Louis slipped something into my beer.*

The festival blared only a meter away from her bed and, in seconds, sleep piloted her into dreams where, on the shore of a tropical lagoon, she ate peppermint candies.

CHAPTER 9

In the parking lot at the Lima airport, Gatsby staggered out of Hardy's Jeep, convinced she had survived a ride that made the Devil Mouse roller coaster in the East Chicago fun center look like a Sunday picnic. He had taken one corner so hard that she'd smacked her head on the roll bar and lost her sunglasses.

Hardy had showed up at the taverna at half past ten the day before—she had found him much blonder, a little tanner, and just as loud as at their first meeting. With his death-wish driving, he had gotten her to Lima just in time to make her plane.

"Well, Mr. Hardy." Gatsby swallowed as she straightened her clothes, smoothed down the spikes in her hair, and wriggled one foot back into the sandal that had rocketed off when he'd swerved to avoid a herd of pigs. "I want to thank you for your assistance. Really."

Hardy gave her a wide grin and cuffed her on the shoulder hard enough to raise a dust-cloud from her jacket. "My pleasure." He winked conspiratorially. "I 'ope you found what you came 'ere for." He hopped back into his Jeep and gunned the engine. "Give my best to old Traussbery, Ms. Donovan. Vaya con Dios!" With a roar, he sped away, singing in Spanish.

Good gods! Gatsby heaved a huge sigh and, in spite of her weariness, had to smile as she strode into the airport terminal to find her gate.

There were no Arabs on the flight back to London; in fact, being a late evening departure, the plane was only half full. Gatsby had an entire row of seats to herself. She lay back with her head below the window and pulled out the journal she had kept during the trip. In less than five minutes, the notebook was balanced on the bridge of her nose, muffling the sounds of snoring.

A blonde steward rustled her a few hours later to offer her dinner. Gatsby declined the Poulet á la AeroPeru and opted for a liquid supper that was less nutritious but infinitely more satisfying.

CHAPTER 10

With a thump and the screech of air rushing over wing flaps, the 747 touched down and taxied to its gate.

Gatsby roused herself, tossed her dusty pack over her back, and shuffled down the aisle. As she reached the front exit, the blonde steward who vaguely reminded her of Boy Wonder smiled and chirped, "Thank you for flying with us today!" She flashed him her "marvelous-now-get-out-of-my-bloody-way" smile and made her way down the ramp and into the waiting area of Gate 36. Heathrow. Home—how good it felt. Even the smog was comforting.

She walked briskly down the crowded corridor toward the desk where she was to turn in her trip itinerary and customs papers. She found herself thinking that the only thing she had to declare from this trip was that either the Peruvians made some nasty hallucinogenic concoctions or she was going to be forced to deal with some challenges to her empiricism.

Finally at the roped-off queue which led around into the customs office, Gatsby dropped her suitcase to the floor and surveyed the line of people in front of her: an American couple, a teenaged boy, a grey-haired gentleman, and a hunched elderly woman holding the hand of a child. The very Western-looking girl didn't look like she belonged with the elderly woman. In a blue dress with white lace trim, tights, and shiny patent shoes, the little girl looked as if she might have just been at a suburban birthday party.

As the hunched woman approached the desk, she held her papers up and jabbered at the black gentleman behind the desk. The child fidgeted, twisting around in the woman's bony grip and scuffing her shoes on the linoleum.

Gatsby watched casually, unsure if she felt more sympathy for the old woman or the squirming kid. The child had turned so that Gatsby could study her face in profile. From the side, Gatsby catalogued brown skin, black hair, and a slightly flattened nose—and felt her body tensing.

My god, she looks...it's that kid I saw outside my window at the taverna! How did...

She craned her neck for a better view. As the old woman turned to reach into a canvas bag, Gatsby saw that she looked Pakistani—there was a bright red bindi dot between her eyebrows. Her face wrinkled even more as she squinted in Gatsby's direction, revealing a gap between her front teeth. Gatsby watched as the customs officer flipped through the woman's passport and then barked in a deep voice, "That's fine, Mrs. Shankar. Have a pleasant holiday." He jerked his thumb toward the door leading into the main courseway.

Gatsby shook her head, muttering to herself. *An Indian kid who looks somewhat South American. How crazy would it be for a raggedy Quechuan girl to end up on the same plane th...no, Gatsby, we don't even want to go there.*

The people standing in line fidgeted. Gatsby stood frozen in her thoughts until the man behind her grumbled, "Pardon, will you move forward?"

Another impenetrable-looking black man in an official, smartly tailored uniform appeared at Gatsby's side. A hot, dry palm slid against her forearm. "Is there a problem here?" he said in a voice that made her think of polished handcuffs.

"Oh! Uh, sorry. No. Nothing. Sorry." Gatsby shuffled forward, feeling blood rushing into her cheeks.

Mr. Impenetrable glowered at her and flared his nostrils for emphasis. "Have your passport ready for inspection when you reach the desk."

Gatsby nodded, absorbed in the weary longing to be back in her own flat, enveloped in the wonderfully tacky familiarity of it and letting the mysteries of Mazilaq dissolve in rosewood bath salts.

CHAPTER 11

Behind the thick lenses, Traussbery's newt-like eyeballs bulged like hard-boiled eggs about to burst. He held the Polaroid photo at the tip of his nose, staring with enough intensity to burn a hole in it.

It had only been two weeks since she had last graced Traussbery's office, but it felt like years. Gatsby fidgeted in her armchair and glanced over her shoulder. The dust mops were there behind her, predictably snoring on their chintz pillows.

Sheesh. He never leaves home without them, she thought.

Traussbery pushed his glasses back up on his nose as his eyes darted, scanning the Polaroid. Afternoon sunlight streamed into his office, throwing bright shafts across the Persian rug.

"Well?" Gatsby finally blurted. "Explanation?"

He plucked off his glasses and rubbed his eyes. Smoke swirled lazily from the pipe resting in the porcelain ashtray on his desk. He pulled out his ever-present hanky and coughed lightly into it. Finally, he murmured, "I see that you had exactly the results—or lack thereof—as I, those many years ago."

"Perhaps not exactly the same. Look at this." Gatsby leaned sideways, pulled a separate packet of commercially developed photos from her leather briefcase, and handed it to Traussbery. "Tell me if you had *these* results."

Most of the photos appeared exactly as would be expected, showing stone walls, the crumbling columns within the Throne Room, the snarling faces of the jaguar Temple guardians. But a handful of the photographs were smeared with ghostly streaks. If she squinted a bit, Gatsby thought that the milky, Rorschach test-like wisps could conceivably be constructed into a nose, chin, eyebrows, and a pair of widely staring eyes...

A gasp escaped from Traussbery's mouth. "My god," he whispered.

The Polaroids Gatsby had strewn across Traussbery's desktop seemed to stare back as belligerently as she and the professor stared at them. They offered shot after shot of crumbling stones and Incan designs, but not one contained a glyph akin to the one on the wall of Nefertari's tomb—or anywhere else in the world.

Gatsby leaned back in her chair and sighed. "And, as you found yourself, when I tried to draw this glyph, I and my equipment took an immediate detour into the Twilight Zone where perfectly functional pens and pencils are incapable of transferring ink to paper. But—" She pulled a sheet of paper from her briefcase and laid it on the stack of Polaroids. "I did manage this." On the paper was a pencil sketch of the double-triangle glyph.

Traussbery gasped. "That's it! The very image that I saw! But how? I assumed it could not be drawn!"

As he spoke, Gatsby saw Traussbery's body trembling. His cheeks blanched and she thought she could actually observe his pupils dilating, like black roses blooming in a high-speed film. Something about the glyph had rattled him—badly. What? She filed the question away for future examination.

"It couldn't," she continued. "Not at Mazilaq, anyway. I did this when I got home. Drew it from memory in my living room, the night I got back." Her eyebrows lifted. "How and why the glyph can be drawn in London but not in Mazilaq— and why it can't be photographed—is still beyond me. For the moment, I'm more interested in what these symbols might mean."

Even as she heard the words come out of her mouth, she felt an imperceptible tug within her, deep in a long-forgotten place. A flag swayed in the slow winds of her psyche, murmuring that she was heading toward the edge of a world, an *ultima Thule,* and that unknown dangers lay beyond. The flag was a beacon, if she chose to pay attention to it.

She chose not to and, instead, said, "I just don't know what to make of this. I've never come across anything this weird in my life."

"Yes, yes," Traussbery said, a tremor rippling his scratchy voice. He picked up his pipe and cradled it in his chubby hand. "That's why I knew I had to send you to Mazilaq to corroborate my experience. *And* I knew that unless you had a firsthand experience yourself, you would never have believed it possible."

"Got that right," Gatsby said, nodding. She blew out a deep lungful of air, still gazing at the photos. "It's not that these glyphs themselves are similar, but could they be part of some unknown language system? And if they aren't, what the hell is behind them? Or who?"

"Pranksters trotting around the globe, scratching undecipherable graffiti at significant archeological sites?" Traussbery shook his head.

Gatsby frowned dismissively. "For the moment, let's put the question of how they appeared on the back burner. Is there a pattern? A connection? What does Egypt have to do with Peru? I've heard theories from Ivan Dickerson and a few of his cohorts that some ancient Middle Eastern civilizations had the nautical technology to travel to the Americas, and that that's why there are such remarkable similarities between the Egyptian pyramids and those in South America. But it's all speculation, no solid evidence to support the claim."

Traussbery sucked generously on the pipe. "Worthy, a worthy thought, something to keep in mind. I heard from Quinn yesterday that he is sending both photographs and videotapes of his discovery. They should arrive in about a week—we can view them together. Perhaps they will shed some light." He sat his pipe down into the tray on the desk—the tremors of his hands caused it to rattle against the edges of the tray.

"Perhaps." Gatsby shook her head, thinking, *What's made him so edgy all of a sudden? Or is it just old age and his far-from-perfect health?* "I have to say," she continued, "I've been to some astounding places. I've seen two-thousand-year-old bowls of fruit preserved in perfect condition in Pompeii. Held in my hands runes that were thrown by Mesopotamian kings. Touched the teeth and smelled the myrrh in the wrappings of four-thousand-year-old mummies. Spent entire days at Stonehenge with those incredible megaliths. But this?" With elbows resting on her knees, she cupped her chin in her hands and stared at him in consternation. "As my uncle in Seattle would say, this takes the cake."

Traussbery retrieved the pipe, relit it, and puffed silently, breathing somewhat heavily. They both stared out the window.

"But before I give up, I want to check the data banks at the museum. For some reason, these glyphs remind me of the East Asian systems. I think there are some references in the computer databases that I haven't reviewed in quite some time. After I've checked them out, perhaps we could meet in the city and talk."

Traussbery nodded. "Excellent. We'll visit my good friend Nigel at the Punch & Judy at Covent Garden, what do you say? Wednesday? Eleven o'clock?"

"Fine." Gatsby stretched her legs as she rose and gathered up her briefcase and shoulderbag.

The Shih Tzus began to snore.

Gatsby wondered if at any moment one of the dust mops might suddenly morph into a strange new shape—the shape of whatever intelligence was seemingly toying with her and the professor. A mental image came to her of ancient gods, peering down from Olympus at the puny mortals, tossing bolts of lightning from the sky, laughing as the pathetic creatures howled and scrambled to interpret their meaning.

CHAPTER 12

The eighty-five minute drive back to London passed as if a
waking dream, in between worlds, subliminal. Gatsby's
mind reeled from the interview—Traussbery's sudden
twitchiness, the inexplicability of the glyphs and, still, the
warm Tenerife beaches that would have to wait until next
year. But the question burning in the engine of her brain was
meaning. Something was at the bottom of these mysterious
symbols.

Some*one*.

As kilometers of countryside flew past her window,
Gatsby's vision glazed. She sank deep into her thoughts,
never noticing her left hand moving on the top of her thigh,
tapping against the denim of her Levi's with the same sort of
pattern it had that afternoon in her office, weeks ago.

Even if she had noticed it, she would have simply taken
it as substitute toe-tapping, keeping in the groove with
Morrison's version of "L.A. Woman." Nothing more.

Nothing that had a remote connection to a grassy field in
a Seattle suburb.

Turning off the A56, in the warm afternoon sunshine,
speeding eastward toward London, her thoughts turned to
still-undeciphered languages. The Easter Island glyphs, the
pictographic etchings found in the Lascaux caves in France,
an Eskimo hand-alphabet to which no one but Aleutian
shamans were privy. The meticulous work that went into
deciphering a language could take years, sometimes
decades. Jean-François Champollion's decryption of the
Rosetta Stone, now housed at the British Museum, took most
of his life. But his achievement had added his name to every
history book in every classroom. Recalling the images of the
inverted-cross glyph and the double-triangle glyph, Gatsby
allowed herself a thirty-second visual of a spot lit podium,
brandishing the texts where her name appeared next to
drawings of those glyphs and the rest of the newly
discovered language of which they were part. Notoriety had
its secret place in archeolinguistics, she thought, just as in

any other science or art. Professionals—such as her—made self-effacing comments, maintaining that they labored for the enhancement of mankind, but beneath, buried like the most precious of all archeological treasures, there was always an ego waiting to be unearthed and polished to a high sheen.

Would this strange adventure, come to her from a slip of fax paper, become the glittering jewel that she willed to the museum of history? She wondered.

Without warning, a dark shadow stored in a corner of her mind rustled, began to creep ominously, tiptoeing toward the lamp of her conscious thoughts. The mental shadow took the form of a beast, imprisoned at the back of her psyche...or was it a sign?...intelligent?...knowing that there would be a day when the cage door would swing open and it would escape?

Gatsby's hand traveled nimbly across the fabric of her pants, moving in rhythmic patterns. An onlooker might have thought that she was a pianist, practicing scales or arpeggios in her mind while driving along the motorway.

She *was* practicing, rehearsing a meaningful set of rhythms and dexterous movements, but she didn't know it.

CHAPTER 13

As planned, Gatsby found herself sitting at a linen-covered table at the Punch & Judy Pub in the breezeway at Covent Garden. It was Wednesday morning; Traussbery had arrived precisely at eleven o'clock and was now chin-deep into a foamy glass of Black Rabbit ale and the story of the Sudan excavation he'd led the year before.

Outside the smoky ambience of his Cambridge office, and sans the mutts, he seemed somehow less vital. Considering his health, Gatsby wondered if the Sudan story would be the last chapter in the annals of his treks.

She sipped her beer while Traussbery finished a plate of linguine and chattered over the noise of the crowd.

Nigel, the stoic maitre d' and Traussbery's longtime friend, stopped by their table. They were fine; he nodded mutely and slipped away.

The last tangy swallow of her beer slid down Gatsby's throat. She said, "I helped catalog artifacts when new remains were found at Herculaneum—the bodies of those who tried to escape by running toward the sea but never made it—and over a summer break from SUNY, I ended up in New Mexico at a pueblo site where Anasazi stick-notch letters were excavated. No one from NMSU knew how to read them, so they called my department. I went."

"Capital!" Traussbery hunched over the table in rapt attention. "That's how you acquired your knowledge of their ritual drawings?"

She nodded. "And you know, of all the places I've traveled, including Peru," her eyebrows rose, "the one that intrigues me the most is only two hours from here."

Traussbery smiled knowingly, his eyes twinkling.

She folded her hands together. "I don't know how many times I've visited it since coming to London. Fifteen, sixteen times. There's something compelling about Stonehenge. As a kid, my father read stories to me about strange places around the world, and when I saw pictures of Stonehenge, I knew I had to see it firsthand. Especially because of the theories."

Traussbery speared a black olive on his fork and popped it into his mouth. "You may have only heard the most popular of those theories. The folklore is terrifically colorful indeed. Everything from kidney stones of the gods to a landing strip for extraterrestrial spaceships." He chuckled and then coughed.

"According to the experts," she continued, "five thousand years ago, centuries before the pyramids, the Neolithic farmers of southern Britain took it into their heads to build this structure that would take unbelievable labor to finish. I've read that just moving the sarsen stones from Wiltshire would have taken six hundred men, continuously working for more than a year! And in that case, they would have had to work day and night, leaving others to attend to the necessities of survival. I've heard of creative obsession, but that's really over the top." She laughed, raising her empty beer glass so that Nigel could see and nod in her direction.

"From the legitimate surveys," Traussbery replied, chewing, "it does seem to have been built with astronomical uses in mind. The alignment of the stones with the seasonal sunrises and sunsets clearly point to that. And it is speculated that it was used as a temple of worship. The thread that's complete codswallop is that it was built by the Druids. John Aubrey, the antiquarian, helped to fabricate that myth, as you know. But Druidic practices were only flourishing at the time of the Roman conquest, and by that time, Stonehenge had been standing for two thousand years. The Druid priests may have claimed a special type of natural magic, but they would have been immortal to have had anything to do with Stonehenge. Besides, the Druids built no temples; they held their ceremonies in forests."

He coughed, spitting an olive pit onto his plate.

Gatsby said, "And how the site was constructed is bloody unparalleled. Some of those sarsen stones weigh forty-five tonnes! Can you imagine what it took to drag them from the Preseli Mountains, across land and water, to Salisbury Plain?

And then to dress them to shape with stone hammers? And the mortice-and-tenon joints of the lintel stones? That's a refinement found at no other prehistoric stones monument anywhere in Europe."

"A phenomenal undertaking indeed. Indeed." Traussbery reposed in his chair, fished out an engraved silver tin from his jacket pocket and took out his pipe. He lit it and puffed thoughtfully.

The once-bustling lunch crowd was starting to thin, conversations to lull. Like a bald, well-tailored ghost, Nigel had silently wafted by and refilled Gatsby's glass.

She raised it, sipped, savoring the bite of the hops. "Even more phenomenal when you consider that it had nothing to do with survival. It was purely for—well, for whatever reason our barbarian ancestors imagined was important enough to put that much effort into." Setting her glass on the tablecloth, she watched the beads of water on the bottom of the glass seep into the linen, forming a fuzzy ring.

"Perhaps not as barbarian as one might imagine," Traussbery murmured, fingers laced under his chin.

Gatsby peered at him quizzically. "What are you getting at?"

The look that had possessed Traussbery during their first meeting, when he'd told her the story of his glyph sighting in Peru, had returned. "Ms. Donovan, what do you know about quantum shifting?"

She shook her head. "That's a strange question. If you mean quantum physics, the answer is I passed my one-oh-one courses but I haven't had any lunches with Steven Hawking recently. Why?" Guarded skepticism moved into her mind—she could almost hear it tacking up posters.

"I will explain. Shifting is an aspect of quantum physics. A field which has only come to light in the last decade, the time frame in which I have been pursuing my own studies into quantum phenomena."

Gatsby took a long swallow from her glass and let him continue. The skepticism was now dry walling a nursery.

"You see, scientists, persons just as ourselves, are generally the hard-edged sort. Logical. Methodical. Driven to acquire factual knowledge and eschew grey areas, or soft science, such as human perception and behavior. And, in their opinions, with good reason. Life is chaotic—it may operate with mathematical precision and it may not. There are no straight lines in nature." He took a deep breath. "But science stands on principles of predictability and order. The paradox is evident; we hunt for absolute answers when the only tool we have to seek out those answers is our own fallible brain. So when a dyed-in-the-wool empiricist drifts into those grey areas, trouble is on the way. Or incredible discovery. Take the research done by David Bohm, physicist at our own University of London. I read that his work led him to an understanding of the physical universe that is quite extraordinary."

Now genuinely intrigued, she leaned forward. "Go on."

"I have made extensive studies of Bohm's research; he was a protégé of Einstein. In the last twenty years, he proposed a new understanding of the universe, a Newtonian leap, you might say. An understanding which Einstein and his colleagues, Podolsky and Rosen, disputed in their argument now known as the Einstein-Podolsky-Rosen Paradox. Case in point: a causal universe operates on logical principles? Of course. From Aristotle to Einstein, we have operated on that principle. Yet, now that we are able to travel in the realm of the quantum, the particle and the wave, we find that in this universe, the rules go out the window. Quantum particles act like children playing hide and seek. A quantum particle, when struck by another, may go off in one direction, may go in another, may not move at all, may suddenly disappear and then reappear in a random location, may instantaneously turn into another type of particle—a veritable heyday for Heisenberg!"

He puffed on his pipe.

"In the sixties, when delving into the subject of cosmic order, Bohm saw a device on a television program, a jar containing a rotating cylinder and filled with glycerin. Within the clear glycerin, a single drop of ink would appear as solid when a handle was rotated one direction and disappear from view when the handle was turned the other direction. This event led Bohm to reexamine the theories of Niels Bohr, Einstein, Podolsky, and all the rest, and the tricksterish abilities of subatomic particles to shift from particle form to wave form. He brought to light compelling evidence that quanta only appear as particles when we are looking at them! The form that quanta might take—or rather, the form that the observer sees, and the difference is worth noting—is dependent on perception!"

Gatsby blinked a few times, absorbing the information. *What the bugger does this have to do with anything?*

He seemed to read her expression and murmured, "You must be wondering what this has to do with our previous discussion." She nodded.

"You see, the territory of how our perceptions are directed is mostly unexplored. If we really understand it at all, that is. The larger question being, *are* they directed? Or does perception direct? If a particle is only a particle when it is being observed, where does it go or how does it act when it is outside observation?

"There is terminology for these ideas. The world of causal, logical phenomena, the world where the quanta are observed, the world of consensus reality, is termed the surface structure or the unfolded universe. Where the quanta go when not observed, the unknown and imperceptible realm, that is the deep structure. The enfolded universe. And as the bits of the consensus-reality universe shape-shift, we have historically attributed these events to myth, to the supernatural, to the paranormal, to deities, to coincidence, to fate, or simply to unsolved mystery."

By this time, Gatsby was swimming in fascination and bemusement. "So excuse me for saying so, but where the hell are you going with this?" She sipped her beer. "Are you now going to tell me that Stonehenge isn't really there? That it only exists when a visitor climbs out of his miniwagon and crosses the highway to look at it? That it's a configuration of wanton particles that come and go as they bloody please?" She groaned, rolling her eyes. "If that's what you're tr—"

"You've studied the inexplicable aspects of Stonehenge yourself," he interrupted, energetically spearing another olive. "The plausible explanations of time and labor, and the mystifying *reasons* behind them, are beyond modern-day comprehension. Yet when we look five thousand years into our past, we see with the eyes of *presumed* wisdom, *assuming* that ancient civilizations are our younger siblings. *Us* at a younger age, less developed. But the opposite may be true! The people who created Stonehenge and other inexplicable ancient accomplishments could well have been *more* advanced than we are now! What if they had conscious understanding of the cosmology's deeper structures and a power of consciousness that gave them abilities to shape those structures, to wield them as a painter uses brush and ink to manifest his visualization in tangible form?"

"To manifest...his visualization...in tangible form..." Gatsby repeated slowly. "Sounds like undergrad philosophy. Plato's Cave—illusion versus reality, we see but the shadows of the real world. But you're not talking about philosophy, you're talking about the shape, or creation, of *physical* reality."

Traussbery stabbed the mouthpiece of his pipe toward her, making her jerk backward. "I'm talking about *both*, Ms. Donovan. I'm talking about the hypothesis that, whether consciously or unconsciously, we mold what we think of as physical reality. I—" He took a few shallow breaths, obviously winded. The white hanky appeared from his pocket and he coughed into it and took a long drink from his water glass. "I do not discuss my ideas on this subject with just anyone. But I have reason—good reason—to believe in them."

"Such as?"

Traussbery stared at her blankly and then stuck his pipe firmly back in his mouth. She saw that his hands were jittering. "It...ahm, I don't wish to go into that. Suffice it to...to say that, ahm, personal experience is reason enough." He waved a hand to call for Nigel and the bill.

Gatsby filed the comment, and his reaction, for further thought. There was obviously some artifact in Traussbery's past that he was guarding tenaciously and unwilling to dig up.

"Well, if shape-shifting particles weren't involved in the construction of Stonehenge, my bet is on pulleys, levers, timber packing, and simple human labor. At least, that's how the supposed experts explain it." She leaned back in her chair, ready to move to a more immediate topic. "By the way, I should give you the update on my glyph-sleuthing."

"Yes! Yes!"

"I spent most of yesterday reading the computer codices on file at the museum. Luckily I was also able to download them to my home computer."

"And?"

"On the positive side, there are languages that these symbols could be part of."

Traussbery's grey eyes brightened as a smile spread across his face.

"On the down side, the number of possible languages is at least fifty."

They slumped simultaneously.

"So far, I've looked through translation files on Elamitic, Grantha, Iberian, Lycian, Moso, Yu-Chen and, well, I can't remember, a few others. But with only two symbols to go by, it's impossible to exactly identify them or to surmise if they are language at all." Gatsby stirred her beer with one finger and emptied the glass with two loud gulps. "I don't know what to tell you, Professor. I'm not optimistic that it will be possible to decipher them. I have one more program to try, one called Logos, but I'll have to go to my office to access it."

Traussbery frowned furiously. "Well. Yes, well..." He sputtered as he pulled out a frayed wallet. "If there is any help I can offer, let me know, my dear."

Once again beside their table, serviette draped elegantly over his arm, Nigel spoke briefly with Traussbery. They shook hands generously, patted backs. After paying, Traussbery and Gatsby made their way to the front door and meandered through Covent Garden to the street.

"I must get into the city more often," Traussbery said as they strolled, passing the storefronts and kiosks on Berkshire Avenue, moving through the flurry of midday pedestrians.

"My lovely wife, Elise, used to love to visit the parks and museums. Ah, I miss her so." He stopped in front of a sedate blue Bentley. "Here we are. Do you need a lift, Ms. Donovan? I'll be glad to drive you."

Having watched Traussbery careen down the road when he had arrived at the restaurant, Gatsby couldn't help thinking of Eric Hardy. She shook her head vigorously. "No, thank you. It's beautiful today, and I feel like walking." That much was true. The afternoon sun shone gloriously on the bustling city streets, and her flat was less than a kilometer away.

"Very well." Traussbery struggled with the door and climbed into his driver's seat. "Do keep me apprised of your efforts, even the smallest detail. I will call you in a day or so." The engine roared to life, and as he slowly drove off, Gatsby could see the white hanky pressed to his lips.

She turned and started down the sidewalk, mentally revisiting the impromptu physics lecture. Traussbery's passionate convictions on shape-shifting quanta.

Personal experience, he had said.

Headed toward Piccadilly Circus, hands stuffed into her pockets, loose hair flying in the breeze, Gatsby thought of the photographs she'd brought back from Mazilaq. Those milky streaks, the ghostly images that almost looked like a startled face, staring at her. Into her.

She walked faster, toward the subway.

CHAPTER 14

Pushing the door open, Gatsby stepped inside her flat. No barking dog leaped to greet her; no mewing cat purred against her leg. No flatmate shouted greetings. She had lived alone since college and had only occasionally found it lonely. Whenever she needed company, she rang her friend and informal therapist, Celia Devereaux, who also happened to be a therapist by trade.

She hung her jacket in the hall closet and walked into the living room. The red light on her answering machine blinked rhythmically; she touched the play button. A due-for-a-follow up call from Dr. Berger. The machine clicked off, and Gatsby made her way to the kitchen. Little more than an overwide closet with slat-louvered French doors, it was made for the person who needed little more than a microwave, a can opener, and a few forks.

Opening the mini-refrigerator, Gatsby pulled out a carton of milk. *Intriguing*, she thought, reaching up to the cabinet for a glass. *Old Traussbery's like a rainbow marble. Every time you turn him over, you see a different color.*

The memory of the headlines in the papers, about the WHF conference ten years back, stole through her mind. Had *that* been him? Now that she'd met him, it seemed more likely that he was the person who had been almost literally thrown out of the conference for causing some kind of furor. Maybe he'd tried to convince the panelists of the legitimacy of—who knows what. But she could easily visualize a conservative international bureaucracy's reaction to Traussbery; five minutes with him and they'd go for his quantum jugular.

She sipped the cold milk and went to her study to check for e-mail messages. The PC on her desk grunted as she booted it up and stared at the screen. No new messages.

"Good," she said aloud and knew it was a lie. For some reason that evening, she really did want some company—someone besides the hacking professor and his snoring dogs. The frustrations of the last several weeks growled in her like a burgeoning ulcer. Her diet had become erratic. She'd neglected going to her health club, which had always been the best way to work out the mental stresses that tended to congeal in her muscles.

Nestled on the living room couch, feeling as bland as the milk in the glass, the quiet of the room weighed down on her. Because she hated things that clicked or tocked, she kept a purely digital and silent household. A car roared by on King's Road. She took another long sip, looking inward to stir the stew of emotions that simmered inside.

Since the trip to Peru, she had sensed herself becoming more and more entranced with the puzzle of the glyphs—and couldn't explain the intrigue. Yet while they fascinated her, they brought something that evaded labeling, a feeling that would slide past the window of her consciousness, peek in through the spy hole, and then mist away. Like an itch that you can't get at to save your life, it would begin to rise, just enough to almost get her attention, and then recede. An iceberg tip.

She sipped, wondering where such a feeling could come from—it was an entirely unique experience. How ironic that, that very morning, Traussbery had rambled on about scientific dogma. Avoidance of the grey areas. Her interior world had been, as far back as she could remember, shaped by a strict governess named Logic. As soon as she had been old enough to grasp the concept of scientific inquiry, she had fallen into its embrace. Sometime in grade school, she had come to the realization that there were things that people made up in their imaginations, and there were provable things that could be tried and found to be true. The truth came in the proving, not in the trying.

She thought back to the first time she came across a new language. The intrigue had taken her hostage. Sixteen years old, in her last year of middle school, she'd befriended an exchange student from Japan. Kimi had shown her the basics of written Japanese, and Gatsby had instantly wanted to learn the language. The foreignness of the strange characters that looked like spiderwebs had struck a spark inside her, created a feeling that words were much more than a puzzle. They were magical entities, sprites that could flit, soar, move right through you or change form at any time. The magic of the game was finding them out—being able to outwit the tricksters.

And the way to outwitting was through deliberation. Attention to minute, empirical detail.

A smile came to her face as a picture formed in her mind—her soft-spoken father reading to her when she was small enough to fit in his lap. Through Edith Hamilton's books, he had introduced her to the entire Greek and Roman pantheon of dramatis personae. A smattering of Shakespeare; she remembered laughing riotously as they'd read *A Midsummer Night's Dream* together and puzzled over the play within a play in *Hamlet*. Then he'd brought home C. S. Lewis and they were venturing into Narnia.

When she left home for her freshman year at Blake, she'd learned more and better ways to use her intellect and develop her reasoning abilities. Platonic discourse and Nietzschean deconstruction became the hammers that chipped away at things fanciful—or improvable. She had signed up for classes in world religions, anticipating that she would find more mythology, like the stories her gentle, loving father had read to her, and was not surprised to encounter the tales she had heard before.

Her father, Thomas Donovan, had ensured that his children would keep a lifelong eye toward literature by virtue of their names; Penelope, from classic myth, and his youngest, Gatsby, from the modern storyteller Fitzgerald. All her life, she'd gotten mixed reactions to her name; both her parents were fond of it, her sister thought it weird but neat, and her childhood friends had either thought it was wonderful or bizarre. More than once she'd been called "tomboy" or "girly boy" by a few of the less well read of her peers. But she had always liked it. It felt adventurous just to say it; its unusualness made her feel unique in a suburban Seattle neighborhood of Kathys, Lindas, and Susans.

She remembered, fondly, her love for languages sprouting from those early experiences with Kimi. Through high school and then college, she had studied French, then

Latin. By her junior year at Blake, mired in double majors of linguistics and philosophy, she had developed what she knew even then was a philological passion. She remembered in vivid detail the specific evening when the magic of words had become so real, so cerebrally intense, that she had to go into her dorm room, close the door, and lay down to hyperventilate with her eyes closed. Words were her soul mates; they were on terms with her more intimate than any real-world lover. With one possible exception: that dashing anthropology student, Woodrow Sanderson...

She looked down between her feet at the flat Berber carpet, the color of applesauce. Glanced up at the clock on the microwave. 6:14. She could catch the last of the evening's news. Setting her glass on the teak coffee table, the images from memory misting away, she rose and walked to the corner of the living room where a media center held her worn television. She found the remote beside the TV and clicked the power button.

The BBC4 news program winked on in the middle of a story on a government official accused of drug smuggling. Gatsby turned up the volume, went back to the couch with the remote, and sipped the milk while she watched. Another story on the economy and rising unemployment. Then something about a major EU Internet provider on the edge of bankruptcy. A few commercials, and then the last story of the program, which was usually some odd or funny bit. The dog who swam the English Channel, the boy who was added to the Guinness Book of World Records for receiving the most get-well cards—things like that.

A coifed, blonde anchorwoman (Janet Wright, the blue caption under her chin read) introduced it. "And now, our spotlight story. India is very much a country of mystic beliefs, and today, a story came in from Calcutta of an unusual man. Many of the rural towns in India have street healers and fakirs, or street magicians, who perform so-called miracles and claim to heal the sick. This man, who gives his name as Siranya, is a street fakir. He lives on the streets of Behala." On the screen was an image of a dirt road in the central market—dusty chickens and goats roamed about through a crowd of Hindu people, some in Western clothing, some in traditional Indian saris. In the middle of the crowd, a thin, bearded man squatted over a square of black fabric, rubbing his hands together and tossing something into the air that looked like pink flour.

Gatsby leaned forward, staring into the electronic images.

"Siranya claims to be able to diagnose and heal illnesses, to perform exorcisms, and to see the future. He also charms snakes, and each day he entertains a regular crowd of people in the market of his town by enchanting a cobra out of a wicker basket as he plays on a shehnai, a double-reed flute."

She's not doing a very good job hiding that smirk, Gatsby thought, watching the smile playing on the anchorwoman's carefully painted lips.

"This morning, however, the performer's show took a dangerous turn. While performing his snake charming, a mass of snakes emerged from the basket. The shocked fakir scrambled for safety, as did the frightened onlookers. Obviously, *that* part of the performance had not been planned. The snakes moved together into the middle of the dirt road and, as the spectators—and the fakir—watched, the snakes created a shape."

Gatsby felt hairs rising on her arms, her skin break into gooseflesh.

On the screen, she saw a mass of hissing snakes, their bodies twisting over and around each other. The camera view moved up to about six feet off the ground, above the snakes, and a distinct circular shape could be seen in the cumulative arrangement of their dark, slithering bodies. On either side of the circle, two distinct shapes emerged: two curved, wing-like shapes emerging from the upper and lower poles of the circle.

"The spectators, the fakir, and the members of the television crew, who had been covering another story, were all asked about the event, but no one had any idea how it could have happened." The camera moved to a close-up of the wiry fakir's face as he spoke rapidly in Hindi, his white turban bobbing. "Siranya insists that he does not know where the snakes came from. He keeps only one in his basket, a favorite black-spotted cobra that he has had for five years. Where the others came from, and how they could have all emerged from his basket and formed the shape, is a mystery even to him. As a performer of spectacles, which many of the people of the region still believe to be actual miracles, Siranya himself is the most amazed of all. He says that he believes it is an omen from Ganesha."

Gatsby swallowed. Her mouth tasted like a hangover.

Janet Wright's cover-girl face came back on the screen, smiling pleasantly. As she continued with her closing comments, her unnaturally white teeth sparkled in a smile that looked wry.

Godandmothermary, Gatsby thought, jerking to her feet. Her knee caught the edge of the coffee table and tipped the glass over, splashing milk onto the carpet. She barely had enough time to throw out a few choice words and remote-click the TV off as she ran to the desk in her study and grabbed a pen and a piece of paper.

Leaning over the desk, Gatsby concentrated and began to draw. She completed a circle, and then drew an upper and lower curve, originating at the twelve and six positions on a clock face.

She stared at it, breathing hard, the quiet of her flat so total that she could hear the bubbles of milk pop as they seeped into the carpet.

Nothing about the shape she had just drawn indicated that it should or could have anything to do with the two other glyphs. Yet she knew, viscerally, that it did. She knew.

"There's no way to prove that." Out loud, her own voice startled her. "The truth comes in the proving, not in the trying. We all know that, don't we?"

Don't we?

Visually tracing the curves she'd scrawled, Gatsby felt something drip down from her temple to her neck and then fall onto the paper. A bead of sweat. Yet the room was cool.

Watching the small dark circle spread through the paper fibers, she felt adrenaline racing through her body and into the core of her being. One drop, so small, yet it could affect an entire system. One small drawing on a piece of paper amid piles of papers and books—yet she knew that it was significant.

Three glyphs. Thebes. Mazilaq. And now this image created by snakes. Out of how many symbols? Meaning what? Coming from where? From what?

Standing over her desk, panting as if she'd just outrun an assailant, she thought frantically of how she would present the story of the Indian fakir's symbol-forming snakes to Traussbery. What his reaction would be, if he hadn't already read about it. If anything could cause a riot at an international scientific symposium, something like *this* would do it.

The pang of fear flaming in her chest was unmistakable. It poked against her lungs like the tip of a razor. It flared as she realized that *she'd seen this symbol before.*

This game of words isn't a game anymore, she thought.

CHAPTER 15

Her biceps screamed but she kept lifting; a twenty-pound weight didn't seem like much until the eighty-third rep.

Gatsby wheezed through her teeth, her shoulder blades pressing into the vinyl pad of the bench press. Her arm muscles shook so hard that the free weights hanging on each side of the bench rattled against each other, and she kept going, eyes squeezed shut.

Eighty-six, eighty-seven, eighty-eight...

The Chelsea Club was air conditioned in the summer, and even though cool air breezed across her skin, she was sweating like a bastard. Vaguely aware of the other people in the weight room, and more than vaguely aware of the two muscular guys blatantly staring at her, she pressed on toward one hundred, now grunting with each upward push. Streams of sweat ran down her temples.

The world disappeared in a fog of pain and panting, and all she heard was the jackhammer of her heart as she counted toward the finish: *Ninety-eight, ninety-nine, one hundred!*

The weighted bar clanged as she dropped it back into the cradles above her head. Her fingers seemed unable to let go of the steel bar; with slow deliberation, she peeled them off, one at a time. Swiping one forearm across her brow, she swallowed and lay still, letting her breathing slowly return to normal.

Not bad for a middle-aged desk-jobber, she thought, slowly sitting up on the bench. The two guys were still staring and smiling lecherously. She stared back until they lumbered back to their rowing machines.

Gatsby stood, finding her legs shaky, and wandered over to the stretching area of the weight room where padded mats were laid out on the floor. She found the closest one and dropped onto it, slid into a hurdler's position and leaned forward, feeling her hamstrings sigh with relief as they relaxed from the intense workout she'd just given them.

It had been weeks since she'd worked out. Instead of her usual fifty minutes on the stairstepper, she'd only managed twenty minutes, and her regular weight-lifting routines had all been cut short. Nonetheless, a good, sweaty workout had helped to work out some of the tension that had plagued her since the first day of her sabbatical and to take her mind off the mysterious events with which she'd been wrestling.

Sitting up and breathing in slowly through her nose and out through her mouth, Gatsby looked around the room. In the early afternoon, the club was mostly empty. The after-work crowd didn't come in until around six, so there were more college students and soccer-moms at the moment. The room was packed with equipment to work every muscle of the body, plus some treadmills, rowers, and step machines. The overhead lights reflected in their polished curves, and their steel parts clanged against each other rhythmically as they were pushed or pressed in a noisy orchestration that made Gatsby think of burly steel workers swinging sledgehammers. To her right, two women trudged eagerly on side-by-side treadmills, chattering as they fast-walked on the electronic platforms.

God, that felt good, Gatsby thought. *I know myself, too easily caught up in work, too mental. A good workout always relaxes me. A sound mind in a sound body, as Mom used to tell us.*

Out of nowhere, an image of Traussbery in weightlifter's trunks and with chalk on his hands bloomed in her head, and she burst out laughing as she stretched her quads.

After a few minutes, thoroughly sweat-dried and limp, she grabbed her towel and headed down the stairs at the back of the weight room to find Celia and the hot tub, where they had planned to rendezvous at 2:30.

"Ms. Devereaux." Gatsby gave a throaty laugh. "I can always find you by that perfume."

Reclining in the Jacuzzi tub, Celia smiled impishly. "Gatsby Donovan, imagine meeting you here at the Chelsea."

Even more tan than usual, Celia Devereaux looked as enticing as usual. Trim and petite, she was a woman whose natural beauty required little make-up, whose eyelashes were thick and dark without mascara, whose black, pageboy-styled hair needed little primping. She had a coltish demeanor, a mischievous smile that attracted men like a potent pheromone, and a sex drive that kept them. The young ones anyway. Summer was the peak of her mating season, and she was in full heat. From their conversations, Gatsby often wondered if a different pair of trousers hung over the foot of Celia's bed on any given night of the week.

Celia was one of the first people whom Gatsby had met in London, and they had immediately become good friends. She loved to cook, had a handful of lovers and the metabolism and stamina of a racehorse. She had a private therapy practice in Kensington and made a point of getting together with Gatsby a couple times a month to relate how she had blessed the male of the species with her tantric talents. She had no children and, apparently, no plans of ever settling.

A bright smile beamed from her tanned face. "Pop on in, dahling!"

Gatsby tossed her towel onto a wooden bench beside the tub and eased her naked body into the steaming, swirling water.

"Mmmmmmm." She slipped down opposite Celia with a long sigh.

"Bloody good to see you, Gats. We haven't talked in such a long time—I think it was Victoria Day! How have you been?"

More than a little confused, Gatsby thought. "Busy," she answered.

"Over your vacation?" A smirk stole into Celia's hazel eyes. "Doing what? Or should I say whom?"

Gatsby smiled wearily. "Nothing *that* interesting. You know me, I always take work home. I'm involved in a strange project."

Celia's eyebrows rose. "Do tell."

Gatsby related the events of the last few weeks: the phone call from Traussbery, their meeting and Quinn's photos, the impromptu trip to Peru, the news story from

India, and the unnerving feeling that while the strange glyphs might not have any meaning at all, for some reason, she felt that they did.

She let her head rest against the side of the tiled tub and let her clipped-back hair dip into the water. "It's the damnedest thing, Celia. We've known each other for six years, right? You know what a hardcore empiricist I am, how skeptical I am of anything that even faintly smells of mythology. I need proof, I need facts to be convinced of something. And I don't have any proof that these symbols mean anything, barely have proof that they buggering exist. But...I have this *feeling* that there's something in them, some...I don't know. Something I need to pay attention to."

The sides of Celia's refined French nose flared slightly. "If some part of you were to guess what that something might be—"

"Oh, stop, I can hear psychotherapy a mile away. Don't start analyzing me, I'm your friend, remember, not a client." Her tone was harsher than she had intended, and Gatsby realized how it would be taken. "Sorry. You know how much I like you, Celia. You're my best friend. But I've never felt comfortable about your profession."

Amusement moved over Celia's face. "Few people do, Gatsby dear. The ones who dig their heels in the deepest are my most regular clients."

Gatsby nodded, lips pursed. She moved her hands through the water, washing it up on her neck. "Maybe it comes from the one experience I *did* have with therapy."

"Oh?" Celia nodded, her eyes watchful.

The hot water felt soothing on her neck and shoulder muscles, and Gatsby tipped her head back again, moving down a dark corridor in her mind that she hadn't visited in many years. Long enough to have forgotten what lay behind the closed doors. Long enough to have allowed forgetfulness to partially erase the knowledge that the doors—or the corridor itself—existed.

She ran her tongue over her lower lip.

"My parents took me to a therapist when I was a kid. It was—well, I was nine or ten years old, and I remember going into a small office with nothing in it but some cushy chairs and fake plants. And a big window, and the smell of...god, what was it? Cologne, like British Sterling. I can't even remember the man's name. I went once a week for, oh, eight or nine weeks. It was fifth grade, I remember that. Penelope had started middle school, playing the violin in the school orchestra, and I was a regular fifth-grade troublemaker, pretending to be Harriet the spy, like the book, playing with my friends, making mud pies and picking wild peppermint in the field behind our house, and becoming interested in languages."

Celia nodded as Gatsby moved her hands in slow figure eights through the water. They were alone in the spa room, and the few women in the adjacent locker room were out of hearing range.

Gatsby breathed in deeply, staring into the water. "There was nothing...disconcerting about the experience, except..."

Celia let silence answer for her, her eyes telling Gatsby that she had all the time in the world and didn't mind getting pruney.

"That's...well, the heart of the matter," Gatsby said, all too conscious of her ragged sentences, "is that I don't really remember why they took me to see him."

"You don't remember?" Celia sounded suspicious.

"No, I just remember going to his office and talking about what I was doing in school, and who my friends were, and my favorite books. I...there didn't seem to be any problem that we discussed. At least any that I can remember." She cleared her throat, aware of the tightness in her stomach.

God, I haven't thought about this in close to a decade. Nothing to think about, really. But I never mentioned it to Celia until now...

"So I went to see, whatever his name was, for a while and that was it. It wasn't anything traumatic. That's the thing. I had a great childhood. Loving, happy family, no wacko dysfunctions, alcohol, violence, anything like that. The mystery is why I went at all." She shrugged noncommittally. "I can't fathom what it was about."

"Have you talked to your parents about it?"

Gatsby shrugged again. "Not in years. It just never came up. Not much to discuss, apparently."

In her mind, Gatsby watched the doors in that time-removed corridor closing, once again sheltering whatever might lie behind them. As the last door closed with a soft snick, her focus shifted back to the hot tub, her friend's worried face, and her aching muscles.

"But that's ancient history and not very interesting. I want to know what you have been up to, you she-devil." She grinned and splashed water.

Celia playfully splashed her back. "Old tricks."

They sniggered like naughty schoolgirls.

Celia rolled her eyes. "Oh, I've been seeing a Carlo. He's actually the son of one of my clients. Yes, I know, I do go for the young ones. And is he beautiful, like a Spanish matador. Graceful and so macho that I'm convinced he swills testosterone on the rocks. He's rotten and rough and a nasty bully—and I think I'm in love." She laughed until she gasped for air. "Of course I'm joking, Gats, don't look at me that way! I'm hardly in jeopardy. The day that I squeeze a gold band around my finger and pop out a litter of brats is the day you have permission to put me down, I swear to god."

Gatsby put on her best serious face. "Which do you prefer, wench, arsenic or pistol?"

Laughing riotously, they both scrambled out of the tub to hit the showers.

The subway ride home, for once, was almost serene. Most of the seats were empty—unheard of late on a Thursday afternoon. Gatsby mused on how the workout, hot soak, and chat with Celia had had a fantastically tranquilizing effect, like a good stiff drink or a vigorous bout of lovemaking.

Been even longer in that department. Guess it's up to Celia to compensate for me there. I work too damn much, Gatsby thought, closing her eyes, the rhythmic bumping and swaying of the subway car lulling her. She stared out the window, watching the station signs roll by. King's Road was six minutes away.

As her stop rolled into view, she grabbed her gym bag, rose, and made her way through the hissing car doors out onto the platform.

A five-minute walk and she was back in her flat, checking the answering machine.

Gatsby dumped her sweaty workout clothes into the plastic laundry bin in her bedroom and then hefted the basket onto one hip. In a flat built for maximum economy, her hall closet held a stacking washer and dryer, each no wider than a briefcase. They sat beside a rack of storage shelves and the cranky water heater.

The image of Nigel, silently pouring her beer at the Punch & Judy, came to her mind as she tugged T-shirts and underwear out of the basket and began tossing them into the maw of the washer. The conversation with Traussbery about Stonehenge had been fermenting in her mind, the bubbles of consternation popping like the fizz of a carbonated soft drink.

Unballing a tangle of socks, Gatsby watched a vivid picture of Stonehenge form on her internal screen. She'd been there so many times that it was easy to do. The parking lot, with restrooms and snack bar. The entrance booth, where the plump Italian woman named Rosalie had sold entrance tickets for years. The tunnel that took you underneath the A334 motorway and then up, out onto the plain. The pathway, roped off to keep visitors at least five meters away from the stones. The outer ditch, Aubrey holes, station stones, and north and south barrows. The remains of what was left of the outer circle of great trilithons. Within that, the outer bluestone circle. The remaining uprights of the horseshoe of sarsen trilithons—the pieces that remained, while the others had fallen, broken, or been scavenged away. Then, finally, the innermost horseshoe or bluestones and the fallen Alter Stone. Toward the southeast, directly in line with the sunrise on the summer solstice, the fallen Slaughter Stone, the tipped Heel Stone, and beyond, the Avenue, leading away from the site into the distance, a pathway that almost seemed to pull the observer from the present back in time to millennia before.

The image was so clear that she could almost hear the chirps of the swallows that roosted in cracks where the mortices had eroded away. Almost smell the clover grass that grew at the base of the sarsens. Almost see the dagger-shaped carvings on one of the five great trilithons.

Carvings. Gatsby stopped, gripping a T-shirt, her arm in midair.

Were they dagger-shaped? Were there any triangles? Any cross shapes? Frowning, she dropped the laundry basket to the carpet and made her way into her study.

Scanning her shelves of books, she located the corner that had been given to titles on Stonehenge. There were seventeen of them, everything from the astronomy and archeological studies to the mythology and folklore. Which one had the full-page color photo she was thinking of? She perused the spines and finally spotted it: *Britain's Mysterious Monuments* by Caitlin McNeil.

Gatsby reached up to the hardbound book and pulled it down. She sat the book on the polished surface of her mahogany desk and flipped through it.

The photograph she'd remembered was in the middle of the book—a two-page, color spread. It was a fairly close shot, taken perhaps two to three meters from the closest stones, which happened to be the second trilithon, Stones 53 and 54.

That's it, and I remembered correctly, they are dagger-sh...

Her focus zeroed in as she pulled in a soft gasp. On the plane of the adjacent Stone 56 was an unfamiliar carving. But it didn't quite look like a carving, more like something drawn on the stone. It had a vertical bar and, from the right side of the bar, a short horizontal bar emerged and ended in a crescent shape, like a quarter moon.

What th...

She felt herself backpedaling from the onslaught of contradictions, in the face of another instance, like those she'd faced in the last several weeks, where rational thought was challenged or discarded entirely.

I have read this book dozens of times and seen dozens of photos in dozens of other books but never seen this in any of them!

The muscles that she had worked loose were contracting; her heart thundered in her chest.

Am...I...losing...

The thought would not give full answer, would not.

She spun and pulled down the sixteen other books—Mavens, Stafford, Drebek, Addison, Killee, Padennoy, and others. Pawed through each one, searching for photos of Stone 56. There were dozens of examples of the same shot, from slightly different angles, under different conditions—summer, winter, at morning, at dusk, with visitors, without. Drawings, sketches, outlines of the formations, artists' renderings of the site in its formative stages.

Nowhere, in any of the sixteen, did she see Stone 56 with the shape—a sideways T attached to a crescent moon—that appeared in McNeil's book.

Going back to the open text, Gatsby felt her left arm raise, her hand creep toward the photo. Felt her fingers slide toward it and a deep urgent need to touch that image, an aching to caress it with her fingertips. As if the book contained a negative magnet and her finger a positive, her hand moved on its own, until the tip of her index finger rested on the crescent shape that had never appeared anywhere, in any photograph of Stonehenge, in any time.

Or had it?

Has it? HAS IT?? A voice shrieked inside Gatsby's head, a voice she didn't recognize but couldn't ignore. *Where did this shape come from? And WHAT is it doing in a photograph where it's NEVER appeared before!?*

The muscles of both hands jerked violently, acrid sweat seeped into the armpits of her blouse.

Close the book.

She tried. She wanted to. She tried again. But messages from the brain weren't being received. The *deus ex machina* leapt about, poking its tongue out at her, mocking her. Her finger was stuck, paralyzed in a locked position, unable to move from the symbol on which it rested, the glyph that couldn't possibly exist.

Shaking and barely able to pull in air, Gatsby felt the frustration and horror inside her spasm into a new entity: anger. It became a fireball in her stomach, lurching up like bile through her body and into her brain, transmuted, as if by alchemy, into rage.

"What—what the FUCK is GOING ON!?!" The cry ripped at her throat. She tore her left hand away, almost expecting it to rip a swatch of paper up with it. Holding her hand in front of her face, the terror she'd felt back in her office—when her left hand had defected from the commonwealth of Donovan—poured back into her. Glassy-eyed, she stared at her hand and then at the photograph in McNeil's book. With her right hand, she slowly closed the book and turned it over, cover face down on the desk.

Nothing magical happened. The digital clock on the microwave blinked greenly—5:58.

She sank into the chair next to her desk, breathing hard through her nose, in and out, rhythmically, unconsciously falling into a breath-control technique that she'd learned in a yoga class. It was the only method currently available to cope with the chaos of thoughts that clamored, every one demanding *an answer, an answer, an answer.*

One huge breath sucked in, held for five seconds, and then released brought momentary calm. She licked her lips, swallowed past a dry throat, and walked to the kitchen, leaving a pile of books scattered across her desktop.

Her hands had almost stopped shaking.

They weren't completely steady as she tossed shots of Kahlua and brandy into a glass, splashed them with milk, and raised it to her lips. But, gratefully, they did the job.

I do NOT want to do this anymore. It's making me loony. I don't want to think about this anymore. I just want to drop this whole fucking thing and forget about it and get out of town, like I had planned in the first place. I want off this train—next stop.

She downed the drink in one eye-watering gulp and walked down the hallway to return to loading the clothes washer. By the time she had closed the avocado-green lid and turned the dial to start, she had already decided to drive to Stonehenge the next morning.

CHAPTER 16

For reasons unknown, Gatsby downed a completely uncharacteristic breakfast—a huge plateful of eggs, potatoes, and fruit salad. With Sumatran espresso rocketing across her synapses, she loaded her daypack with research journals, a notepad, pens, and a camera.

Her Volvo was particularly cranky as she got on the motorway, heading west from London, but by the time she flew through Guildford and Farnham on A31, it hummed along without a hitch.

Although she hadn't been to Stonehenge in almost a year, she knew that the drive took the better part of two hours. She settled back in the driver's seat and stuck her right arm out the window to capture the June breeze.

The sparsely populated towns sleeping beside the motorway soon turned into rolling hills and farmland. She saw fields dotted with small structures that she knew were akin to kennels for pigs. And all around, there were barrows—earthen burial mounds, the ones for which Great Britain was famous.

The day was good for photographs—warm sunshine and clear skies—and Gatsby thought, *If my camera is inexplicably unable to photograph whatever is out there, then I'm going to throw in the towel and become a scuba instructor.*

She found a parking spot and pulled up the brake, staring, her chin slack.

Whatever had happened, it had attracted a media crowd. Minivans sporting the logos of all four British television networks had jammed the parking lot at the Visitor's Centre, their side doors open and electronic guts spilling out. A half-dozen cameramen were hoisting gear onto their shoulders or had already made their way through the entrance gate and into the pedestrian tunnel. The air sizzled with electricity and brusque shouts as field reporters tamped down their cowlicks and checked their teeth in their rearview mirrors. Above the din of engines and snapping cables, Gatsby heard shouting. At the entrance gate, a portly woman was waving her arms to ward off a group of three reporters as another group pushed through the turnstile.

There's Rosalie. Gatsby grabbed her pack, locked her car door, and wove her way through the automotive chaos.

"Rosalie!" she shouted as she neared. The woman peered in her direction, and her plump face slowly registered recognition.

"Ms. Donovan?"

"That's right." Gatsby strolled up beside her, pushing an errant strand of hair off her face. "Gatsby Donovan. I remember you from the British Museum. You volunteered there a few years ago, right?"

The Italian woman's dark eyes brightened and she pulled her hands from the pockets of her blue uniform to wave them enthusiastically. "Yes! And you worked in, ooh, Conservatory?"

"Manuscripts," Gatsby said. "Rosalie, what the hell's going on? What are the media doing here?"

The woman pressed both hands to her cheeks and then did a strange thing; she crossed herself. The gold hoops dangling from her earlobes glittered as she drew Gatsby close and whispered, "You better see for yourself, Ms. Donovan."

Pulling out of Rosalie's grasp, Gatsby stepped back, threw the strap of her pack over one shoulder and said, "I'll do just that. May I?" She gestured toward the entrance gate, just to the left of a snack bar counter where a tall, blue-jacketed reporter was ordering a Pepsi.

Rosalie nodded energetically, her eyes wide and her red lips pressed tightly.

"Thanks." Gatsby bumped the reporter's paper cup as she pushed through the turnstile. The path ahead of her led into a tunnel that dipped underneath the motorway, the A334, and rose up to ground level again on the other side. It then became an asphalt walking trail that curved around the perimeter of Stonehenge.

The tunnel was cool and dark, damp as a sea cave, and when she emerged on the other side, the bright sunlight made her squint until her eyes adjusted. She stared out onto Salisbury Plain and was almost knocked over as a man carrying a floodlight barreled by on her right.

"...obvious that it happened sometime last night," a reporter, a few meters in front of her, was saying, facing the lens of a camcorder. Behind him, a throng of journalists shoved and scrambled for better views. He continued, "Investigators from the Yard have been called to see if they can identify the party responsible for this un—ooof!—this unbelievable deed." A policeman had abruptly elbowed the reporter in the jaw as he hurried by; the reporter rubbed his cheek with a sardonic look.

The atmosphere was a state as opposite to its normal serenity as it could have possibly been. In addition to the vans full of newscasters filling the parking lot, a clamoring crowd of tourists and academics had now filled the curved walkway around the site. The squeal of a police whistle cut the air; reporters tried to shove their way into or at least closer to the restricted area, each one followed by a sweating cameraman who jogged along with television equipment bouncing on his shoulder.

Gatsby walked up to the nearest reporter, who had finished his take and was now sipping from a sports bottle.

"Can you tell me what this is all about?"

He turned toward her, derisively. "Who are you?"

Returning his sarcastic look, she said, "I'm with the British Museum."

He took a sip of water and pointed. "Then you'll be very interested by what you see out there."

As her gaze followed the direction of the reporter's hand, Gatsby felt her eyes widen. She started down the path, swerving to avoid other journalists, cameramen, lighting crews, and onlookers.

The stones came into view.

Her eyes followed the upward lines of the sarsens and then traced the lines of the few remaining horizontal lintels.

Staring at the world-renowned stones, she felt, as she had on so many other occasions, a visceral surge of awe.

At the location of the tallest sarsen, Stone 56, the remaining upright of the great central trilithon, there was a gaping hole ripped in the earth.

Gatsby swallowed, eyes darting. Near the south edge of the perimeter ditch, she spotted a closely huddled group. As she walked toward them, she saw what they were looking at and a groan moved in her throat.

"No," she whispered hoarsely.

Stone 56, twenty-two feet high and forty-five tonnes, was now twenty meters south of the location it had occupied for four thousand years. Adjacent to the South Barrow and tipped at a steep angle, it jutted upward from the ground as if it had been tossed like a javelin. Two-thirds of the sarsen were still visible—the *upper* two thirds. The rounded tenon shape attested to its unchanged uprightness. It had not been upended, it had simply been relocated.

Simply.

The crowd standing around the stone, Gatsby noted, seemed to be scholarly types: archeologists, geologists, professors. Numb with shock, she moved toward them to listen in on what their conversation, to find out if they had any straw of logic to explain what she could not believe even though looking right at it. But the chatter of the media crowd drowned out their murmurings—she caught only snippets, units of measurement, speculation on the time of day, chemical and textural changes in the grass and soil abutting the rock. Gatsby imagined that what she was hearing was akin to the conversations of murder scene investigators as they hovered over a cooling body.

"Hey! Out of the way so we can get a shot!" a cameraman shouted from somewhere to the right.

The group of scholars turned. It became apparent that none of them would do what they were all thinking, so Gatsby did it for them and raised a middle finger. With a disgusted expression, the cameraman turned and started talking to one of the other reporters.

She sighed and tugged at the sleeve of the man nearest her, a lanky, long-faced gentleman in a tweed jacket, holding a thick notebook. "Excuse me, does anyone have a clue as to...uhm..." She stopped, flustered.

His blue eyes turned on her as he made a despondent sound. "My dear, just look at it. By all reports, as of yesterday afternoon, Stonehenge was as it has been since the Bronze Age. Early this morning, it was found thus. What do you suggest? Dust for fingerprints? If you have any brilliant ideas, enlighten us."

Gatsby cleared her throat, toying with the straps of her pack. "Sorry." She moved in closer to examine the front of the stone, and then walked around to peer at the backside. Both sides showed the dents and scratches where the stone had been chiseled to shape with heavy stone hammers, millennia ago. And at the top, the curved tenon projected up toward the sky. It was exactly as it had appeared since the age of the construction of the Pyramids. Twenty meters from where it belonged.

She stared hard, her eyes scanning across the rough grey surface, looking for anything even vaguely crescent- or moon-shaped.

Nothing.

"Son of a bitch," Gatsby heard herself murmur. The scholars glanced at her; heads nodded, chins were scratched.

She slipped away and made her way toward a private path that was reserved for researchers. It wound her around the site to its northeast point, near where the Slaughter Stone stood close to the motorway, and then to the easternmost side of the site. From that angle, she had the best view of the second trilithon. Gatsby sat her pack down on the asphalt walkway and took a long look at the stones.

It dawned on her then that on the second trilithon, Stones 53 and 54, triangular carvings had been found. These glyphs had been studied exhaustively since the first legitimate studies of Stonehenge in the 1600s by John Aubrey. Most of the markings were arrow- or dagger-shaped and were thought to represent weapons in use at the time of

Stonehenge's second construction phase: the early Bronze Age, about 1800 BC.

She thought back to the night before, sitting at her mahogany desk, slamming her fist on the pages of McNeil's book as frustration had rolled through her. The same sensation began to move in her again, and she swept it away in weary resignation. It wouldn't do any good. There was nothing there to see, no strange symbol that anyone had ever seen, except for her. And here at the site, even her. Anger wouldn't change that one iota.

She pulled her camera out anyway, sighted Stone 56, and took a sequence of shots.

A whoosh made her whirl around—a caravan of cars, all with the English Heritage emblem on their sides, zoomed by on the motorway. She watched as they screeched into the parking lot at the Visitor's Centre like ambulances hell-bent for chalk outlines.

Gatsby slowly made her way back to the public pathway and stood mutely gazing at the chaos around her. At the entrance to the underground tunnel, she stopped. The media people, increasing in number by the minute, raced around, shouting, tripping over their cables and scribbling in their notebooks, all jousting for positions where they could get the best view of the relocated stone. She felt a little sickened by their frenzied opportunism but, at the same time, felt the import of getting a story like this into the public awareness.

Gatsby stared back at the monument, blankly, not really seeing it. The still-shot of Stonehenge as it used to look burned in her deep memory. She'd seen pictures of it all the way back to childhood, and it was *supposed* to look a certain way. The way that the Mona Lisa was *supposed* to look like the Mona Lisa or the Eiffel Tower was *supposed* to look like the Eiffel Tower. Now Stonehenge looked *wrong*. It wasn't Stonehenge anymore. And in its altered state, it was both damaged and defiled. It had lost something essential.

There were some things in this world that were supposed to be unchangeable. Fixed, forever.

Someone had indeed painted a big, black mustache on the Mona Lisa.

The knot in her stomach tightened as she turned her back on the crowd and the violated site and walked into the black mouth of the tunnel.

During the drive back to London, Gatsby stared vacantly through the front windshield. She left the radio off.

In Ovington, she stopped at a grocery store and nodded wordlessly at the cashier as she paid for a can of iced tea.

It was almost seven by the time she turned onto King's Road and pulled into her garage.

Sprawled on her couch, Gatsby stared at the eggshell-colored ceiling. With hands that felt heavy as lead, she turned over, picked up the phone, and called Traussbery. She heard three rings and then a scratchy voice.

"Traussbery? It's Gatsb—"

"I heard—the whole bloody world knows by now!" he blurted. She heard him cough hoarsely. "Dear god. Now I hear that English Heritage has shut down the site, no one will be allowed in for the next two weeks. Blast all! This cannot be hushed up like a Household scandal!"

Good god, he's raving, Gatsby thought. "Traussbery, what's the matter with you? You sound as if you were personally responsible." She sighed. "It's rattled me too, you know. I was there today, I saw the looks on the faces, talked with the archeologists at the site. It's a complete violation. That's clear. But we can't act like the buggering Virgin Mary has appeared at Zeitoun or we've been serenaded by extraterrestrials. We're scientists, for...Traussbery? Are you there?"

She heard ragged breathing. Then, softly, "Forgive my outburst. Rattled. Yes, that's the word. Rattled. It is most unnerving. *Most* unnerving. A place so deeply entrenched in the global psychology is changed. Perhaps irreparably. And—" She heard him swallow. "It is such a shock. A mystery. The place is such a mystery to begin with, as you and I both know—we spoke of its mystery just the other day, did we not! And now something has changed the visage of Stonehenge forever."

Gatsby heard the quiver in his voice and wondered if he was about to burst into tears. In a moment, she heard him take a shaky breath. "A tragedy." He was silent.

After a pause, Gatsby said, "Professor, I understand. Just like the sun needs to rise every morning, Stonehenge needs to look like Stonehenge. And now it doesn't. I would think that the stone will somehow be unearthed and moved back, but that doesn't change the fact that somehow, someone took it upon himself to diddle with one of the world's most important archeological sites." She heard more ragged breathing and coughing. "Professor? Are you all right?" Suddenly panicked, she thought, *Don't have a bloody heart attack and die on the phone, you old bastard!*

"I'm just exhausted. The whole thing has overwhelmed me. I must get some sleep. I haven't...felt well all day. I'll speak with you tomorrow, Ms. Donovan."

"All right. Good night."

She hung up the phone with a deep sigh.

I don't know how much more of this I can take, she thought. Her frontal lobe throbbed miserably. She pressed her fingers to her temples and massaged; a headache was starting to boil between them. In the frantic phone conversation, she'd forgotten to tell Traussbery about the new and equally inexplicable glyphs: the snakes in India and the image that appeared in McNeil's book. On Stone 56.

She took three aspirin and threw herself on her bed.

CHAPTER 17

Like giant furry Mexican jumping beans, the Shih Tzus hopped frantically as Traussbery shoveled gooey dog food into their bowls. He straightened with a groan, hands to his lower back where the arthritis was singing music hall numbers.

Traussbery shuffled through the small, Spartan flat, cleaning up his evening meal, tidying the daily newspaper. It had been a long day of teaching, office hours, a dry departmental meeting, and the short but bothersome drive home. Because so many of the students and the population of Cambridge traveled by bicycle, it made life rather miserable for motorists.

He settled down on the worn sofa in his living room to review a textbook on ancient China and took a look around the room, noticing, perhaps for the first time, how dreadfully quiet his house—and his life—had become since Elise had died. Each morning, the silver-framed photographs on the walls reminded him of how much he missed her. The fireplace was cold and dark, rarely used. The burgundy curtains she had hung on the windows had been taken down long ago and put into storage.

A lump grew in his throat as memory overtook him: the day they celebrated at the beach, after the phone call informing him that he had been offered a professorship at the University of Cambridge.

How we celebrated, he thought with a smile, then a grimace. *And she never knew of my crime.*

In the quiet, he heard the dogs licking up their meal and the click of their nails on the hardwood floor as they trotted toward him. They jumped onto the sofa next to him, panting breath that smelled of tinned beef by-products.

"I never told anyone," Traussbery said to the dogs, which looked up at him, their pink tongues dangling like hooked shrimp. "How could I?" He laid the textbook on the floor, then pulled from the pocket of his cardigan a soft leather pouch containing his pipe and lighter. He lit the pipe and puffed thoughtfully as he spoke out loud. The dogs settled in on either side as if they had heard his stories many times before.

"When I had the opportunity to join the research team in Cuzco—what archeologist could pass that up? I went and climbed the stairs up into the Throne Room, and I saw the strange symbol...yes, the same one that our friend Ms. Donovan has seen. None of my travel companions saw it, and what did I think at the time? That either the altitude had warped my senses or that I had eaten something quite hallucinogenic. In either case, I thought it was a one-time occurrence. Yet the image stuck in my mind. Not only the image, but the mystery of its appearance, as a shadow appears when a cloud moves over the sun."

He puffed at the pipe, then coughed. The dogs dug into the warm trenches beside his scrawny legs. In the dim room, his voice sounded weary, even to himself.

"The experience reconstructed my beliefs about physical phenomena. Process of elimination chiseled at my theories about that symbol. No other person, either at the scene or later, had seen it. Only I. If hallucination, it was mine alone. If real—was it also mine alone? Not a completely preposterous thought. But with no further experiences to confirm the hypothesis, I could do nothing but ruminate on it. Until a year later."

The fatter Shih Tzu sneezed.

"Gesundheit, Seti," Traussbery muttered. The other dog, Khufu, looked up, sleepy and slightly perturbed.

"I was finally considered for Cambridge. Yes. The year Elise and I toured the Balkans. I completed the letters, the interviews. I remember speaking with Hugo Davidson, the kindly old bastard. He took me under his wing, said he'd speak with the committee members, probably when they were in their cups and suggestible. He wanted me to have the appointment, that much I know. And as we walked Billings Commons, he told me that only one other candidate would be considered for the post. Nor—"

Traussbery's voice quivered to a stop; he stared out the window as if searching the heavens for his next syllable.

"Norton. Travis Norton. From Croyden."

The tobacco embers blazed as Traussbery sucked in quick breaths, and the hand holding the pipe trembled.

"Croyden. Schooled in the States and Africa, I heard. I had never met him, of course, until, until—"

He sighed heavily. "Until that day at the WHF conference in Luxembourg. I gave my paper on archaeokinesis, and they threw me from the podium. Toffee-nosed peelers! Blinded with dogma! They wouldn't listen, denied everything. When I'd had enough badgering, I left the room and stumbled down the hall to the book salon. Wandered a bit to calm down, to investigate the recent titles my colleagues had published, and literally backed into Travis Norton."

The dogs rested their chins on Traussbery's knobby knees. He patted one on the head as he continued, his voice now gravelly.

"What fates were at work? Who could know? We introduced ourselves and entered into mundane small talk. But the second that I heard him say his name, unabashed hostility came over me. Perhaps it was suppressed rage, from the torment following my presentation. I had to get that post, I deserved it! Davidson was doing his best for me, but still this *prat* from Croyden was, was in the way. I thought of Elise—what would I tell her if Norton were awarded the post instead of me? The more I thought of it, the angrier I became, my body shook with agitation..."

Traussbery sat the pipe down in a heavy glass ashtray on his end table. Eyes closed, he gingerly massaged his temples.

"Then I realized that the shaking wasn't *me*, it was the bookcase. The huge case just behind Norton, packed with heavy textbooks, shaking as if an earthquake had struck. Nothing else in the room, just the case. The books jittered against the wooden shelves...at first he didn't notice, but as I stared and it increased, he finally turned, turned and saw, shock and horror on his face...I could see what was happening, the case was top-heavy and standing near a runway, not against a wall, and so not braced against anything, and the thought blazed through my mind, *it will fall on him!* Again, the words ran through my fevered mind—*it will fall on him!* What would that mean? What else could it mean? I could see the entire scenario in my head, full-blown, like a still from a film—Norton on the carpet beneath mounds of textbooks, splinters and shards of broken wooden beams, one edge of the case bloodied where it had struck his cranium—I saw the scene, I *saw* it. I concentrated on it, I envisioned it *as if it had already happened.* The picture crystallized in my mind and I watched the case tip— he saw it too but it was too late, he ducked, just as the books from the top of the shelf began to pelt him, but in the blink of an—"

Traussbery opened his eyes, staring blankly. The dogs snored.

"It all fell, case and books, knocking him to the floor, and I, who had seen it coming and said not a word of warning, I dove out of the way. He screamed, and it was lost in the crash and splintering as he was knocked unconscious. And my shouts, my cries for help. Too late. Whatever acuity had allowed me to see the glyph of the Coricancha had also enabled me to use that willed vision to cause the case to fall and crush Norton. To open the door to my Cambridge post. As—"

His hand rose, cradling his double chins.

"As it did, of course. The ambulance came, they took him to Saint Beatrice, bleeding and incoherent. The medics asked what had happened. I told them that it was a disastrous accident from which I had, luckily, escaped."

As Traussbery wheezed to get his wind back, he heard the wail of an ambulance rising from outside.

"Norton is still there, with machines to pump his heart and lungs for him, tubes to feed him. But no life—"

As tears sprang, Traussbery choked back a sob, which brought on a fit of coughing. He dabbed at his eyes with the sleeve of his frayed sweater.

"No life remains. The man's life is gone, he's just a shell of a human being. And I have been at Cambridge for ten years now. Davidson clapped me on the back. Congratulations—As one man's fortune decreases, another's increases. Yet I knew the heinousness of my act, the ruthlessness of my self-centered greed. It cost Norton everything and rewarded me with the position I'd worked for all my life."

Tears rolled down his cheeks, and Traussbery found himself amazed that he could still cry for the past. The incident was a long-buried memory, buried as deeply as it possibly could be, and bringing it all up fresh, speaking the words out loud as he had never done before, brought sobs more gut-wrenching than he had ever known. Not, at least, since Elise's funeral.

The dogs opened their eyes, snuffled at his noises, and pawed at his hands.

"I had caused it. The symbol in Peru appeared only to me, and I knew that somehow I had an ability to literally see things that others couldn't, to physically effect things that others couldn't. I was and am convinced that I had caused that case to tip. To eliminate the competition! Who could suspect—who would suspect an acclaimed professor of archeology? A mild-mannered codger, grey and dickey, with a lovely wife and a summer home in Brighton. Who would suspect such a character?"

He swiped a tear off the end of his nose and then rustled the dogs as he dug into his pants pocket to retrieve his wallet. Inside it, he found a small scrap of paper with a phone number penciled on it. He stared at it, his heart booming cannon fire in his chest. Traussbery cleared his throat, coughed, and looked up at the telephone hanging on the wall by the kitchen. The dogs moaned as he rose and walked toward it.

Fool! he thought, dialing.

The line connected to Saint Beatrice Memorial Hospital and clicked a few times.

Traussbery's palm began to ooze sweat against the plastic shell of the phone; he felt his pulse throbbing in his head.

Another click as the call transferred to Room 502.

He sagged against the doorjamb; the weights on his shoulders were pushing him into the earth.

One ring...two...

I can't! he thought.

The line picked up; there was stertorous breathing.

"Hhhhh..."

He slammed the phone down into its receiver, gasping. He licked his lips.

Traussbery fidgeted with the edges of his sleeves as he walked back to the sofa and repositioned himself between the dogs. He thought of Gatsby Donovan and the conversation they'd had at the Punch & Judy.

I'm a murderer, he thought.

It was 11:28.

CHAPTER 18

An angular face with questing, hazel eyes...in her twelve-year-old voice, Penelope asks, "Gats, want another M & M?" She giggles, reaching her hand into an orange and black bag, retrieving a handful of wrapped goodies...

She's walking through a field, knee-deep in wet weeds, and as the weeds thin to soft grass, the field becomes a quad, a giant square of lawn divided by footpaths at forty-five-degree angles and full of students, hurrying toward their fall term classes. Tang in the air, crisp, leaves underfoot, the glint of the sun low in the sky...Carver Hall, the lounge for architecture students and the best place on campus to study because of the deafening silence that makes even coffee slurps unbearable...the face of her favorite professor, Joanna Hunt, German and elegant, proper but not averse to a few of life's pleasurable vices. In her office, reviewing the paper on Kant...Professor Hunt settles into her chair, pulls a large volume from her bookshelf, places it on the desk in front of Gatsby...what images does the book hold? She peers down into the pages, to see...

...a box...more like a sarcophagus, and inside it a woman lies naked, eyes closed. Her skin glows with a golden sheen, almost as if she has been airbrushed head to foot with gold paint. Her almond-shaped eyes open, black pupils. She slowly rises, stands, and opens her mouth, about to speak, but then simply raises her hand and presses an index finger over her lips...no sound. No words. No language...

Gatsby moaned softly and rolled over; the dream continued...

A small office with a long green couch, an overstuffed chair, fake plants and tall windows. Outside, a parking lot, a post office, and apple trees. The quiet man with round glasses seats himself in the chair, folds his hands in his lap, and smiles. "Gatsby, you're pretty good at this!"

Her small body, ten years old, still in pigtails, still brown with a summer tan, lean from swimming in Alton Lake. She tosses back, "Yeah, I am."

"You know how to start."

She sits back on the couch, palms down on its velour, playing with the nap. Quiet hands, quiet eyes...her eyes close. "The beach, when it's the end of summer and no one's there." A prepubescent voice, later to drop to a rich alto. Fingertips still rubbing the nap back and forth, a scratch on her neck and then both hands come to rest in her lap, on jean-covered legs. Swallow. "No one's there. Seagulls and seashells. Waves that splash on my toes. Playing Frisbee with Penelope, and Mom and Dad bring sandwiches and the sand gets in your teeth when you eat them."

She smiles. The memory is vibrant enough to heat her cheeks with remembered sunburn.

"Ritz crackers and peanut butter...Penelope likes Dr. Pepper and I get a cup of lemonade."

The man in the chair is wearing a cotton T-shirt and drawstring pants, has small gold glasses and very white teeth. A dark mustache, short beard. A soothing, quiet voice, a good voice for telling bedtime stories. He tells her a lot of jokes and they're all pretty dumb but he's nice. He takes a long, slow breath and as he exhales, he says, "That's right. Crackers and peanut butter. The waves. The end of summer." Another long breath, and as he breathes in, he says, "Remember breathing in the air at the beach, the warm air that smells like the beach...that's right..."

She feels herself taking in a slow breath. Her hands feel heavier in her lap, her body heavier on the couch.

"And perhaps you brought a friend with you...do you have a friend who might have come with you on your trip to the beach?"

"Sometimes Dana comes with us to the beach. Or she stays over at my house."

"Stays over at your house...good...and when she stays over at your house..."

Eyes closed. Body sinking into the cushions of the green couch, the sun warm, coming through the window. Smell of *the cologne, the kind grownup men wear. Her head tips, hair pressed against the back of the couch. Another long slow breath...more questions...it feels like she's falling asleep but it isn't sleep, just imagining and talking to the nice man...*

"Do you like to read books? What's your favorite book?"

"Uhmmm...Harriet the Spy..."

"Did you read that in school?"

Car pulling up outside, in the parking lot. The man asks more questions. She feels sleepy and warm, the smell of cologne...did someone else come with her to the beach?

"...and who else do you like to play with?"

Seagulls flying overhead, screeching.

She opens her eyes, stands up and looks across the room...the far wall of the room has vanished and just beyond the grey carpeting she sees grass. She walks toward the grass, behind her the man and the room and the fake plants fade away and she's walking in tall grass, hot sun overhead. Mixed in with the grasses are brambles that stick in her socks...a barren patch over to the right where neighborhood kids are building a fort, digging into the dirt to make a sunken secret fort, covered over with plywood stolen from the construction site...ten years old, running through the field. It's summertime, and her field is where the queen lives and the dragon follows her. The field is where gigantic trees grow and you can eat the bark because it's peppermint bark. The field is where all the animals talk to her and are her friends, the mice, the lions, the squirrels, the monkey and the hippo named Mopey who's miserable all the time but likes to hang around with her...

Skipping through the grass, she reaches out and takes the girl's hand...they look at each other, smiling and laughing...the girl's eyes twinkle mischievously as she raises a finger to her lips to quiet Gatsby, and then the girl's hands begin to move in the air, quick gestures with the right hand, slower, intermittent movements with the left...Gatsby stares, watching the movements, and then repeats the movements with her own hands...they laugh together under their breath, dash through the meadow toward the tall peppermint tree where the dragon lives, and surprise him out of his sleep...

The two girls climb up into the tree, settling in a crotch of thick branches...Gatsby turns to look at the girl and notices something different about her...her eyes suddenly look darker, more almond shaped...her hair is now long and black, her teeth beautifully white against her soft brown cheeks...a slightly flattened nose...

Gatsby raises her hands in front of her face and completes a short burst of gestures...the girl smiles back at Gatsby, props her feet up on the tree trunk, closing her eyes and soaking in the warmth of the sun...they pull strips of peppermint bark off the tree branches and slurp on them like candy suckers, laughing...Gatsby grins, leans forward, her hand reaching forward, up, toward the girl's soft cheek...

She bolted upright, gasping, glanced at the quilt and sheets twisted in her hands, her pillows kicked off onto the floor, her clock-radio blasting Strauss. Gatsby took a long breath and let it out slowly. She had learned that when she was on vacation, she would have convoluted dreams that seemed to last the entire night—could have been three full-length motion pictures all strung together.

That was a doozy, she thought. The images were fuzzy in her mind, a journey back into her past...

"Hmm," she murmured and threw the covers back.

She took a hot shower, brushed her teeth, and made a pot of strong coffee.

Terrycloth-robed and with steaming coffee in hand, she strolled to her study and turned on the computer. It made its lovely chiming sound as the OS kicked in and brought up her main menu. She dropped in her chair, sat the mug on the mahogany desk, clicked her way into the Internet and, momentarily, was able to bring up the daily news service. She scanned through the links to three days before when she had seen the television news program about the Behala fakir and his snakes. The English version of the Bombay daily,

The Times of India, had carried an article on the story, along with three grainy photographs.

"Yes!" Gatsby blurted and downloaded the file.

The computer's guts whirred, lights blinked. A bell sound told her that the file was successfully transferred. She hit "Print" and waited, sipping, while the printer grunted rhythmically.

When it was done, she held up the printout to scan through the text. Her eyes focused on the pictures.

A sphere with upper and lower wings, like a yin-yang folding itself inside out.

Her left hand moved up until the tip of her finger touched the image on the paper. The undeniable feeling of connection moved through her again as when, before, she had touched the image—or the *alleged* image—of a glyph on the face of Stone 56 in the photograph in *Britain's Mysterious Monuments*, authored by Caitlin McNeil.

McNeil's book still lay face down on the corner of the desk where Gatsby had left it. She reached out and turned the book over. Gazed at the two-page spread, pages sixteen and seventeen. The impossible glyph was still there. A vertical bar, a crescent moon.

I'll call the publisher. The author. Anyone who knows who took this photograph and when, and how the hell it can contain a nonexistent glyph.

She turned the book face down, again, on the desktop. That seemed best, for the time being. Sighing, she looked back at the printout in her hand.

Four symbols? she thought.

She rose and shuffled back to the coffee pot for a refill, and to ponder on the questionable nature of reality and the significantly more unsettling thought that her model of reality had never before been in question.

CHAPTER 19

Juggling her shoulderbag and an armful of books, Gatsby slid her ID card through the slot scanner. Momentarily, the panel's red light blinked to green and the door to the Manuscripts wing unlocked.

She stepped inside. At nine o'clock, virtually all of the staff was gone; a few security guards milled around in the lobbies. A handful of lights showed in offices, but the building was mostly vacant.

You call this a sabbatical? she thought with a deep sigh, starting down the familiar hallway toward her office door.

She slipped her key into the lock, stepped inside, and turned on the light. Everything was just as she had left it—in ubiquitous and voluminous piles. A single-cup espresso maker sat on the wood laminate surface of her desk; as she walked to it, she dug in her leather shoulderbag and pulled out a plastic bag full of coffee grounds.

A few minutes later, as the espresso maker sizzled and steamed, Gatsby turned on her computer and sat in front of it. She took a deep breath, aware of how loud her breathing sounded in the silent room. Outside in the black night, a misty rain fell, tapping lightly against the glass window. She ran her hands through her hair and then brought both hands up in front of her face. Memories of the first day of her so-called sabbatical, weeks ago, before the trip to Peru, loomed in her mind—the bizarre episode of her hand, spasming, fluttering in the air like a crippled bird. She turned her hands over, front and back, staring at them as if they might metamorphose into alien beings, then shook her head and poured the espresso into a white mug that bore the imprinted logo UMBRAINIACS.

As the computer booted up and the colors on the monitor splashed into view, she tipped back in her chair and pulled four items from her shoulderbag: the sketch she had made of the Peruvian symbol, the photos that Quinn had sent of the symbol in Thebes, the computer printout of the snake-glyph in India, and McNeil's book on Stonehenge. She spread the materials out on her desk and grabbed a pen and piece of paper, thinking as she scribbled notes.

An inverted cross with a waving line to the left. A double triangle, diamond shaped. A sphere with upper and lower wings. A sideways T with a crescent moon, facing right. Start at the beginning. Could these symbols be pictographic? They don't look like objects, at least anything easily identifiable. No ox heads, lightning bolts, stalks of wheat. The crescent shape could be a moon, as it's drawn in many ancient inscriptions, but who knows if these symbols are ancient or modern? Ideographic? Possible. Each symbol standing for an abstract concept, such as Sumerian, Cretan, or Egyptian hieroglyphs. Syllabic? Possible. Each symbol could stand for a phonetic syllable, like Japanese kana. Alphabetic? Each symbol could stand for individual phonemes that combine into morphemes and meaningful words. Then there would be the question of syntax; what would the grammatical rules be? In what order should each element be placed?

She stopped writing to rub her cheek, thinking, If there's an order at all. *Oh christ, this is ridiculous, these symbols could be anything, bloody anything, or nothing!*

She spun her chair toward the window where, on a low desk, a flatbed scanner sat. One by one, she laid the drawings and photos on the glass scanning surface and waited while the machine hummed and flashed. In less than two minutes, she had digitized images of each symbol on the screen of her monitor.

If these are ancient, here's where paleography meets the microchip, she thought, and glared at the symbols. They shimmered in the light grey background of her image-processing program. With a few keystrokes, she tapped into the museum's network and found her way to the languages directories. The software bank included a program called Logos, which could analyze data or images and match them with reference files of over eight thousand languages. She initialized the program, waiting for its masthead to form, and then got into its primary folders.

The program prompted her for input. She downloaded the scanned images of the symbols and, while waiting, warmed up her espresso with a fresh shot.

Rocking in her swivel chair, she thought, *How long...oh.* The program shot a message box up on the screen: Complete analysis: 230 minutes.

Ugh. I don't plan to sleep over, she thought.

While the program started to work, she watched its text and graphics moving on the screen, letting herself retreat in speculation as she visually scrutinized the glyphs.

Location? Hmmm. Peru, Egypt, India, and Stonehenge— well, inside a book about Stonehenge published in the UK. The first three are known for their ancient civilizations, as far back as 3000 BC, though Stonehenge predates the Egyptian pyramids and any known civilizations in Peru. The pictorial nature of the symbols seems to point to proto- civilizations, cultures without representations for abstract concepts. But for a language to have evolved across continents without being discovered until now? Impossible!

She made more espresso, checked her watch, and returned to the computer. Using her mouse, she rearranged the symbols horizontally, left to right, in the order in which they were discovered, and a blip of intuition nudged at her.

Maybe I'm going about this all wrong...

She reminded herself that there were many ways, not necessarily linear, that symbols could be connected. Few languages were written left to right—some were written right to left, vertically, boustrophedon or inverted by line like the Easter Island Rongorongo script, even in a spiral fashion as on the Phaistos Disk.

She began shifting the glyphs around, creating different shapes—circle, square, diamond, diagonal, crescent. Then she moved them into a triangular configuration: the flag to the right; the crescent top center, the double-diamond left and even with the flag, the sphere/wings directly below the flag. The configuration felt right, although she had no idea why it should feel wrong or right or any other way.

Her left hand slowly rose; the tip of her index finger moved to the surface of the computer screen, aligned with the double-diamond glyph.

Her other hand then raised itself and her right index finger moved to the waving line of the flag. Now both hands were before her, fingertips pressed against the glass of the monitor.

There's NO reason that these symbols should mean anything, to me or anyone else, but I KNOW that they do! And I KNOW I've seen them before! But where?! How?

Shaking her head, she reached for her mug and brought it to her lips, taking a sip of the mint tea...

Tea?!?

She stared into the mug, mouth agape. The liquid inside it was thick and dark brown, just as espresso should be. Cautiously, she took another sip and breathed the steam deep into her lungs. It was rich Arabica, spiced with vanilla.

Good god, now olfactory hallucinations?!?

She sighed and drained the mug, carefully noting that it was indeed coffee, and went back to staring at the symbols. The program churned data.

Her mind drifted back to Traussbery, his story of his trip to Peru eleven years ago, and the appearance of the first glyph.

Why him? Of all the people in the world, why would these symbols seem significant to him? Or to me, for that matter? What's the connection? And the quantum theories he went on about...manipulating a medium the way a painter uses brush and pigment to recreate his visions...what is creating these symbols? What imagination is behind them? What is it trying to say? Or is this simply the work of miscreants, having a wizard good laugh watching two scientists going loony, trying to decipher utter gibberish? It's not that far-fetched; the crop circle makers eventually showed themselves and exactly how they had fooled the world into thinking that we were being visited by exceptionally artistic aliens.

Another message popped onto the screen; the program had flagged two possible matches: Iberian, a mixed syllabic-alphabetic European language, and Lycian, an alphabetic Greek derivative. Both undeciphered.

And miles to go before I sleep, Gatsby thought, noting that the program was one hundred and eighty-three minutes away from completing the analysis. Time to get out of here.

She packed the materials back into her shoulderbag, wiped out the coffee mug with a paper towel, and stood with a yawn and a stretch. With the computer still churning through its commands, she walked to the door, turned off the light, and stepped into the hall.

Her tennis shoes squeaked softly as she padded down the dark hallway, glancing around as if one of the guards might halt her at any moment. It was close to midnight; most of the guards had gone.

She slid her card through the security plate at the end of the hall, stepped outside, pulled the door closed behind her, and started toward her car.

As she drove slowly through the dark London streets, back toward Sloane, something made her nose wrinkle—a tart smell that she couldn't quite identify.

Must have dropped a throat lozenge under the seat, she thought absently as she turned onto King's Road.

CHAPTER 20

"Ms. Donovan, how many times must I repeat myself? McNeil's book is in its fourth reprint, and let me assure you, there is no symbol such as you describe in this edition or any previous edition. Have I made myself *very* clear?"

The female voice on the line was tearing at the seams.

Gatsby rolled her eyes and held the phone away from her mouth to compose a phrase of choice Anglo-Saxon oaths concerning the character, lineage, and intelligence quotient of the managing editor with whom she was speaking, Judith Ladbrooke.

"Quite clear. Now what's the name of the photographer?"

"Absolutely not. Harris-Pernfield Publishing owns the rights to the images in that book, and the photographer in question left our firm years ago. You've wasted enough of my time, Ms. Donovan. Good day."

"But Ms. Ladbrooke, don't—"

The line broke with a loud click and then the dial tone.

"Shit!" Gatsby slammed the phone down. She rubbed her eyes until she saw stars. "I'm not going to get anywhere with her. I'll just have to go over Dame Judith's head." She sighed. "But first things first."

Rising from behind her desk, Gatsby walked to the hall closet and got her jacket and shoulderbag. Lunch had been several hours ago, and she was starting to feel her stomach grumbling. The image of a hot croissant wafted through her imagination. The bakery was just down the street.

As she walked down the stairs to the lobby of her building, and then made her way out the front door to King's Road, she mentally went over the morning's work. The software program, Logos, had finally yielded results. From her home computer, she'd been able to retrieve the report that Logos had generated. It had flagged only four matches and reported that the theoretical reliability on all four was less than six percent. Along with Iberian and Lycian, it had flagged Cretan and Harappa: the former, a mixed ideographic and alphabetic language in use about 2000 B.C. and undeciphered; the latter, even older, originating with the Indus civilizations, mixed. Undeciphered.

As she strolled along the sidewalk, sidestepping passersby, Gatsby shook her head, her thoughts dark with frustration.

In other words, nada. Rien. Zip. Bugger all. And in keeping with this crusade of lunacy. Appearing symbols that exist but don't. Equipment that mysteriously fails. Talented cobras. A forty-five-tonne rock that relocates itself to a new spot—what, just to see the view? Is there a bigger picture here, some kind of message? Perhaps that either you, dear, are losing your hold on reality, or reality is monkey-banging itself?

She turned onto a side street and was at the front door of her favorite cafe, Amitas, inhaling the aromas of hot yeast and heady caffeine. The pain au chocolate in the glass case looked marvelous; it had just emerged from the oven. Gatsby stepped up, asked the punkish girl behind the counter for a croissant and a double French espresso, take-away. With paper bag in hand, she paid, took her change, and headed out the door.

As she stepped onto the sidewalk, something out of the corner of her eye made her do a double take. Gatsby turned her head sharply to see, about ten feet away, a girl turning the corner off Sloane Street. She was dark-skinned, wore a blue jumper-dress, and had her long, black hair pulled back in a ponytail. In the fraction of an instant before the girl disappeared from view, Gatsby felt a vague but disquieting sense of alarm.

Stopped in her tracks, the paper bag gripped in a tight fist by her side, Gatsby thought hard, wondering what was making her stop. A girl walking on the street—certainly nothing unusual about that. But...

Association *clicked.*

A girl who peered in her window at the taverna in Cuzco.

A girl at Heathrow, standing in the queue.

The child she'd just seen had looked something like the other two, but there had only been a split second to discern.

It wasn't the details of the girl, it was more of an overall impression, a vague sense of...

Familiarity.

Followed by a deeper but even more mysterious emotion.

A snort burst from her lips. "Phh! Yeah, right," Gatsby laughed out loud, taking a deep breath and starting down the sidewalk. Glancing in the dress windows of the shops along the way, she checked out the latest London fashions, new arrivals at the shoe shop, the Gucci bags and La Croix jewelry at Harrods—items she never perused or bought.

Late afternoon subway passengers flocked by her, chattering, as she walked past the Tube station entrance at Sloane Square and, in less than a minute, she was at the front door of her building.

After dinner and the evening news, she turned on her computer, dropped into the chair at her desk and, with the "Four Seasons" playing in the background, began to type.

This sabbatical is taking me, literally and metaphorically, into new territory. Peru, for a start. But these symbols have caused such a bizarre ruckus in my life, and I can't figure out why they have and yet feel utterly compelled to do just that. How and why do I know I've seen these symbols before, in the face of all logic? I don't know, but I feel it. There's no reasonable explanation, just as there's no explanation for that episode with my hand. So why am I spending my sabbatical trying to decode glyphs that are probably meaningless? And what is making me see a girl on the streets and believe that not only have I seen her before but that I ought to know who she is? The moved sarsen at Stonehenge—why does this event happen at the same time that bizarre glyphs are appearing around the globe? The misplacement of a forty-five-tonne rock is impossible to deny; if I began to think that was just my personal hallucination, then...Is it odd, somehow more than slightly ironic that, after sixteen years of scientific work, the strangest process going on here is that I'm scrutinizing my own logic? What do you do when your slide rule can't measure a thing? How do you conceptualize inexplicable evidence? Is there some event horizon at which even the most die-hard empiricist is forced to lay down the standard tools? But when all scientific options are ruled out, is metaphysics the only choice? And if there are realms beyond the scope of scientific inquiry and natural law—observable, measurable, quantifiable law—where does that road lead? Back to skull-holes and witch burning? To see myself even consider moving in this direction is the most frightening of all. But...

She stopped, fingers poised over the keys, feeling her heart thudding hard in her rib cage, staring blankly at the blue sea of the monitor before her. An image had popped into her mind, out of nowhere—a scene she had never recalled until that moment.

Running with her sister along a bright beach in the Pacific Northwest, eating Ritz crackers and peanut butter. Drinking lemonade. Sand crunching in her teeth.

Where did that come from?

But more importantly, what was the darker image secreted behind it?

It was like trying to look closely at a venomous animal— knowing that if you got close enough, you'd get hurt but having to look anyway, *needing* to see it up close and personal. If there were a way to move around to the other side...

Gatsby closed her eyes, breathing fast and loud through her nose. Her ears started to ring; she swallowed hard, noticing how dry her mouth had become. She looked down at her hands, still poised, frozen, over the keyboard, shaking uncontrollably.

"Ritz crackers and peanut butter," she whispered. The guttural edge in her voice made it thick, sludgy, monotone. Her head tipped back; her body sank into the chair, as if she were falling asleep on the spot, and in a few seconds, she realized that she might have been falling asleep or at least on the edge of sleep.

For no reason at all, she remembered running through a grassy meadow behind her parents' house, laughing and playing with her friends.

Her eyes popped open. Running shaking fingers through her hair, she took a deep breath and looked back at the computer screen.

This direction is the most frightening of all.

Her fingers flew over the keys.

With a heavy sigh, she saved and closed the file, turned off the computer and stereo, and went to brush her teeth.

She crawled into her bed with the packet of photos she'd brought back from Peru. Images of the stone walls—and the ghostly streaks in the images, like wisps of white cotton candy. Gatsby stared at them until her vision doubled and her chin bumped her chest. She laid the photographs on the night table, turned out the light, and turned on the projector of dreams.

CHAPTER 21

The phone rang, waking Gatsby out of a strange dream. She fumbled about the nightstand, knocked over the phone base, and finally found the handset.

"Hullo?"

"Do you sleep all day?"

"Celia?"

"Who else would ring you at the crack of noon?"

Gatsby rolled over, squinted at the clock-radio, and groaned. "Oh god." She sat up and pressed the phone to her ear. "What's up?"

"Well, when you get your lazy bum out of bed, would you like to have lunch at Poppi's?"

"Uh, sure."

"I hadn't heard from you, so I'd assumed that you must have run off to a foreign country with Mr. Tall, Dark, and Handsome."

An image of Traussbery in floral swim trunks bloomed in Gatsby's mind, and she burst into guffaws. "Ooh, not even close, but Poppi's sounds great. I'll meet you."

"Supah," Celia said. "See you at two."

Gatsby hung up the phone and stumbled into the bathroom. Standing under the spray of steaming water, she sniffed at her shampoo bottle. There was a tangy smell to it that she was sure hadn't been there before.

The maitre d' glowered over the tops of his bifocals and motioned for her to follow. Gatsby stepped into the cool, lush ambiance of London's most famous Greek restaurant and glanced around, looking for her friend.

"Gats!"

Celia was sitting in a booth next to the solarium. She rose, looking coltish and seductive in a white stretch catsuit that left little of her shape and even less of her cleavage to the imagination. She gave Gatsby kisses on both cheeks and returned to her seat, her eyes sparkling, her fire-engine-red lipstick glistening, her perfume wafting around them.

"You look fantastic," Gatsby said, suddenly feeling ungainly in khaki pants, a white polo shirt, penny loafers, and a distinct absence of glamour.

"So I've heard."

They brayed laughter and tried to muffle their giggles as the maitre d', a man who looked as if he had suffered constipation for decades, coasted to their table. Gatsby ordered Greek salad; Celia, dolmathes, spanakopita, tabbouleh, and a bottle of ouzo.

"I never met a woman who could eat or drink like you," Gatsby said, shaking her head as she sipped lemonade.

Sunlight glinted off Celia's highly polished nails as she raised her own glass in a toast. "Dahling, I work it off." She winked. "Aerobics."

The food arrived and Celia filled Gatsby in on recent events: a visit from her nosey Bostonian mother and a weekend trip with her new flame to see the Mona Lisa at the Louvre.

"We never did get to see the old girl." Celia gave a sigh that sounded satisfied rather than disappointed. "Never got beyond the front door of the hotel. And you, you tireless workhorse, when's the last time you got laid? The Ice Age? When are you going to meet some nice rich archeologist and finally allow yourself a good shag?"

Gatsby smiled. "Probably in the next Ice Age." She gazed into her lemonade. "It's been a while. You know me, married to my job. The only—" She stopped, staring across the room, through the fronds of the palm trees. "The only love affair of any real consequence was back at Blake. Remember Woody Sanderson?"

Celia's eyes widened; she grinned. "God, how could I forget? You went on like he was descended from Olympus. For a while, anyway."

She swallowed and leaned back into the padding of the booth. "We had a real bond. I almost felt that he was more of a brother, because he cared about me so much, but he was no brother in the sack." She rolled her eyes, grinning mischievously. "Dios mio."

"What happened?"

"He wrote twice after graduation, from Paris, then Greece. Saying he'd be back in a few months and planned to come back and spend the next interim with me." She grabbed a chunk of bread from the plate before her and buttered methodically. "But I never heard from him again."

Celia's expression was rueful. "So tell me," she asked, waving the skewered dolmathe on her fork, "how's your research coming?"

Gatsby relayed the details of the mysterious glyph in the photo book and the even more mysteriously shifted stone at Stonehenge. Celia listened with rapt attention and wide eyes.

When she was done, Gatsby finished off her lemonade and flagged the waiter to order a White Russian. The conversation had unnerved her.

Celia leaned back in her booth seat and stared at Gatsby with a nonplussed look. "It's—well, what are the chances that all of this is just some yobbo's idea of a bally joke?"

Gatsby shook her head. "Celia, at the Coricancha in the Andes, I was holding a pencil in my hand, squatting in a ruined temple, and all of my equipment failed me. The writing implements didn't work. The camera didn't record what I saw right in front of me, a glyph as real as this table." Her hand trembled, making the ice in her glass tinkle faintly. "The book on my own bookshelf? I've looked at the photographs in it dozens of times and there has never been a glyph in the image. And then someone moves that rock at Stonehenge? Overnight?! Without leaving a trace?! It's incomprehensible, even wackier than how the stones got there in the first place. It still hasn't been explained— investigative teams have been out there scouring every pebble and leaf of grass, and not being able to explain it is what's scaring the hell out of me."

Celia poured more ouzo, nodding.

"What are you going to do?"

"Well, I don't imagine that I'm going to get much of a tan this summer, because I'm going to be holed up either in the basement of the museum or in my flat, with my head buried in musty books." She sighed. "Not very exciting. But this is the most perplexing thing I've ever run up against, and I have to know what it is. It means something. I can feel it."

Celia stared hard at her, then speared the last dolmathe and devoured it. "Any minute now you're going to scoop your lunch into a tower shape, look at me with crazed eyes, and mutter, 'This means something.'"

The reference was clear. The main character in the film *Close Encounters of the Third Kind* had done exactly that with a plate full of mashed potatoes while his family looked on in stunned terror.

"Don't worry." Gatsby grinned a little. "When I go that far off the deep end, you have my permission to haul me over to St. Beatrice."

"You know—" Celia started with a guarded expression.

"What?"

"Perhaps no one but your best friend could tell you this but, sweetie, you are looking ragged. Are you sure you aren't letting this work get to you?"

Gatsby snorted. "What? I'm fine. What do you mean, ragged?"

"Well, those are some dandy circles under your eyes. Not sleeping well?"

Out of nowhere, an image of a dragon wafted through Gatsby's mind.

"I'm...well, I have had some strange dreams lately, but I'll be damned if I can remember them, and I'm sleeping just fine, and thank you so much for your tact."

They smiled weakly at each other over the table as the thought crept through Celia's head that for the first time, her friend was hiding something from her. More accurately, from herself.

"Just take care of yourself, and remember, if you need someone to talk to, I'm there."

"Celia, you're always therapizing."

"Well, it is my job!"

The waiter appeared and asked if they would care for dessert. Gatsby ordered lemon sorbet; Celia, a chunk of baklava. They ate with gusto, groaning over their full stomachs. Celia called for the bill, paid for the meal and, before they were out the front door, had a tentative date with the waiter.

CHAPTER 22

As his last sentence sank in, she stared at Traussbery, thinking, *This man is unbalanced.*

"You did it," she said flatly. Rhetorical.

Traussbery sat across from her in his armchair, bent forward, elbows on his knees, gasping as if he might be sick. His office was lit with thin morning light and, hidden in the dark corners of the room, the jeweled green eyes of the Egyptian statues stared down as if rendering punitive verdicts.

The soliloquy he'd just given—of a tipped-bookcase accident involving a man named Travis Norton, and his vehement accusation that he had used some "metaconscious" power to cause the bookcase to crush the man and effect an eleven-year coma—still hung in Gatsby's head, dementedly surreal as a glow-in-the-dark Dali painting of Elvis with the head of a goat. Hung upside down.

He pulled his handkerchief from the breast pocket of his jacket and blew his nose with a loud honk. Looking up at her with bloodshot eyes, he croaked, "I know you don't believe me, and why should you? How should anyone! But Ms. Donovan, I had to tell someone, and you were the only person—even though I know that you must think I've gone mad!" He wiped at his eyes as he leaned back in the chair. "Mad! The only word we have for these phenomena, because we cannot understand them with reason. Like dreams, they are outside conscious understanding—" His voice trailed off.

Gatsby rubbed her eyes wearily. "Traussbery, you're trying to convince me of telekinesis? Is that it? Not just spoon-bending or floating tables but the ability to move anything using the mind?" A sigh escaped her. "I...well, I...I mean, you have the look of a respectable and *lucid* scientist, but this? I'm sorry to say it, but you've lost me. I can believe that images can *seem* to materialize. I can believe that the eye is subject to all kinds of optical illusion. I am starting to wonder if a bunch of damn snakes can wriggle around and create a potentially meaningful shape. Or if the builders of

Stonehenge perhaps did have some kind of technology that we have yet to discover. But if you think you can convince me that you were responsible for moving—" She spread her hands in entreaty. "Are you listening to yourself, Professor?"

Crumpled and wheezing in his chair, Traussbery covered his wet cheeks with his hands. "Of *course* it's unbelievable; that's what makes it even more horrible! Ms. Donovan, I didn't *want* to see the glyph in Peru! I was just there and it *appeared*! No other on the face of the earth has seen it except you, and I realize that you don't believe there are supraphysical elements involved. The conscious faculties have been subjected to scientific examination for centuries and still their full scope is untenable. Still the realm of faith, or mysticism, or mythology, or whatever term one wishes to use." He leaned forward, eyes bulging, heaving hot pipe-tobacco-flavored breath into her face. "I swear to you, Ms. Donovan, if the events had not happened to me personally, I would be sitting where you are now, opposite a person you undoubtedly believe has gone barking mad. Am I right?"

Gatsby stared out his office window and folded her hands in her lap. The ticks of Traussbery's wristwatch seemed as loud as gongs in the mortuary-like quiet of the office. The lawns were deserted; the city of Cambridge seemed to have vanished for a holiday.

Where am I supposed to go with this information, she thought miserably, *the World Heritage Foundation?* She murmured, "Traussbery, you know how intrigued I am by the glyphs. That I am committing myself—no pun intended—to learn their meaning. That I am forced to give some credence to acts of intuition. Believe me, that's the only way I can explain my own obsession with these bloody things. And I've had experiences of my own that fall far off the beaten path of my scientific background. Far off. But I am not ready to accept the leap you have made or to accept that a forty-five-tonne rock can be moved by a thought. In fairy tales, in mythology and fantasy, yes, but in the tangible world? Mass and dimension shifted by human thought? That's not reality! That's not science! It's magic!"

"You know as well as I, Ms. Donovan," Traussbery replied softly, "that what is now called physics was once called magic." He splayed his hands flat against the tops of his legs and looked her in the eye. "All right. Can we agree that the understanding, the consensus-reality understanding, of the capacity of the mind has changed throughout time? Has adapted as our understandings deepen?" He held her with a hard stare.

Gatsby watched her hand move over the curve of her leather boot, propped atop the opposite knee. "Reasonable enough." Frowning, she ran her hands through her hair. "But let's go back. Tell me again how you say that it happened."

Traussbery reached for his pipe. "As I said, I had recently been thinking of Travis Norton. The malevolence I had done him—yes, I can see what you're thinking. Put it this way, Ms. Donovan: at the very least, I stood by and watched the accident happen. Through inaction, I caused harm to come to him and expedited my own advancement. I took up my telephone one evening and actually rang his room but lacked the courage to speak. I couldn't. What could I say? I hung up. In any event, the night after the WHF conference, I had gone to the local for dinner and then come home. My belly was full, my head even more so with thoughts and memories—the appearance of the Peruvian glyph, eleven years ago—when I began to wonder, was I possessed with some sort of power of consciousness? That was when I began my research into the theories of Bohm, Grof, Pribram, and Sheldrake. The untapped potentials of human evolution, the evolution of consciousness! The unexplored frontier of the mind! I began to imagine, for the first time, that it was possible for one to possess ability beyond the range of normal understanding, beyond consensus reality, and I understood for the first time that although I hated myself for what had happened to Norton, I—"

His body shuddered. Gatsby looked closely at his face as he stared at the rug—the shadow of his unshaven chin, the puffiness around his melancholy eyes, the pallor of his skin—and thought, *He's eating himself alive over this! Is it turning into delusion? Mental breakdown?*

"I still craved it. *Lusted* for it, Ms. Donovan, in the most diabolical insinuation of the word. The simple monosyllable if became all to me. *If* it were true. *If* I had enacted a quantum force upon the universe, causing that bookcase to topple. *If* the enfolded structures of the cosmos were somehow breaking through into the unfolded world—like the tip of a needle piercing through cloth. *If* tangible reality, as most perceive it, truly was a mutable, a malleable characteristic of our universe rather than something we perceive as solid," he pounded on the arm of his chair, "as this! *If* with attenuation or resonance of consciousness, my hand could move through this chair rather than being stopped by its delusive solidity..."

Moving closer to Gatsby, Traussbery drew his hands, balled into fists, in front of his face. "Do you comprehend what that would be, Ms. Donovan? Do you have any inkling of what such capacity would bring? If such attenuation can be achieved, then we have entered the world of magic. Supraconsciousness! In all respects, the concept of God."

Gatsby stared, blinked.

"And all the wizards of history, all the shamans and witches and saints and demon-possessed, have not been mad but have been particle physicists beyond all measure!"

She swallowed.

Traussbery tipped back in his chair and lit his pipe. "What does a scientist do when presented with *that* bundle of ifs, accompanied by power lust? Test it! The discovery of a lifetime—ha! of all humankind!—was the prize! I had to do it, no matter what the cost. If it cost everything, if it cost the planet, if it brought another Big Bang! I had to know! So I decided to devise an experiment. I would attempt to cause another observable event.

"The next morning, I went back to the local. Took my usual seat and ordered a usual breakfast, pastry, jam, and tea. I then saw my experiment before my eyes. I would effect some kind of a change there in the pub and note whether or not others observed it.

"Remembering the day at the WHF conference, I attempted to recreate, mentally, emotionally, and viscerally, the state I had been in at the moment that the bookcase fell.

To relive it entirely. I thought of my sense of injustice, my rage at Norton for even daring to occupy the same room as I! As the agitation came over me, my body shook so hard that I felt the legs of my chair clattering against the floor! I closed my eyes, and the sensation mounted. I thought...dear god, I thought of Elise, as I had that day, saw in my mind a picture of her face as she might look had I been forced to tell her that Norton had received the appointment instead of me. Such emotion surged through me! As if I had grabbed hold of electric fencing! It overwhelmed me, I cried out, my eyes flew open and the first thing I cast my gaze on was the teacup. It—"

He paused, breathing hard. Gatsby watched him, transfixed.

"In that instant, my vision blurred or, rather, changed. The dimensionality of the teacup metamorphosed and I saw, or believed that I saw, its elements, its particles! The very molecules of the container and the water inside it! A feeling came over me...the only way I can describe it is as if the cup absorbed me. I became a part of its constituent elements! I felt the heat of the boiling water all around me! And then! A sharp shock, like a hard slap in the face, and perhaps my eyes closed, I'm not quite sure, but I was momentarily in darkness. I drew in a breath and looked around myself. The teacup lay shattered on the floor."

They sat silently as Traussbery coughed and blew his nose again.

Gatsby rubbed her chin as she watched him labor to get his wind back, wondering where the story would go. She felt mostly pity for the man, but laced in with it was a current of unease.

He continued slowly. "I had not moved my arms. My hands were cupped together in my lap, as they had been prior. Nothing else had changed or moved, no one had come near me. But a cup was now broken on the floor, tea spilt everywhere." Traussbery looked up at Gatsby with red, blazing eyes. "The server had heard it break and was on his way to my table. As he approached, the young man said, 'Nothing to worry about, sir, I'll have it cleaned right up,' something to that effect. I nodded, I couldn't speak. As he mopped the floor and threw out the broken pieces, an unearthly euphoria came upon me. Had I *caused* particle to shift to wave? My thought-experiment had indeed, it seemed, produced an observable result! I wanted to weep and shout at the same time!"

Gatsby took a long breath.

"The enormity of it rocked me. Rocked me, Ms. Donovan! I felt unstoppable, omnipotent! It was a, well, a moment that I can't describe. There is no vocabulary for it. But there was one thing I knew: somehow, I had to repeat the experiment."

"And?" she asked with wary precognition.

Traussbery puffed out his cheeks before replying. "Something even more undeniable. A shattered teacup is a tangible event, yes, obviously! But if I truly were endowed with a power of consciousness, how powerful could it be? How far reaching? How godlike could I become?

"I tell you, Ms. Donovan, the temptations in my life have been few. I led a quiet existence with Elise for many years, as an academician and an introverted scholar. I have not often experienced powerful emotion. Hatred, lust. But something happened to me the day of Norton's tragedy, a deep change in my psyche. For the first time, I felt unadulterated, self-indulgent desire. Perhaps it was a crisis of personae, a necessary part of maturity, releasing a mantle of inhibition? Perhaps it was not. Perhaps it was, in actuality, a transformation on a cosmic level, on a quantum level!

"But to the story. I paid my bill and left. It was ten o'clock and I should have been tired but instead was burning with incredible energy. In my car, I started out onto the motorway and the next thing I knew, a fanatical obsession had overtaken me to go to Stonehenge! My night vision is so bad nowadays that I took several wrong exits—it took over three hours—I distinctly remember checking my watch as I pulled off to the shoulder of the A344. It was past one o'clock in the morning. I cut the motor but left the lights on, shining toward the stones. I stood there in the darkness, very much alone; there's certainly no traffic on that road in the middle of the night. I knew that entrance to the site was impossible, never mind the fact that my presence there was pure madness. I have no rational explanation for my actions. I simply knew that I had to be there. Something, some crazed thought, was already starting to brew in my mind, but I—"

He licked his lips, pressed his palms together.

"I stared out into the darkness at the site. I could see the outlines of the stones fairly well, with my headlights directed on them. It's one thing to stand in the presence of those sarsens in the light of day, but in the middle of the night it's quite ghostly. But there I was, alone on the side of the motorway, in the dark, peering like some kind of macabre creature drawn by the scent of blood. Suddenly, the enormity of what I was doing overcame me. I *knew* that I must be going mad! There could be no other explanation. All my wild speculation about quantum shifting, the absurd blathering on particle shifting and the deep structure of the universe and its malleability—the lunacy of it all struck me! Suddenly weak, as if many years of aging had come upon me all at once, I grabbed onto the fencing beside the road. How far gone was I with these delusions? Had I really lost my sensibility? What in god's name am I doing here? I cried to the sky, to the night, perhaps to the stones, begging them for wisdom. What has happened to me? Have I allowed god-complex to consume me? Should I believe myself—

"I stopped, because I began to feel the electric sensations I had experienced in the pub! A rushing wave-like feeling, as if I were being swept up in a storm of unbelievable force. But I was not wishing it or attempting to create it! It came of its own accord! And grew! And again, my vision changed—I spotted the nearest stone, about ten meters off the roadside where I stood and, staring at it, I felt the same absorbing experience. As if the rock had grown to the size of a continent and engulfed me as one clump of soil in its enormity! A mote—a molecule!—within it! With the sensation came a sound, starting out as a deep, grating rumbling and soon growing to a monstrous roar! I felt my knees buckle, and the only physical sensation I was aware of was the gravel biting into my knees.

"I had not voiced aloud the last of my thought, but I had thought it: *Should I believe myself capable of moving a monolith?* A flash of an image, a microsecond of a vision had burst into my mind—of the stones moving!

"The noise grew! Good god, it was like a mountain erupting! I shrieked, leapt for my car, started the engine. The rumbling, grating noise continued! Finally I had the courage to open my eyes and look toward the site, into the darkness, where the sound seemed to be coming from, my entire body tingling and quivering, like the bolt of energy I had felt in the pub but even more vibrational. My eyes slowly adjusted, and—"

Deep wrinkles gathered as Traussbery's eyes squeezed shut and a tear trickled down his cheek. He said thickly, "I saw the sarsen, Stone 56. Sh-shifted to...to the side of the site, jutting upwards but angled like some monstrous javelin. In my mind's eye, I had been envisioning Stonehenge in its familiar formation, complete, all its stones in their original places, but...but what I s-saw—"

He sobbed for a moment; Gatsby watched, wishing to comfort him but not knowing how or, ultimately, if she should. She sat quietly with her chin in her hand.

"Like the phenomenon with Norton, there was no one I could tell, no one who wouldn't simply believe me insane and whisk me to an asylum." He dropped his head into his hands.

They may yet. She cleared her throat and said gently, "You realize, of course, that none of this can be corroborated. You don't have a shred of reasonable proof of what you're saying."

He sniffed, nodding, staring at the floor.

Gatsby ran her hands through her hair. "And you know how all this sounds, Traussbery. Do you want to start with stories of the Loch Ness monster? Yetis? UFOs? Goatsuckers? Three-headed babies? Stigmata?" She leaned her elbows onto her knees. "Even if you believe in the truth of what you're saying, and you obviously do, how do you expect anyone else to believe it?"

Traussbery wiped his eyes with his handkerchief and took a deep breath. "I don't. If I were a courageous man, I suppose I would go to the police and give them the answer to their investigation. But I'm not courageous, and naturally they would brush me off as a fanatic. And god knows they are already dealing with enough of those." The morose expression on his face began to change. "But I can't live with the knowledge that I have destroyed one of the most significant sites in the world. I know what I must do next."

Mother of god, Gatsby thought. She asked cautiously, "What?"

"Put the stone back."

She gasped. *What do I do? Humor him?*

Traussbery's voice lowered to a conspiratorial hush. "Ms. Donovan, since that night—what has it been, two weeks now?—I have made every effort I can imagine to, ahm, correct what I've done. Hypnotic trance, visualization, construction of models, everything short of ritual sacrifice and, obviously, I have not been successful. But I have conceived of an experiment that will focus and perhaps harness an immense source of power. Perhaps enough power to put Stone 56 back in its rightful place."

She raised her eyebrows. "Go on."

"As you know, the summer solstice is approaching, and because of what has happened at the site, there will surely be a confrontation between English Heritage and the SOE."

"SOE? The Society of Earth?"

"Yes. The association of modern Druidism, which gathers each twenty-first of June for a mass ritual at Stonehenge. You've no doubt heard about these annual gatherings?"

"Pretty hard to overlook a gathering of seven thousand Druids," Gatsby said, rolling her eyes.

"Indeed. The SOE will badger English Heritage for their customary grant-of-entrance to the site on the solstice. But English Heritage, and the police, will want to keep everyone out. If the SOE is granted access, this is what I'll do. I'll attend the ritual, and I will solicit the cooperation of the participants."

"Cooperation? How? For what?"

Traussbery's eyes began to gleam. "To focus their thought-energy—their deep particles, as it were. To fashion an image in their minds, to re-envision Stonehenge as it was, as it should be! To visualize—and effect—Stone 56 back to where it belongs, in the center of the site!" He slapped his palms against his thighs. "If a single person can do what I believe I have done, imagine the energy of a group, numbering in the thousands, of psychically sensitive persons! The power of mass consciousness has moved mountains, Ms. Donovan, built pyramids, erected cathedrals, overthrown empires!"

Gatsby hoped her expression didn't reveal the gnawing unease that she felt. "I see."

Traussbery retrieved his pipe and sucked on it thoughtfully. Puffs of smoke began to circle his head. "Ms. Donovan, think of it this way. If I conduct this experiment and nothing happens, what is lost? Nothing. The investigators will continue to look for clues, English Heritage will eventually bring in large machinery of some kind and restore Stone 56 to its rightful place, and the world will go on turning round. But if anything does happen—"

He steepled his fingers together in front of his chest and wormed his glasses upward by wriggling his nose. Poking the mouthpiece of his pipe toward her, he said, "There will be corroboration such as the world has never seen before."

CHAPTER 23

"More coffee, madam?" The waiter's voice broke her daydream.

Gatsby looked up. "Please. And cream, if you would."

He nodded and strode away.

The lunch crowd at the Regent Arms was sparse; most of the customers were at the bar, chatting boisterously and watching the Wolverhampton-Hammersmith football game blaring from the television mounted adjacent to the glass backwall.

Gatsby sipped her coffee and stared out the window at the flow of Friday afternoon shoppers. She was working on a bowl of the pub's signature dish, a redolent soup of vegetables and barley, thick with basil and thyme. She raised a spoonful from her bowl and into her mouth. Wolverhampton scored a goal and the pub spectators cheered in unison.

All morning, she'd been mulling over the conversation of the day before in Traussbery's office and wondering what to do next.

He's over the edge. I don't think any level of rational discussion will help now. God, the look on the man's face, the way he broke into tears! No matter what other weirdness he spouts, it's clear he's killing himself with guilt over something. He absolutely believes he snagged his position at Cambridge through misdeed. And the incident with Travis Norton, which he has convinced himself that he caused by telekinesis—is it just self-incrimination stemming from some other, more malicious act? Maybe he simply pulled the case down on Norton, or even assaulted him, and has blocked out the memory. But this business with Stonehenge, holy—

The waiter appeared and refilled her cup with espresso. She nodded in thanks and he disappeared. Gatsby absentmindedly stirred figure eights through her soup.

Now he wants to crash the Druids' party at Stonehenge and somehow persuade them to use their mental forces to move a forty-five-tonne rock back to where the original builders put it in the Bronze Age. She sighed. What the bugger am I going to do? Go along with his lunatic ideas? Tell him he's lost his mind and to get stuffed? Turn him in to the police?

She stirred figure eights.

Maybe the only thing to do is keep focused on these glyphs and let Traussbery do whatever the hell he wants. If telekinesis is his vice of choice, well, everyone needs a hobby.

The viewers at the bar erupted again, and Gatsby looked up at the screen. She frowned.

The television screen had gone blank; it was now solid blue. The sounds of the game were gone.

She watched the crowd. They all stared up at the screen, commenting on plays, clapping each other's backs, and chatting about the referee.

What were they seeing?!

What the hell? she thought frantically.

An image was emerging from the blue background—a dark curve, a crescent moon. The crescent shape shifted, rotating to the right until both tips pointed downward. A dot appeared between the two points and then spread horizontally, becoming a line. The shape now looked like a capital letter D lying on its back.

A commercial? But they're not—

Watching the crowd continue to cheer and argue over corner kicks, lousy passes, and offside violations that they apparently were seeing on a screen where Gatsby saw only a strange symbol in a blue background, she began to breathe harder. Her fingers suddenly felt sticky against her spoon. She sat frozen, eyes glued to the screen but peripherally watching the rest of the crowd.

Another small dot appeared in the center of the D—it slowly morphed into a circle that changed into an upside-down teardrop.

Panic raced through her and before she could stop herself, she shouted, "What's that on the screen?" As soon as the words passed her lips, she felt her face flush with embarrassment.

A portly gentleman sitting at the bar turned toward her from his pint of ale. "Hammersmith, Wolverhampton. And the Wolvers are getting their arses kicked." He chuckled and returned to his glass, his gaze moving upward and fixing on the screen.

Two blonde twenty-something men, also on stools at the bar, suddenly banged their fists on the counter, swearing vehemently. "Did you see that? Jesus! The bloody ref is blind! Nielson was five yards from being offside, the effing moron!"

While the viewers at the bar pointed at the screen and clamored over plays, Gatsby broke into a sweat and felt her stomach contracting into a hot, hard ball. She squeezed her eyes shut, took a few deep breaths, sat perfectly still for a moment, and then looked back up at the screen.

A capital D on its back, an upside-down teardrop inside. A deep blue background. No sound.

The men at the bar whooped again, pointed, and cheered as though a goal had just been scored.

"Madam?"

The voice at her elbow made her jump. She looked up into the waiter's fresh, scrubbed face. He looked down at her questioningly with blonde eyebrows raised.

"Anything else I can get you?"

"Wh—" Gatsby opened her mouth and a wisp of air came out. She cleared her throat and tried again. "Uh, I...the television, up there," she pointed toward the corner above the bar, "wh...what's on right now?"

The waiter looked up at the screen. "Football match, madam. Are you a fan?" He stuck his hands into the pockets of his Regent Arms apron and stared at her with a bland, bored expression.

Gatsby shook her head and asked for the bill. He pulled her ticket from his pocket, laid it on the table next to her bowl, and strutted off toward the kitchen.

She pulled bills out of her shoulderbag and laid them on the table. Frantic inspiration seized her, and she jumped up, scrambled toward the bar, reached up, and pushed the channel button.

Just as the D-shaped image flickered out and then back again, the men on their barstools shouted in unison.

"'ey, there!"

"What're ya doing?"

"Leave it alone!"

"'ang on there, lady!"

Under their growls of protest, she apologized tersely and slid away.

At the exit door, she stopped and turned. The television screen was still silent, the image on it still a D shape with a teardrop. The viewers at the bar still sat with their eyes glued to the screen, lost in a world where Wolverhampton and Hammersmith battled away at each other.

Dizzy and decidedly nauseous, she pushed the door open and walked out.

As the subway shook and bumped toward King's Road, she pulled a pen and a grocery receipt from her bag. She drew the D-shaped image with trembling fingers and stared at it, her heart pounding loudly.

Like the others, the shape was unnervingly *familiar*.

Beyond conscious awareness, her left hand moved on the fabric of her pant leg.

She shoved the receipt into her bag and, sighing loudly, laid her head back against the worn padding of the train seat. She thought, *Traussbery's craziness is rubbing off on me.*

A creature spewed bile and panic at her core.

CHAPTER 24

Gatsby closed her front door and stepped into the chilly darkness. Gripping a thermos of espresso in one hand and her shoulderbag in the other, she stumbled down her front steps toward the curb where Traussbery's Bentley sat rumbling.

Sliding into the passenger seat, she muttered, "Ready for the Great Annual Druid Gathering and Cook-Off, Traussbery? Where's your cloak and barbecue sauce?"

Traussbery glared from behind his steering wheel. "I grant that you are unable to take this experiment as seriously as I, but sarcasm is uncalled for."

She buckled her seat belt with a sigh. "Well, what am I supposed to say? Good luck with the telekinetic boulder-tossing?"

Traussbery frowned in response as he glanced at his watch. "Twenty past three. We should be there in just in time for the sunrise or any other cosmic events at exactly one minute past five o'clock." He roared the engine, pulled away from the curb, and headed down the darkness of King's Road.

She rubbed her eyes and yawned. "Good god, the last time I was up this early was four years ago on a flight to the Yucatan. Want some coffee?" She held out the thermos.

Traussbery shook his head and, sounding annoyingly alert, replied, "Never touch the stuff, thank you."

As they entered the motorway, heading southeast, Traussbery said, "I spoke yesterday with a Mr. William Stableford of English Heritage. My prediction was bang-on. When English Heritage was contacted by the SOE, requesting access to the site for the solstice, Heritage adamantly refused. The SOE appealed to the Salisbury District Council, making a case that they were being denied the right to practice their ritual, victims of religious censorship and so forth. Finally, a High Court magistrate was called in and decided to allow a thousand people to attend the ceremony, plus a handful of scholars. You and I included."

"Thank god for that," Gatsby said, rolling her eyes.

"By all means. I'm sure the media will be there, chumming."

"What do you think they're going to capture on film for the evening news?" Gatsby asked, staring out the window into the darkness.

"I can only imagine," he said, a smile playing on his lips, "but here's my plan. It's very simple and will not call much attention. I have these leaflets—here—that explain my idea. All I will attempt to do is encourage the participants to create a picture in their minds. An image of Stonehenge with Stone 56 in its rightful place. Focus on it, concentrate on it, see it. They will want to see it that way, restored, just as you and I do. Their visualizations will be directed by their desire, and that is a fantastically powerful combination. If the cosmos is in a mood to carry on its routine habits, then the sun will rise over the Heel Stone as it has for thousands of years, songs will be chanted, and we'll all go back to London for tea and biscuits. But if one molecule of matter is altered by conscious energy, then—" His voice trailed off.

"Then?" Gatsby prodded.

"Then!" Traussbery nodded vigorously, wide eyed. "Then!" He pursed his lips to indicate how perfectly obvious the rest was.

Gatsby shook her head and stared out the window. The shadows of rolling hills, mounds, and burrows of the countryside began to appear as she nodded off.

A kilometer before the exit to Salisbury, they were stopped dead in traffic.

Gatsby rolled down her window and stuck her head out. "Bumpers as far as I can see." She pulled back inside the car. "Look at this, Traussbery—it's insane! We'd get there faster by walking."

He nodded and said, "Then let's walk. Are you up for it?"

As long as you don't croak on the way, she thought. She grabbed her coat. He parked the car by the side of the road, and they clambered out.

"This is unbelievable," Gatsby said as they walked along and gawked at the cars as they passed. "Look at these cars with designs painted on them. Zodiac signs on that one. Why do I feel I'm about to smell incense and dope?"

"Don't be surprised by anything today, Ms. Donovan," he retorted mysteriously.

As he scuffed along the asphalt, his black overcoat flapping, Traussbery coughed periodically but seemed enlivened by the honking cars, shouting drivers, and clouds of exhaust. The look on his face was one Gatsby had never seen before, and she recognized it momentarily. He looked like a six-year-old boy with a new toy. He gripped his bundle of leaflets tightly under his left arm and looked positively radiant.

The bumper-to-bumper motorway, stuffed with cars of every imaginable variety, reminded her of the rock concerts of her teenage years. Many of the drivers were following suit with her and Traussbery and were packing their rucksacks to finish the journey on foot. Of all sizes and shapes, male and female, young and old, most wore cloaks or long robes of white or green. A few carried musical instruments—lutes, drums, guitars, bells. In the darkness, the sounds of shouts, tires, crying babies, and honking horns enveloped them. As they merged with the stream of pedestrians, Gatsby felt like a New Age pilgrim headed toward a prehistoric Mecca.

"Woodstock at Wiltshire," she muttered.

"What's that?" Traussbery popped up.

"Nothing." She shook her head and kept walking.

As they ascended the last crest of the A344 motorway, the Visitor's Centre, an outcrop of fluorescent lights, and a bustling throng of people came into view. They trudged along the dark highway until they finally entered the parking lot that was jammed with cars and awash in incandescent glare.

"No turning back now," Gatsby said. Traussbery nodded energetically as they made their way toward the entrance gate where a blue-uniformed officer stood with a clipboard and a pen.

He asked brusquely as they approached, "Group?"

"British Museum," Gatsby said.

Traussbery coughed and said, "Cambridge."

The officer made checkmarks on his pad. "Right. Hands up, please, we must search everyone."

Traussbery and Gatsby exchanged annoyed glances as they raised their arms and were gruffly patted down from shoulders to ankles. Gatsby spied out of the corner of her eye while the officer searched Traussbery, wondering what he had done with his bundle of leaflets. She realized that he had stuffed them down his shirt and, spread across his middle, they became an inconspicuous layer of his abundant stomach.

The officer straightened with a soft groan, muttered, "Right," and pushed the gate open to let them through.

As they walked through the tunnel passage that dipped under the highway and then emerged at ground level, Gatsby saw that the site was already bulging with crowds. A contingency of solemn, white-robed Druids had commandeered the central circle of the stones. The entire monument was circled by police, and while the television crews hadn't yet arrived, many celebrants had brought their handheld videorecorders. Tall, portable lights resembling studio lamps had been erected all around, casting a spooky, artificial glow across the stones and eerie shadows behind them.

"What do we do now?" Gatsby whispered as they stepped off the asphalt walkway and onto the grass.

"You don't need to do anything, Ms. Donovan," Traussbery replied. "In fact, wander as you like. We'll meet up later. I'm off." He slipped away, his overcoat flapping behind him.

"Wonderful. Bloody wonderful," Gatsby sighed to herself. She looked at her watch and wandered toward the southwest area of the site. From that vantage point, on the northeast axis of the site, she faced the Slaughter Stone and the Heel Stone. If she moved to the center of the site and peered between Stones 1 and 30, she would be able to see the sun when it peeked over the horizon and rose just to the left of the Heel Stone.

She glanced to the spot where Stone 56 never should have been at all and now was angled into the earth in complete aberrance. An elfin woman in a flowing white robe stood next to the isolated stone, slowly moving her hands in the air as if in synchrony with music she alone heard. As it had the last time she'd been at the site, the utterly wrong position of the stone tugged at Gatsby's sense of cosmic propriety. The giant mustache on the Mona Lisa.

Gatsby shivered and hugged her arms across her chest.

Moving silently along the gradually lightening paths, the vermicular line of robed worshippers seemed a procession of ghosts—phantasms floating through the night, weaving a dark web of mystic incantations around the ancient temple. Although she felt some sympathy for Traussbery, who had done nothing but set himself up for a disappointment of global proportion, she also recognized awe moving inside her. She'd visited the site only during the daytime and never in the company of a thousand robed pagans. She glanced around at the growing crowd, which seemed to be meandering into a circle around the perimeter of the stones, following the curve of the Z holes.

Where was Traussbery? Squinting into the darkness, she finally recognized the lumpy figure scuttling through the crowd, approaching shadowy figures one by one and talking briefly with each person as he handed them a flyer.

She looked at her watch. 4:51. Ten minutes.

The circle of worshippers surrounding the perimeter uprights was complete, and within the horseshoe-shape of the inner trilithons, a dozen or so Druid elders had assembled and were adjusting their white head-scarves or standing quietly with hands clasped. Except for two elderly women, their group was composed of young or middle-aged men. As they slowly formed a semicircle, facing the Heel Stone, each lit a white candle and raised it to shoulder height. They began to sing in unison.

Gatsby looked toward the horizon where soft shafts of light were beginning to rise, illuminating the sky to deep purple, turning lithic shadows from black to grey. Police milled aimlessly, looking at their watches and occasionally checking with each other on cellular phones, but there was no ruckus for them to contain or riot to squelch. The crowd of over a thousand was quite reverent.

"Spectacular, isn't it!" A voice behind her made her jump. Traussbery had appeared out of nowhere.

"Damn, Traussbery, don't sneak up on me like that." Gatsby grabbed for her thermos as it almost popped out of her hand. "Spectacularly nuts is more like it. Have you distributed your flyers? Educated everyone in basic telekinetics?" she asked wryly.

"Indeed. Each person I approached promised me that at the moment of sunrise, at exactly 5:01, he or she would fasten upon a visualization of Stonehenge in its original construction and concentrate on it and nothing else. I have also given each person a key word—a trigger, so to speak—to act as a subconscious point of focus." He rubbed his hands briskly together. "Who knows what may happen, Ms. Donovan!?"

"I know what will happen," she muttered, "the sun will come up and we'll go back to London for tea and biscuits, just like you said."

He tugged at her sleeve. "Let's move in closer, shall we."

"Traussb—"

He grabbed her jacket and Gatsby found herself being dragged, like one of his Shih Tzus, toward the middle of the site. They moved in as close as they could to Stone 57, an upright sarsen, where a lot of other people were trying to crowd in as well. Although no longer in direct visual alignment with the Heel Stone, they could still observe the ceremony taking place. Someone crushed against her from behind, and the mane of a scruffy, male neo-hippie whipped across her face. Gatsby elbowed for breathing room and peered toward the center of the circle.

Rays of sunlight were streaming up from the horizon, now turning the clouds gold and orange. Silhouettes of nearby groves and hedges became backlit with gold; the shadows of the hills to the east were now soft hues of green and brown; the details of millennia of weathering could now be seen on the surfaces of the megaliths. The wind picked up, blowing hoods, hair, and jackets, and the Druids cupped their candles. A flock of sparrows whizzed by overhead as the worshippers continued to sing.

Gatsby found herself thinking, *With everything else that's happened, what if...* There was no answer to the if and, before she could speculate further, Traussbery tugged at her sleeve again.

"Look, Ms. Donovan!" he hissed in a stage whisper. "Look!" His neck craned as he looked around them.

Squinting, she saw Traussbery's yellow leaflets everywhere, gripped between fingers, protruding from pockets, sticking out of backpacks.

He's right on one count, she thought, *they do want to see Stonehenge as it has been for five thousand years. That's a lot of consensus consciousness.*

She knew that she wanted to see it restored too. Willingly or not, she was part of that consensus consciousness.

The sky brightened, glowing in rich golden colors as the bottom edges of the clouds reflected the imminent arrival of the sun. Birds began to fly and sing.

5:00.

Traussbery leaned over and whispered, "I believe, Ms. Donovan, that this is, as they say, it."

The Druids fell silent. They blew out their candles en masse and stood as still as the sarsens. A white-robed man moved to the center of their group, holding a drum. Slowly and measuredly, he brought his palm down on the skin of the drum, once every five seconds.

A thousand people turned to gaze east toward the Heel Stone.

Gatsby swallowed, watching intently, all too aware of her heart racing between her ribs. There were no words for the moment, but it felt imbued with an unearthly power, reverence for the unfathomable and mysterious architects who had created the monument, wonder at the timelessness of stone and the earth itself, of the enigma of eternity.

A gold corona, like the Bailey's Beads of an eclipse, wavered on the horizon line. Thousands of eyes focused on the spot above and just to the left of the Heel Stone.

The drummer stopped.

Breathless.

The corona bridged the horizon line, and the disk of the run rose, a brilliant crescent of the world's first fire.

"Now," Traussbery whispered.

Something chimed.

Traussbery and Gatsby jumped, turning quickly to see that the drummer had raised a silver bell into the air and struck it with a small mallet. A moment later, he struck again. The single, high tone sang out, clear, floating through the night like the call of an ancient clarion, lost in an ocean of darkness.

A strange, copper-orange glow began to bathe the site, spreading up and toward the stones like an ocherous flood. The stones themselves seemed to radiate as vibrantly as the spot on the wall of the Coricancha where the double-diamond glyph had glowed into existence before Gatsby's eyes. The glowing newborn sun inched upward.

Gatsby glanced toward Traussbery; he was shaking violently, his skin blanched white. Before she could speak, she noticed the woman who had been standing near Stone 56. The woman pointed westward and shouted, "My god!!"

All eyes turned.

Stone 56 was trembling.

The woman darted away into the crowd, and everyone within ten meters scurried backward. Cries and shouts erupted.

The police began to rush forward, shoving people out of their way, as the stone vibrated.

"Traussbery—" Gatsby started.

Traussbery had frozen in terror.

Someone yelled, "Shit, LOOK OUT!" as the stone began to tip.

Pandemonium broke loose; the worshippers scattered, screaming, darting toward the embankment ditch or the fence near the motorway. Even the police turned and sprinted.

A huge, crushing, groaning, grinding sound filled the air as the forty-five-tonne boulder began to drop. Meter-wide hunks of earth and rock flew as the buried end of the rock churned through soil toward the surface. With the swiftness of a head-on collision, the stone crashed to the ground with the eardrum-blasting boom of a hundred cannons. The ground shook violently; chunks of rock flew; people ducked, screaming, running and crying as they were pelted with shards. The raining bits of stone dissipated and dust clouds swirled into the sky and over the crowd.

Gatsby felt her knees buckling. She reached out for Traussbery's arm and looked into his face. His chin trembled as he turned toward her, a portrait of incalculable misery.

"Are you all right?" Gatsby whispered.

"No," Traussbery croaked, coughing. "Entirely not all right."

A stout policeman bustled up near them. "You folks okay here? Anyone hurt?"

Heads shook, noses were blown, and shaking voices reported that for all the potential for catastrophic injury, the worst effects seemed to be cuts from rocketing pebbles.

Forming an authoritative frontline, the policemen began herding people toward the Visitor's Centre. Cries rose from those who were determined to continue their ceremony. The police assured everyone that as soon as they had confirmed that no one was injured or major damage done, the rite could continue.

The white-robed Druids who had been circled inside the stones cautiously reassembled near the pedestrian walkway. In shaking but melodious voices, they began to sing in a tongue that, after a moment, Gatsby recognized as old Gaelic.

"Can you see it, Ms. Donovan?" Traussbery asked as he stumbled toward a nearby bench and dropped onto it with a sigh. "How bad is the damage?"

She craned to look. A noisy group of policemen had circled around the stone, but she could still see most of it. What had been upright for millennia was now horizontal. Bits of the tooled edges had broken off but, worse than that, a jagged break had appeared at its midpoint—one that, if aggravated, would split the stone in half.

With a heavyhearted sigh, she said, "A bad crack at the middle."

Traussbery slumped. "Dear god. And I had hoped for..." He sighed deeply and stood. "It's cold and we have a long trip back."

Gatsby nodded wearily, limp with the fatigue that comes after cataclysmic disaster, the numb weariness that remains when the adrenaline has been exhausted. She looked around at the carnage—police hustled about, groups of people huddled together on the cold ground, rocking, calling out, crying, moaning. It was like the numb-with-shock aftermath of a terrorist bombing or massacre.

"Let's go," she whispered.

Traussbery nodded and started to push past the huddled toward the entrance tunnel.

The epitome of a failed experiment, and an incomprehensible disaster. Gatsby stumbled along in the wake of Traussbery's flapping overcoat. She knew what he had wanted. The same thing that she and a thousand other fervent souls had wished for. Restoration.

If wishing could make it so...

She let her mind ruminate on that thought until it started to bother her; then they were at the entrance gate, the blue-uniformed officer, the glare of lights, and a kilometer's dreary walk back to Traussbery's car.

As they started down the highway—now a graveyard of deserted cars, their owners still at the site—they talked little. Gatsby remembered the shock, several days back, of seeing an igloo-shaped glyph on the television screen at the Regent Arms, but she didn't tell Traussbery about it. Traussbery muttered to himself about particles and whether or how perception altered their behavior. Then, perhaps reminded of the state of Travis Norton's particles, he fell silent.

Back in the warmth of the Bentley, Traussbery squinted fiercely at the road signs as he drove. With her empty thermos of espresso in hand, Gatsby was snoring within minutes.

CHAPTER 25

She jerked awake and looked at the clock. Ten.

Eleven hours? Gatsby threw back the covers and trudged to the kitchen.

While the espresso machine gurgled and hissed, she ambled to her desk, turned on the computer, and logged onto her ISP.

International news; the latest space shuttle mission, new military crisis in Iran, tragic death of a country western singer. Scanning through the stories, she clicked the icon for local news.

A headline, capitals in a blue textbox, read, STONEHENGE MYSTERY EXPLODES!

Her heart skipped as she clicked the mouse to bring up the article. Reading the first line brought a thick, cold feeling as if a prehistoric sarsen had sunk into her body.

London (AP News International)—English Heritage staff arriving this morning at Stonehenge to investigate the mysterious repositioning of one of the central stones were aghast to find that the fallen stone has been removed. The organization president could not be reached for comment, but at the site, Chief Inspector Davis Lansing said, "Someone was extremely sophisticated about it. Estimates of the weight of the stone range up to forty-five tonnes, but we have seen no evidence of machinery, no trampling, ruts or drag marks. It has been suggested that the stone could have been lifted from the air, but no known aircraft could support that weight or the equipment that would be required. Heritage staff, a large crowd, and police forces were here just yesterday morning for an annual gathering. How could someone come out here during the night, by aircraft, carrying the kind of equipment that could raise this stone into the air, and make off with it? It's inexplicable, not to mention a truly heinous crime. This is a one-of-a-kind monument. Before fencing was put up, people would scrawl graffiti on the stones, or chip off pieces, or otherwise damage them. But to steal one?"

The story ended, appropriately, with that question.

"Bloody bastards!!" Gatsby swore at her computer. She dropped her head into her hands and closed her eyes, breathing hard. "What's English Heritage doing out there, contemplating their buggering navels? How could this happen?!?" *Christ, I suppose Traussbery is going to try to tell me that he's responsible!*

She slammed her mug on the desk and ran downstairs to her front door to retrieve the morning newspaper. The story was there on the front page.

Back in her flat, she headed to the phone. She muttered under her breath as she dialed and listened to the ring on the other end, "Come on, Traussbery, pick up." Her fingers drummed against the beige casing.

The line connected, and she heard the old man's raspy voice. "Yes?"

"Traussbery? Gatsby Donovan."

"Ms. Donovan, how marvelous to—"

"Have you read this morning's paper?" she cut in, knowing from his cheery tone that he hadn't.

"No, I'm grading exams. Why?"

"I think you should read it for yourself. Front page."

Traussbery harrumphed discontentedly. "Ms. Donovan, I don't have time for guessing games. Why don't you—"

"Just get your paper and look at it!"

Another harumph, then the sound of the phone clattering on a hard surface. Gatsby sighed as she heard scuffling noises, a door being closed, a few high-pitched barks, and the sound of crinkling newspaper.

Then silence.

Traussbery began coughing violently.

This is it, he's going to have a bloody heart attack while I'm on the line, she thought. "Traussbery, are you there? Answer me!"

After a fit of horrible coughing, Traussbery finally caught his breath and said, "Here, Ms. Donovan. Incredulous but...this is—"

"Do you see it? Stone 56, Traussbery! Stone 56 is bloody GONE! What did it, Traussbery, miscreant particles? Did you visualize this?!?"

Traussbery's voice shook as he whispered, "I had nothing to do with this." He asked softly, "Dear god, what are we dabbling with, Ms. Donovan?"

"You tell me!" Closing her eyes, she threw herself on her couch with the phone pressed hard against her left ear. "This is it, Traussbery, the end of the line. Not only have I wasted most of my sabbatical chasing some undecipherable glyphs and listening to your crazy theories about particle physics and moving boulders with your mind, but I think this whole situation is getting dangerous—do you know what I am saying? First someone rearranges Stonehenge and now they are trying to destroy it! What kind of criminals are we dealing with?"

She heard more paper rustling sounds and a quivering sigh. "If I knew the answer to that, Ms. Donovan, you never would have gone to Mazilaq. Perhaps none of this would have ever happened and we might not even be having this conversation. But when the stakes in a dangerous game have risen, that does not mean that the players throw down their hand, does it? We can't give up now!"

She understood his meaning: was she in or out?

She was quiet for a long time as she stared out the living room window at the sky, the birds making lazy circles above the streetlights, and listened to the gurgling of the espresso machine.

All I want is OUT, but I'll be damned if I can let these glyphs go. There's something there, something I'm supposed to know. Or figure out.

Finally she said, "I don't know, Traussbery. I'm not sure what it means for me, but I'm not going anywhere near Stonehenge. Whoever has removed that stone possesses technology that will baffle the scientific world, and I don't want to get in the way if they decide they want to start removing *people*."

"Of course, Ms. Donovan, I understand. General consensus as to responsibility will probably point to one of the fringe groups. But the Society of Earth, the World Peace Builders, the Stonehenge Campaign, or any of the other groups that showed themselves there would not have the sophistication to achieve this, let alone the motivation."

"Well, as they say, there's one in every crowd, Traussbery. You put a thousand cultists and fanatics in one place, and a critical event is bound to take place." She snorted, flipping through the newspaper article. "My god, this story implicates every group from Earth First, the Anarchist Teapot, the Rainbow Gatherings, the Atlanteans, and the Vegan Society to the Crop Circle Connector, for godssake! Crisis is what these people live for! What if they start some sort of Stonehenge jihad? A political event? Take and shoot hostages if the stones aren't all liberated?"

"I couldn't answer that, Ms. Donovan." Traussbery coughed miserably. "But let me ask, has your research into our glyphs unearthed any information that might speak to this catastrophe?"

Gatsby threw her head back on the arm of the couch and closed her eyes. "No. I don't have any more information." The image she had seen in the Regent Arms—should she tell Traussbery? She decided not to, at least not at the moment. Its impact seemed absurd in light of the disappearance of an irreplaceable piece of world history.

With a start, she noticed her left hand trembling violently; her heart started to race.

"I have to go," she blurted. "I'll call you later."

"Please do. And in the—"

Unceremoniously slamming the phone into its cradle, she breathed hard, staring at her hand. It jittered on her terrycloth robe. She watched her hand as, trembling, it moved upward. Then holding it at eye level, palm away, she watched it moving slowly; the thumb dipped forward, then pulled back as the wrist rotated and the third and fourth fingers tipped downward. It was the same movement she had observed over a month before, in her office, just before Nelson Clevis had knocked on her door and scared the hell out of her.

Fear bit into her vitals, forcing her to get up and go to the kitchen. She filled her mug with strong espresso and then, for no reason at all, looked in the cupboard for peanut butter. Her hand had almost stopped shaking.

Scooping out dollops of the peanut butter with her index finger and slowly sluicing them around in her mouth, she stared glassy-eyed out the living room window, expecting a glyph or the face of the Virgin Mary or some other inexplicable sign to appear in the clouds.

A thousand Druids within arm's reach of Stone 56 and, within twenty-four hours, it's gone. The next thought melded irony and despair. *Is there a connection?*

CHAPTER 26

At the St. James station, the train screeched to a stop. The doors opened with a pneumatic wheeze, and Gatsby threw her gym bag over her shoulder and made her way onto the platform.

Cracking good workout, Gats, she thought, using the argot she'd picked up from Celia, *really capital.*

The flow of late afternoon Tube passengers was beginning to swell to rush-hour levels, and Gatsby had to dodge and swerve as she made her way down the advert-crammed corridors toward the Sloane Street exit.

As she whizzed around a corner, a blue rectangular sign for the women's bathroom caught her eye. She stopped, caught between the tired aching to get home in time for the evening news and the demands of her bladder. The bladder won.

Stepping inside the empty lavatory, she dashed into the first stall, inspected the floor before setting her bag on the tiles, and unzipped her jeans.

Once adjusted to the bite of the cold seat, she let her eyes wander over the tangle of graffiti scrawled over the steel walls—the usual statements on romance, identity, politics and sex, who loved whom, who didn't love, who will never love, who cannot love. Who can love whom. Why love sucks. Why women and men are the way they are. Reproductive rights, Gertrude Stein, a quote from a horror film, and where, how, and when the reader could get laid by someone identified only as Z.

Amazing, Gatsby thought as she perused, *someday I'll do a book on graffiti as modern cuneiform, comparisons with hist—*

Up and to her left, a drawing on the wall caught her eye. It was a dark circle about the size of a 50p coin; within the circle, at a forty-five-degree angle, she saw a cross resembling a tilted, lowercase "t."

That's...I've seen it before...what is that shape? Almost like something on the Phaistos Disk but somehow different, or...or is it...no...

Her Levi's bunched around her ankles, Gatsby gazed at the drawing. As if in a dream, her left hand rose and moved toward it until her fingertip met the cold metal and lightly stroked the curves of the shape.

The hairs on the back of her neck rose.

Where have I seen this before? Where? I know what it...do I know what it means?

She rummaged through her gym bag, finally finding a ballpoint pen at the bottom. Then she searched for a piece of scratch paper and came up with a bank deposit slip. She sketched the symbol onto the back of the slip and, stuffing the drawing into her bag, thought, *God, am I going to spend the rest of my life hunting for glyphs in TV screens and public bathrooms? Christ, this has got—*

Pain sizzled through her left arm, making her yelp at the shock. Her left hand twitched, and before she could look down at it, it thrust up into the air before her eyes, fluttering, repeating the same gesture it had before: the thumb dipped down, then the second, third, and fourth fingers pulled downward as the thumb flipped upward, over and over.

Incredibly, her right hand moved upward to chest height, while Gatsby stared, goggle-eyed, wheezing through her teeth, helpless with terror as her hands moved outside of conscious control.

The right hand splayed itself out flat and the fingers began to wriggle up and down, as if moving across an invisible keyboard. Beads of sweat formed on her face as she tried with every molecule of will and muscle control to stop them, but her hands kept fluttering, and the panic brought tears to her eyes, choking in her throat.

I've got to get help!

Flexing her shoulder muscles, she was able to get both hands down to her lap, to press her wrist bones hard against her hips, and tug her jeans up as she stood. Then there was the problem of the zipper. As she stood frozen, terrified and wondering what to do, her left hand stopped spasming for a split second, and she was able to grab the zipper tab and yank it up in one motion. Panting, she watched her hands—both now hung motionless except for occasional twitches. Awkwardly but successfully snatching up her gym bag, she threw the stall door open with a bang that made the mirrors over the sinks shake, and rushed out of the bathroom.

Lurching down the corridor toward her exit, swearing and still on the verge of tears, she bumped into an elderly woman. Gatsby turned, reaching to steady the woman by her arm, and stammered, "Oh, I'm do, excuse do, sorry—"

The woman clutched at her purse, frowning, and croaked, "Young lady, what did you say?"

Gatsby had already turned the corner and was bounding up the escalator. Then at street level, at the Sloane Street entrance, she headed down the sidewalk toward her flat.

"Son of a bloody buggering bitch," she hissed, the ball of terror in her stomach molting into nausea. "I should have seen Berger!...epilepsy as Parkinson's...are kind of stroke...something neurological..." Muttering vehemently, she ignored the passersby who quickly moved out of her way, likely imagining her to be a lunatic, transient, or Tourette's sufferer. "Goddamn it! Why didn't I call him? Now see probably do late! I've probably—"

Turning the corner onto King's Road, Gatsby smacked hard into a small body.

"Shit! Why d—" she started and then took a good look at the person: a girl who peered up at her with dark, almond-shaped eyes, standing silently in a blue jumpsuit. Her clay-brown skin and slightly flattened nose gave her an exotic look, and her long black hair had been swept back into a ponytail. She gazed up at Gatsby with a solemn, inquisitive expression and then raised both hands in front of her face and made a series of gestures.

"Y...y..." Gatsby sputtered, incomprehensibility reeling in her. "Did you—"

The girl blinked and repeated the hand signals faster, more emphatically.

"Who are you?!" Gatsby heard the rising panic in her voice, felt her lungs lurching for air, and then a strong smell assaulted her: a head-clearing scent that shot through her nostrils like a wash of ice water and, instantly, she knew what it was. The same smell she'd encountered in peculiar places ever since the trip to Peru. In her car. In her shampoo bottle. In the bizarre espresso which had suddenly and magically tasted like tea.

Peppermint.

"God," she heard herself whisper.

The girl opened her mouth and spoke in an unfamiliar language. Her hands fluttering crazily, she repeated the gestures over and over, more emphatically, as she spoke louder.

"Wait, I can't...I don't understand!" As Gatsby reached out to grab her, the girl turned and fled down the street.

"Shit! Wait!" Gatsby shouted and ran after her. After chasing for a block, the girl had vanished into the crowds of pedestrians.

"Wait!" she shouted once more, ignoring the perturbed stares around her. She flopped back against the side of a building, panting, "Damn it!" Cars drove by as the street light changed to green; a girl walking a Corgi strolled past and gave her a disgusted look. Gatsby took a shaky breath and shouldered her bag. On quivering legs, hoping she wouldn't be sick in the gutter, she slowly walked home.

She stirred the cream in with one finger and tossed it all down in one swallow. Lying back on her couch, with a stiff drink in her bloodstream, a pillow over her face, and no uncanny, unintelligible children in sight, she was starting to feel marginally better.

What the hell can it mean...

Thinking over the day's events, she asked herself the same question again and again.

Then she picked up the phone next to the couch. Dialed.

"Hello?"

"Celia?"

"Gats, dahling! How—"

"Celia, I have to see you." She took a deep breath. "Professionally."

There was a pause, then Celia's subdued voice. "Do you want to tell me what it's about now or later?"

"Later." Gatsby took another sip and swallowed. "I've got to talk to somebody, things are happening to me, Celia, that...that I can't explain, and I'm starting to feel like I...I'm losing my grip."

"I have a, let's see, a two o'clock cancellation tomorrow, will that work?"

"Fine." She sighed and pulled the pillow off her head. "Thanks, Celia."

"Are you...okay? You're not—"

"What, a danger to myself?" She snorted. "Hardly. I'm going to take a hot bath and go to bed."

Celia's tone sounded anxious. "All right, but you know, if you want to call for anything, anything Gats, just ring me at home."

"Thanks. I'll just see you tomorrow."

"Goodnight, hon."

She hung up, then called the office of Jerome Berger, MD, and left an urgent message, demanding an appointment as soon as possible. Then, dropping the hand piece into the receiver, she pulled the pillow back over her head and closed her eyes.

My body has gone AWOL and taken my mind with it...That girl! How the hell do I keep running into dark-skinned girls who all look the same? If I'm hallucinating her, it's become a bloody realistic hallucination...she did try to talk to me, but not in a language I've ever heard. And the gestures...were they...were they? Something like the kinds of patterns that MY hands made?! I just didn't get a good enough look...and the smell coming off her! Christ! Peppermint! The most memorable smell from my childhood...that field of wild peppermint in back of our house!

The nerved-wracked state she'd been spinning in since dashing from the Tube lavatory dissolved into a wash of self-pity, followed by nostalgia for the golden age of her childhood; free of anxiety, protected, loved. The memory of a box popped into her mind—a box of childhood memorabilia she had stashed in her bedroom—and after a moment, she pushed herself from the couch.

She flicked on her bedroom light, went to the closet, and found the box, tucked in a corner and piled with other boxes of forgotten clothing. With a bit of rearranging, she had the worn cardboard box in hand and let her eyes wander across the words she'd scrawled on it with a black felt-tip pen, kid stuff.

Looking at it brought a weary smile to her face. She dropped to the carpet, sitting cross-legged, and pulled the top flaps open. Plunging her hands inside, she dug through the treasures of years gone by. High school report cards. Photographs of friends, signed on the back. Yellowed yearbooks. A necklace from a forgotten beau. The ID tag she'd had made for her dog, Bagel. A pressed corsage. Her favorite elementary school books, *Charlotte's Web, Harriet the Spy*, and *A Wrinkle in Time*.

And a diary.

She picked up the frayed book, fingering the strap that had at one time been attached to a miniature lock. Torn, it now hung loose. Gatsby ran her fingers over the dusty green vinyl covering and then opened it.

It was the diary she'd kept when she was ten. *Sixth grade,* she thought, reading some of the entries. Many of them were terse: *Turned in science projects. Karen and I went to Dairy Freez on our bikes, got choc melts, she stayed over. Some were more descriptive: Kristy wants to be friends with me, but she doesn't see that every time I'm around her and her pack of uptight friends, she ignores me and treats me like dirt. I should tell her to get lost. Or I can tell her new boyfriend that she doesn't like HIM anymore. Ha!*

She flipped through more pages, through the months of that year and then stopped at May.

May was blank. June, July. Blank.

Nothing? Gatsby thought, frowning. *I don't remember going to summer camp or anything, how come I skipped thr...wait, that must h—*

She pulled in a deep breath. *When I went to see that counselor. Was that it? It must be...what WAS that all about? Why did Mom and Dad send me to a therapist at age ten, for godssake? You'd have thought that I was...*

Her gaze moved from the blank pages down to the carpet, the weave, the patterns running diagonally, beige, brown, grey. A deep feeling of heaviness moved over her, quiet, stillness. For a moment, her eyes glazed over, her vision doubled.

In a blink, she focused again. She took a deep breath, closed the diary, put it back in the box, and pushed the box back into the far corner of the closet.

Later, as she lay in bed staring at the ceiling, her hands twitched, making small, repetitive patterns. She finally jammed them underneath her, hoping, somehow, to make it stop—wanting and at the same time not wanting to know why it had started.

CHAPTER 27

Gatsby froze at the door, her eyes moving over the name carved on a wooden plaque: Celia R. Devereaux, MSW.

Millennial Sense Worker? Missing Sanity Wizard?

The corridor was empty except for a ficus at the far end under a glowing red exit sign. The other doors were closed—in fact, the clinic seemed deserted. The suburb itself—Kensington, about ten minutes from Gatsby's flat on King's Road—was strangely quiet.

Can I really go through with this? Looking down at her hands, the imperative surfaced loud in her head: Now, before you lose whatever thread of nerve you've got left!

She flashed back to the day before—the elderly woman she had bumped into as she had bolted from the women's bathroom—and knocked. The door swung open.

In her professional role, Celia's look was subdued. Softly elegant in navy blue silk. A blazer, loose slacks, a scoop-neck blouse, gold-rimmed glasses perched on her small nose. Her black hair swung against her neck as she smiled and motioned for Gatsby to step inside.

Although Gatsby had seen Celia's office a handful of times, the visits had never been from the keen perspective of a client. The long, narrow room was lined with shelves and psychological reference books and felt somehow comforting in its mild disarray. At the far end, two well-padded armchairs, oak end tables, and broadleaf plants sat in a pool of sunlight.

"Have a seat," Celia motioned. They settled into the chairs.

Gatsby dropped her shoulderbag to the floor. She took a deep breath before making eye contact. "Celia, this feels, well..."

"Odd to seek therapy with your best friend?" Celia finished. "Uncomfortable? Overexposed?" Her lips raised in a delicate smile as she tilted her head to one side, looking Gatsby in the eye.

Gatsby gave a quick nod.

Celia propped her navy pumps on one of the end tables. "Dahling, if it will make you more at ease, I can take my clothes off and then we'll both feel naked."

The laughter that bubbled from her belly was an instant relaxant. "Thanks, Celia." She sighed heavily. "You're a good friend. That's why I had to see you, and why it feels so difficult to talk about this."

"What exactly is *this*?" Celia nudged quietly.

Gatsby swallowed. "You know about these glyphs I've been trying to decipher. And I told you about Professor Traussbery." She filled Celia in on some of Traussbery's quantum theories and, more recently, his allegations of telekinesis.

"There are two more glyphs, six in all now. Not one of which I would take seriously under normal circumstances, except for the fact that I feel that I've seen them before! That I know what they mean, but...I...can't fathom how or where."

Celia nodded.

Gatsby's shoulders drooped as her voice lowered. She stared into her lap. "And then there's this girl." She tried to laugh but only managed a shallow gasp. "This is *almost* the weirdest part, Celia. When I was in Peru, I saw a Quechuan girl outside the window of a taverna. Nothing wacky about that, right? But back in London, at Heathrow, I saw a girl at the customs desk that looked exactly like her. Her bloody twin. Naturally, I wrote it off—coincidence and jet lag. But just yesterday—"

She swallowed before continuing, retelling her experience in the bathroom, discovering the spherical, T-crossed glyph scrawled on the wall, and how her hands had fluttered out of control. Panic rose in her throat and squeezed her lungs. "It wasn't the first time, either. It happened once before, in my office, the first day of my sabbatical. I...there was nothing I could do, I had no control over my body, it was like an alien presence possessing me, and I should have called Berger immediately, but..." Tears welled in her eyes. "Celia, you can't know how horrifying it was to be so, so useless, sitting there and watching your body flailing around like there's a madwoman inside you, like, like some deranged marionette!" She wiped at her eyes.

Celia leaned forward to rest her hand on her friend's knee. "Describe it as best you can. Slow."

"I panicked and ran out, ran most of the way home. On the corner where King's Road meets Harrington, I ran into this girl, and when I got a good look at her, she...she looked exactly like the girl at the airport *and* the girl in Peru! It was her!" She closed her eyes for a moment, pressing her fingers against her temples. "Now do you understand why I'm here?"

She recounted the girl's unintelligible speech and the hand gestures that might, in some *non compos mentis* universe, resemble the gestures that her own hands had made, outside her will to make them stop or ability to explain them.

Gatsby rubbed her forehead and glanced at her hands cautiously. "Aside from Traussbery trying to tell me that he can flip boulders with his mind, the strangest bit of all is the smell that came off her. Peppermint. I've been smelling it ever since I got back from Peru—in the shower, in my car, even in my buggering dreams. And it's a memory-rich smell for me. When I was a kid, we had a field of wild peppermint in back of the house, and I spent a lot of time out in that field, surrounded by the smell of peppermint."

Celia nodded. "Smell is persistent—the oldest sense, nestled down in the limbic system with basic survival instincts."

Gatsby stared back, wide-eyed.

"Does the smell of peppermint have a particular meaning to you? Specific connotation?"

Gatsby shook her head. "It...well, it doesn't, or...actually, I would say it shouldn't, but for some reason, I don't know," she paused, "it feels like it should mean something. I have this feeling that it's something I should pay attention to but I'll be buggered if I can say why."

Celia watched dust motes drifting through the beams of sunlight coming through the window. "You are paying attention to it. You're here." She leaned forward, elbows resting on her silk pants. "There's more to this. Hidden in your subconscious, maybe trying to emerge but being blocked."

Gatsby leaned back in her chair, staring out the window at the light flow of afternoon traffic, head turned to the side, almost to look away from the feeling that was growing inside her. It was there—something spectral, something pricking at her psyche.

Every time I tell myself there's a reason, a reasonable explanation—a logical explanation!—I get signals that don't have a face or a name...how can everything in my life go upside down so quickly? A spasm moved through her body and with it came tears. She gasped as it possessed her, as the panic she'd carried for weeks spilled out in a hot gush. *God, I'm unraveling...*

"I'm unraveling," she moaned, her voice cracking, looking into her friend's eyes with naked dread in her own, "I'm fucking unraveling."

Celia leaned forward and held her, letting Gatsby drop her head onto her shoulder, letting the tears become dark blots in the blue silk. She held her friend quietly, then drew a tissue from the box sitting on the end table. "No extra charge." She held it out.

Gatsby blew her nose, wiped her eyes, and heaved a huge sigh. "Oh god. I can't even remember the last time I bawled."

Celia shifted her chair so that it faced Gatsby's. "Gatsby, if you're willing, I'd like to try a hypnotherapy process, and we'll see if we can make some friendly associations alongside the frightening feelings you're having. We can do it so that if at any time you feel you're getting too close to those feelings of unraveling, you can come back to a place where you are safe." She laid her hands flat on her thighs. "Do you think you're ready?"

"I have to be." Gatsby heard her voice trembling and roughly cleared her throat. "What do I do?"

Celia took in and then slowly blew out a breath. "It's the easiest thing to do; we all do it many times a day. Every time someone reads a book, watches a movie, or has a conversation, she is in a self-hypnotic state. That's all this is.

A quiet, focused, relaxed state in a safe place, just sitting here in my office with me, no one else here. So let your body be very comfortable, move around in the chair until it feels very comfortable against your back, underneath your legs, supporting your body. Let it hold your body, let it do the work for you. Let yourself be supported by its frame while your body can begin to feel relaxed and quiet..."

Already noticing her breath slowing, Gatsby leaned back into the soft cushions of the chair, let her head rest against the frame and, with a quick dab at her nose with the tissue, let her eyelids drop.

"That's right. And letting your body relax and become quiet, you may even want to let your hands rest on the arms of the chair. That's good. Resting lightly on the arms of the chair, so lightly that you almost can't even feel them. Your legs so comfortable against the seat of the chair that you almost can't even feel it. Your feet so comfortable resting on the floor that you almost can't even feel it..."

She continued working through a slow progression of body relaxation and focusing suggestions, altering her own breathing patterns so that she inhaled and posed questions as Gatsby breathed in, exhaled and offered statements as Gatsby breathed out. She altered her body language to mirror Gatsby's. In five minutes, she had noticed that the movements behind Gatsby's closed eyelids had almost stopped. She could see that Gatsby's skin color had lightened slightly as her pulse, breathing, and micromovements slowed. She adjusted her voice, letting it drop to a deeper alto and consciously timing the spacing and cadence of her phrases.

Inside, eyes closed, moving into the dark space within her mind, Gatsby sensed images...words...voices... sensations and sounds mixing, blending and melting like soft watercolors on a canvas. Scenes from childhood. From the snow-capped vistas in Peru. Classrooms at Blake. Walking around London. Stonehenge. Celia's voice flowed in and around her, guiding her lightly. She felt as if she had slipped into the muted, velvety realm between wake and sleep where conscious and dreamlike subconscious images danced together. She sensed the rise and fall of her lungs and diaphragm in a slow rhythm, her heartbeat pumping peacefully and otherwise was unaware of the room, or the chair, or why she was sitting in it.

"...that's right. Very deep and comfortable. Noticing how easy it is in your mind, to see back to the past...now, imagine that if you were standing on a road at an intersection, which way would the past be? In front or behind you? Left or right?"

Gatsby's head dipped as she replied, her voice monotone, "Over my left shoulder."

"Over your left shoulder. Good. So if you turn to your left and look down the road into your past, how would you describe what you see?"

It took a moment for her to find the word for the feeling. "It feels...open."

"Good. So if you were to take a small step, and start to walk down that path, to watch yourself walking back into your past, would that feel open to you?"

"Yes."

"All right. Let's start this way. I'm right next to you, and as you begin to walk down that path, a part of you will stay at the intersection. At where you and I are now. That part will stay there at the intersection, which we could call the home base, and if at any time you want to get off the path, or feel afraid, you can go back to your home base."

"Mmmm..."

"Good. Now as we start to walk together down this path, you will be able to see yourself at different ages in your past. We're starting to walk back to age thirty...how does it feel?"

Gatsby cleared her throat. Her hands fluttered over the armrests of the chair. "Exciting. Moving to London. New job at the museum."

"That's good. Now I'd like to ask you some other questions...when we get to certain spots on this path, I'll ask you to think of a color that could be around you, or on the road, or in the clothing you're wearing. At thirty, what color would you see around you?"

"Ummm...green."

"Green, good. Okay, let's keep walking down the road, going back into the past, and we're coming to twenty-five...how does it feel?"

"Busy. Grad school. Thesis."

"And is there a color that seems to go with twenty-five?"

Eyes closed, Gatsby smiled, shaking her head, remembering SUNY. "Yellow."

Celia continued, taking Gatsby visually and emotionally back through age twenty, then to fifteen, noting the associations and the colors as well as Gatsby's tone of voice and unconscious gestures. As a trained hypnotherapist, Celia could tell that Gatsby had quite easily reached a deep trance state—she moved her eyes under her lids at certain memories, drummed her fingers or recrossed her feet or cleared her throat at others.

"Okay. That's right. So fifteen is a new and exciting time for you, starting middle school and making new friends. And the color that could go with fifteen is?"

A frown moved over her forehead. "Uhhh...red. Dark."

"A red object? Or a red feeling?"

"Red..." Her fingers twisted into the chair fabric. "A red...light. Red stop sign."

"A red light. A stop sign." Celia leaned toward Gatsby, watching her eyes beneath her lids, watching her smallest movements. She saw tiny muscles twisting along Gatsby's jawline and shoulder. "Like something is coming to a stop? Is the sign for you?"

The frown deepened on Gatsby's forehead—her tongue ran over her lower lip. "I...something had to stop, I think...I...I had to stop, red is to stop...but..."

"To stop. That's good. And remember, if you need to go back to home base, you can do that at any time. That's the safe place. Is this an unsafe place, here at this section of the road at fifteen, where there's a red stop sign?"

Gatsby took a deep breath. "Okay...now...but I'm afraid."

Celia also took a deep breath and let it out. "Okay. All right. So if we were to keep walking, down the path, toward age ten, would you be willing to do that?"

"Hmmm...okay."

Celia noted that Gatsby's voice had moved into a slightly higher register, as if sounding through smaller vocal chords.

"Okay. So now we're going to start walking on the path, toward ten. Is there a color that you begin to see as we walk?"

The frown on Gatsby's face disappeared; her eyebrows peaked upward, her mouth dropped open. "Black." Her hands tensed into fists; she breathed faster.

"Something black?" Celia asked, dropping her voice to a hushed tone, spacing her words slightly farther apart. "Can you describe the black for me?"

Gatsby's eyes scrunched tight, her nose flared. "I...can't see into the...black...around me...nothing, a hole..." Her fingers gripped the armrests tighter. "I can't look there do anymore...can't see it anymore...can't remember why I had to go there...if I don't stop...they want me do stop, keep telling me I can't...I see are, and...but not see do anymore because I have do are stop—"

The words tumbled out, faster and higher. Celia leaned forward anxiously, knowing that something could be revealing itself, and if she ended the process now, it might stay hidden forever.

"Okay," she whispered, "you don't have to look. If you want to stop, we—"

"Can't see it anymore...do as see...it's time to..." Gatsby's head turned back and forth, no. "It's are...it's are, can't have and it do are see anymore...see have to let it go..." Slowly, her head stopped moving, her muscles relaxed. Her fingers spread across the armrests, and she pulled in a deep breath. Celia watched carefully.

"Do you want to go back to home base?"

A tear spilled from one eye and slowly ran down her cheek. Gatsby pressed her lips together tightly. "Let it gohhh..." A collage of images swept through her mind. Fake plants. The beach. A dragon sitting in a tree. Then, vividly, the face of a girl with almond-shaped eyes and dark hair, pulled back in a ponytail. The expression of hope and longing—and loneliness—on the little girl's face brought a stab of pain, of sadness for something treasured. Something sent away. Something let go.

Gatsby opened her eyes.

"Gats?" Celia whispered, confused. She hadn't ended the process.

Something treasured, something let go...

"I had to let it go," Gatsby whispered thickly. "Made me let it go."

Celia knew it was time to ask. Softly, she said, "Let what go?"

Gatsby dropped her head into her hands, wept, and let herself be submerged in loss. Fear. Feelings that had been buried for long, so long...

that could not be spoken

because

Celia's hands gently covered Gatsby's. "I'm here."

Gatsby jerked her hands away, breathing hard, tears swimming in her eyes, and sensed panic surging from all directions.

Tell / don't tell.

Her face flushed and wet, she reached for her bag. "I have to go."

Celia lurched forward. "Gatsby, we're in the middle—"

"I have to go. I can't. I can't talk." She stood abruptly, wiping off the tears with her palm. "I'm sorry, but I have to go, now."

"Gatsby?" Celia followed, confusion arching on her face, as Gatsby headed for the door. "Stop!" She grabbed Gatsby's arm and forced her to turn and face her. "Are you hearing me? We're not through, you need to end this congruently! You can't go!"

Gatsby replied evenly. "I can't do it right now. I have to go. I'll call you later." Sniffing, she pushed the strap of her bag up over her shoulder, turned, and walked out the door.

"Gatsby!" Celia called after her as she watched her friend disappearing down the hall. Gatsby didn't turn or answer but steadfastly headed for the stairwell.

"Christ," Celia whispered.

She quietly closed the door and sighed, crossed the room to her desk, and sat to make some notes in her session log.

She made special notation of the nonsensical sentences: "I see as are, and...but not see do anymore because I have do are stop...can't see it anymore...do as see..."

Staring out the window, Celia shook her head and murmured, "What the hell?"

CHAPTER 28

One more for the road, she thought, and flipped on the computer; it beeped and grunted as it booted up. Gatsby crossed the room to shut her office door and then settled into her chair before her desk. She let her shoulderbag drop to the floor.

She'd driven to the museum late. Only Russ Mackie, the elderly guard with a wingbow mustache, had been at his post to nod at her as she had walked through the main lobby and down the dark corridor to her office.

A ten-week sabbatical and I spend it here. The deciding vote in the case of Gatsby versus sanity, she thought morosely as she wheeled her chair up to her desk and took a deep breath. The Logos program initialized. On the screen, the four glyphs she'd scanned appeared, glowing ethereally in a cobalt blue background.

Reaching into her bag, she brought out two slips of paper, the sketches she had made after lunching at the Regent Arms and in the bathroom of the Tube: the letter D, laying on its back, shaped like an igloo, with a teardrop inside; the circle with a lowercase "t" shape inside, tilted at forty-five degrees.

She raised the lid of the scanner, flipped the power switch on, and laid the sketches on the glass surface. The machine whirred; momentarily, she was looking at all six glyphs, digitized, on the monitor. As she stared at them, the names of the possible matches that the software had identified ran through her head—*Elamitic, Grantha, Moso, Yu-Chen, Iberian, Lycian...*

Why am I here? Really? I keep flogging away at this puzzle as if it can be solved, but am I kidding myself? To what end?

She moved her right hand to the mouse on the pyramid-shaped mouse pad next to her keyboard. Her fingers curled over its plastic shell and began to move it; as she clicked on the digitized glyphs, they moved in accord. First she lined them up, left to right, in the order in which they had appeared. Then right to left.

Something's...just...not...not the right arrangement? But what is?

A hot twinge shook her hand.

She looked down and saw it trembling as if the mouse had turned into a small vibrator.

Don't you DARE!

She forced herself to manipulate the mouse, rearranging the shapes on the screen, and suddenly a click reverberated through her, like the "aha!" of finding a word that fits in a crossword puzzle where no other word can fit. Her thoughts moved in synch with the rolling sound of the mouse's track ball, using the nomenclature she had concocted for the glyphs, sending out placement instructions like a football coach.

"See as in do are a," she whispered, completely unaware that she had spoken aloud.

First glyph, Flag-Cross, on the right of the screen. Second, Double Diamond, opposite it, on the left. Third, Sphere with Wings, on the right, directly below the Flag-Cross. Fourth, Crescent Moon, between the first and second and above them. Fifth, Igloo, on the left, directly below Double Diamond. Sixth, Slanted T, between the third and fifth and below them.

She stared, breathing through her mouth, waiting for the glyphs to voice themselves through the speakers on each side of her monitor, to aspirate their glottals and fricatives and reveal their encrypted message.

see as in...

She blinked, shaking her head to clear the fog-blip that had wisped through her mind.

Where the hell did that come from?

She felt her heart thudding dully but loudly, her mouth dry as bone, her hand shaking.

Follow me!

She quickly glanced around and spotted the phone on the right side of her desk. *If I need to call for help...but what if I'm not able? What if I fall and I can't get up, ha ha...she* thought, realizing that the mocking phrase didn't sound funny at all. It sounded deadly.

Panic flowered in her chest and with it, a barrage of images splashed across the screen of her mind, as if an insane projectionist leaped and gibbered in the booth, forcing her to see...

fake plants...Ritz crackers and peanut butter...

Both hands shook so hard that she lost her grip on the mouse. It skittered out of her fingers and off the mouse pad to hit the desktop with a hollow plastic snick.

Want another M & M, Gats?

"Nooo..." she heard herself moan through clenched teeth.

Her right hand began to rise. Messages racing from her cerebral cortex down her spine to her arm were futile. It rose, like a hypnotized appendage, from the surface of the desk to eye level.

Oh god what's...

Her mouth filled with hot, copper-tasting wetness, a taste like chewing a mouthful of pennies.

The left hand slowly rose from beside her keyboard into the air to meet the other hand, about eight inches from her face. Both hands had moved into a warding gesture, palms facing away from her, fingers spread, shaking violently.

*Epilepsy...stroke...*The voice screamed unthinkable options inside her head while at the same time she would have done anything, even plunge an ice pick into the voice's owner, to make it shut up, shut up, shut up.

Is it better to know or not to know why your mind and body are leaving Normal ha ha... Insane laughter gurgled through her brain and she bit hard on her lower lip to keep from screaming.

The left hand curled into a fist: both hands turned, facing each other like pugilists.

A tree trunk seemed to have lodged in her throat. Her mouth opened and closed as hissing gasps pumped out of it; her heartbeat raced in tachycardia, she could feel it throbbing in the veins in her eyes, in her teeth.

in do are a...

Follow me!

A red stop sign filled her mind's eye...and Celia's voice...hidden in your subconscious, maybe trying to emerge but being blocked...ever been hypnotized?

STOP SIGN! STOP SIGN! The smell of cologne dripped, bitter tasting, down the back of her throat.

The left hand snapped forward, slapping into the palm of her right. Then the fingers of her right hand fell forward, so that the tips of the right-hand fingers rested on the knuckle line of the left. The two thumbs, side by side, pressed up against each other, like twins huddling together in a storm.

God what is it oh don't...

Her vision doubled, the room spun, and she felt herself falling, her body sinking into the padding of her chair...the room grew taller...she was looking up at a ceiling that was now twenty feet above her.

Down the rabbit hole???

The filing cabinet, the computer, the desk, the espresso machine, the fax machine, the scanner—all melted into waking dream. Staring straight ahead but not seeing herself, the perspective often taken in dreams, Gatsby found herself looking at a wide, wild expanse...

Her hands compressed so hard that she wondered if she was close to breaking bones, her lungs locked in convulsive, heaving hitches, her heart gone into arrhythmia and sweat pouring into her T-shirt; she closed her eyes and waited for the worst.

Something snapped. A thousand flashbulbs exploded at once.

She was in Seattle.

Don't...my...is...wha...

Impossible to put one word after another. So clumsy. She then realized how effortless it was to dismiss internal dialogue and let word-images roll over her—as easy as flying in a dream.

There was a knifepoint of fear and underneath it, darkness. Where the red stop sign warned her not to go?

Had to let it goohhhh...
Letting go was the only option. She did and it was there,
all of it, in full rich color, sound, smell, taste, feeling—she
was there, in it, swimming...

The expanse was the field of wild peppermint behind her
parent's house, and she was ten years old, running through
the grasses, laughing...

The middle of July in a quiet suburb just north of Seattle.
The weeks of summer had never been lonely before. They
were always full of trips, summer camp, Scrabble, playing
Red Rover, television shows, hanging out with Lisa and
Dana and the neighborhood kids, and endless hours of the
flights of fancy that are childhood.

But for Gatsby, this summer was already unbearably
boring and becoming desperately lonely.

Penelope, her older sister, had come down with a
terminal case of puberty; she was in the throes of make-up,
first crushes, first kisses. And while she used to be a great
companion to Gatsby, she now acted as if she would rather
die than be caught with her ten-year-old sister. A sneering
tone had crept into her voice, especially when she said "little
sister" with emphasis on the *little*. She'd even learned a few
choice swear words, took great delight in trying them out on
her little sister, and was becoming completely insufferable.

As she sat on the back porch of her house, the backs of
her legs warmed by the sunbathed pine slats, Gatsby kicked
her feet. Her lower lip pushed out defiantly. Penelope was
no fun to hang around with, and her so-called best friends,
Lisa Gilbert and Dana Hannason, had both had the nerve to
be sent to TAG camp for the duration of the summer.
Discovery Camp, it was called.

What am I supposed to do all summer? she thought
miserably, smacking the heels of her tennis shoes hard
against the underside of the slats. *I'm not going to stay
cooped up in the house, and if Dad tries to read one more
mythology book to me, I'll scream!*

She was, it seemed, pretty much left on her own.

Sheila can keep me company.

A year before, when reading a story about a young princess that had saved a kingdom, Gatsby had decided that she wanted a princess friend, one who was beautiful and smart and courageous. The image became alive in her mind. Gatsby's imagination provided all the details needed: dark skin, like an African or Egyptian, long dark hair, solemn eyes, a lilting laugh, and all the time in the world to play.

When she ran out into the field of wild peppermint to chase dragons, hunt down elves, run with the fantasy animals that talked and played with her, and peel strips of edible bark off the towering peppermint trees in the Peppermint Forest, Gatsby ran with Sheila.

Let's go, Sheila, let's go play! she thought and jumped off the porch. She closed her eyes and imagined the girl there, hair pulled back in a ponytail, white teeth flashing, and the girl taking her hand, laughing and running with her into the field. They breathed in afternoon air that buzzed with frogs and neighbor's cats, wavered with the sugary smells of bubblegum wrappers and penny candy.

They spent that morning together, and when the sun rose straight up in the blue sky and Gatsby's stomach started rumbling, she knew it was time to go in for lunch.

"I'll come back and play with you later, Sheila," she said as she skipped along, the bright sun beating down on the top of her head, thinking, *I'll play with YOU all summer since there's no one else around.* With a heavy sigh, she thought, *I wish you were a real girl, not just made up.*

A strange feeling twinged in the middle of her body. She froze, standing still in the grass, the scent of peppermint enveloping her. She blinked a few times, wondering at the feeling—did it hurt? No, it was more like a funny stomach cramp that almost felt good, like the way your stomach would lurch when you rode a roller coaster. Almost made her want to laugh out loud. A smile rose to her freckled face and she giggled a little, then ran the rest of the way home, ready to pester her Mom into making her favorite lunch: a tomato-cheese sandwich and cold lemonade.

By the end of that summer, ten-year-old Gatsby and the Princess Sheila were inseparable. They did everything together, read library books, made papier-mâché animals, experimented with the camera her Dad had given her, played with the neighbor's Manx kitten. But when people were around—parents, siblings, or other lesser or greater authorities—Gatsby instinctively moved her friend-of-fantasy back into the created universe from which she had been born.

"If only I could make you real," Gatsby would find herself saying aloud when she was out of earshot.

The summer dragged on interminably—its length and, for Gatsby Donovan, the unspoken desperation of its solitude as stifling as the heat.

August—a week before school started.

Scampering down the porch stairs, Gatsby raced into the peppermint field to look for buried treasure in the Forest of Peppermint Trees, taking Sheila, the Princess of Elysium, with her. Sheila with the long dark hair, almond-shaped eyes, and dark skin, like a Nubian queen.

"Come on, Sheila, let's find Mopey and Reginald!" She laughed as she ran, grasses whisking against her bare legs. The sun that warmed her face was thinner, as if whispering that new classrooms and new number two pencils were just around the corner.

She stopped before the trunk of the oak tree where Reginald the Blue Dragon lived and plopped down in the dirt for a moment, panting. "We'll take all his gold!" she said out loud, giggling and, in her mind, she saw Sheila nod and answer, "And then we'll bury it where no one can find it!"

Something rustled from behind the tree. Gatsby turned and felt her eyes widen.

She stood there, looking at Gatsby with deep, dark eyes. She wore a blue jumpsuit and flat black canvas shoes. A beaded bracelet encircled one wrist.

Long dark hair, almond-shaped eyes, and dark skin, like a Nubian queen. And with a slightly flattened nose, which made her look South American, although Gatsby knew little about South America at the time.

The image from her imagination—the friend she had fervently wished to be real—was, incomprehensibly, standing next to the Blue Dragon's oak tree and silently staring at her.

She didn't know how to react and just stared.

"Hh...who are you?" Gatsby's voice trembled as she spoke, and at the same time she thought, *You're Sheila, that's who you are, Sheila the Princess of Elysium...but...but...*

Gatsby's young world still teemed with the waving flags and panpipe songs of fantasy but, at ten, she knew the difference between *real* and *make believe*. One was black, the other white. Books and movies on TV weren't real, they were made-up stories. Even stories real people told you didn't make the characters in the story appear.

She knew what magic was and how it worked, and in the real world of ten-year-olds and sisters and parents and teachers, schools and shopping malls, real magic only happened in stories. She had seen magicians at school parties and understood that what a dopey magician at a school party did was a trick. A trick that any person could learn to do. It wasn't *real* magic.

While these formative thoughts rushed through her, Gatsby stared with wide eyes.

The girl smiled, and the expression on her face was one of such gentleness that Gatsby instinctively knew that the girl was friendly. And as children do, those whose innocent nature is intact, the girl walked over to Gatsby and sat down next to her, as if they had been friends forever.

"What's your name?" Gatsby said, her voice a little stronger.

The girl tilted her head slightly, looking at Gatsby as if studying her.

"Can you hear me?" Gatsby asked cautiously and then thought, *Dummy, if she is deaf, she can't hear you asking the question! Geez. Maybe she can teach me sign language...*

The girl sat silently, still scrutinizing her.

"Um, do you want to play a game with me? I'll show you the Forest of Peppermint Trees." Gatsby turned to face her and pointed toward the field.

The girl nodded enthusiastically.

And indeed the new girl—Sheila, for lack of any other name—stayed with Gatsby for the rest of the afternoon, running through the meadow, picking flowers and making daisy chains with them, scooping guppies out of the nearby creek and tossing them back. She pointed and gestured but never spoke.

As they lay on their backs in a clover patch, staring up at the clouds, the girl turned her head and looked at Gatsby. She held her hand out. Gatsby's ten-year-old mind stalled for a moment. Lessons drilled in by adults rose—*don't touch strangers, even* strangers who happen to be kids. Be careful. The girl continued to look at her with a questing expression. Finally, Gatsby slid her hand over and wrapped it around the girl's.

Years into the future, she would have the vocabulary to describe the feeling that moved through her as she took the girl's hand—warm skin, pulsing with a heartbeat as steady as her own. There would be peak experiences that would take her words and her breath away but, at the moment, all she knew was that she felt a hot spark of shock, realizing, *She's a REAL person.* A twinge of fear followed: *Is she with someone else? Someone who could hurt little girls?*

Amazement and quiet acceptance stole over her.

They both lay silently, two girls with dark hair, lying on their backs in a field of soft clover, hand in hand, the summer sun beating down on their faces, eyes closed, gentle smiles on their faces as if they had always been best friends and always would be.

Gatsby opened her eyes, and she was alone.

She sat up, touched the grass that had been tamped down beneath Sheila's body, and found it warm. She had just been there.

And in a split second, she had *disappeared*.

As she wandered through the grass back to her house, sad confusion stole over her. There was no way of knowing if Sheila would ever return.

Gatsby felt the seesaw of truth teetering inside her. It was a prickly, uncomfortable, adult feeling, and she didn't like it.

If I tell Mom and Dad that I made up the Princess Sheila and then I really saw her, they wouldn't like it. Her ten-year-old psyche, never before so challenged by questions of reality and illusion, reshaped as thoughts formed and quick decisions were made as she followed the path that ended at her back porch. *They would say that I was just making up stories or that I fell asleep and dreamed it. But I didn't dream her! She WAS real, I touched her hand and I FELT it.*

She hopped onto the porch and sat, swinging her legs, her elbows on her knees.

Would Penelope believe me? Fat chance. She'd laugh until her eyes popped out and call me names.

She swung her legs hard enough to kick the underside of the porch with her heels and the solution asserted itself. *If she comes back, I'll bring her home with me, and then other people will see her.*

The heaviness gone, the answer to the problem in hand, and the rest of the summer waiting as tranquil as a forest lake, she jumped up and ran inside to get ginger ale and Ritz crackers.

Sheila did come back, almost every day, but she didn't speak. She only pointed.

It seemed that a common language was needed, and with six symbols, the Peppermint Language was born.

The second week of September, Lisa and Dana returned from camp. School started in only three days.

Sixth grade! I hope Sheila will be in my class, Gatsby thought as they lay together on their backs in their favorite clover field, staring up at the clouds. Sheila's origins were still mysterious. Did she have a family? Where did she live? Every time Gatsby had asked Sheila about it, the answer had been nonsensical. Not part of their Peppermint Language. Something foreign.

Sheila sat up, looked at her with questing eyes, smiled and gestured:

Follow me!

Running along behind, Gatsby felt her hair flying out behind her, the whisk of the grasses against her shins. They ran to the oak tree where the dragon lived.

The dark-haired girl started climbing up the tree, tucking a foot into a knothole and pushing herself up branch by branch until she came to a fork that was just wide enough and sturdy enough to hold two children. Grunting a little, Gatsby hauled herself up into the tree behind Sheila and found a spot opposite her in the crotch of the limbs.

They sat facing each other.

Each pulled a folded piece of cardboard from her pocket. On each piece of cardboard, a diagram comprised of six symbols had been drawn. Smaller symbols, some resembling musical notation, were drawn next to each of the six larger images.

They moved their hands and began to talk.

The language required both hands. Each word-symbol and its smaller symbol (years later, Gatsby would learn it was called a determinative) was identified by the left hand and the diagram. The right hand created a moving gesture in the air. By combining hand gestures with the written symbols, they had formulated about sixty words and each day invented a few more.

They had found that, as they had become more proficient and could sign at higher speed, the motions became fluid and both hands moved gracefully, resembling the articulate movements of a pianist at a keyboard.

Gatsby stopped as a thought blazed through her. She made a series of signs that if translated into everyday speech would have approximated *We do not know each other's names*. She pointed at herself and said out loud, "Gatsby."

Sheila stared back at her, ruminating. Then her face brightened and she took Gatsby's hands in hers. She curled Gatsby's left hand into a fist and wrapped the right hand over it so that the fingers of her right hand rested on the fingers of the left.

Puzzled, Gatsby relaxed her muscles, allowing Sheila to move her hands around—she seemed to know what she was doing.

Sheila pushed Gatsby's hands about ten inches apart and then brought them together. There was a smack as the left hand, curled into a fist, struck the palm of the right. Sheila slapped the fingers of the right hand onto the back of the left—a softer, smaller *thud* sound issued.

She did it again.

Smack thump.

Again.

Smack thump.

*It makes...a sound...like...*Gatsby thought, as the strong-weak sounds rolled through her mind.

strong-weak

smack-thump

GATS-bee

Maybe that's it, she thought, and smiled. *It sounds the way my name sounds. GATSby. GATSby.* She repeated her name in her mind as she made the gestures herself, over and over.

"Gatsby!" she said out loud.

They looked at each other and then laughed together.

Gatsby pulled her cardboard diagram onto her lap and looked at the symbols. She signed two words: *get* and *be*.

Close enough, she thought.

Sheila nodded and then gestured, *Watch*.

Gatsby leaned forward to watch Sheila's hand move in the air as she pointed with the other hand to the symbols on the cardboard.

She frowned, the tip of her tongue poking out as she concentrated, and moved her hands slowly over the board. After identifying six symbols, she stopped.

See. As. In. Do. Are. A.

Gatsby stared at her, shaking her head; she signed: *I don't understand.*

Sheila repeated the movements. Six symbols. See, as, in, do, are, a.

"See as in do are a," Gatsby said out loud. "See as in do are a? That's your name?" She signed you and the symbol they both understood to indicate a question.

Sheila nodded, pointed at herself, and repeated the gestures.

"See as in," Gatsby whispered to herself, trying to imagine how those words could be a name, and as the sounds of the words echoed through her mind, she wondered if maybe they weren't complete words but letters...C? S? N?

C S N D R A

Gatsby stared at the symbols, wondering what on earth Sheila was trying to say. It certainly didn't spell Sheila.

But then I named her Sheila...when she...she... A shadow crossed over her mind as the sentence finished itself, *when I made her up.*

The paradox of how it could have happened—how the image of the girl with almond-shaped eyes could have lifted from her imagination and metamorphosed into a living human being—had, of course, never been satisfactorily resolved. Gatsby had known better than to ask her parents, or anyone, about the paradox. Ten-year-old girls could still have dolls and give them names and make up stories while they played, or have make-believe friends and imaginary adventures, but Gatsby knew that she was old enough to understand disbelief. To understand the graves in which Santa Claus, the Easter bunny, and the tooth fairy had made their final resting place after their utility was gone.

When I made her up, she thought again, looking at the girl who sat facing her, on her haunches in the crotch of a tree, her hair fluttering in the breeze. For the first time, Gatsby noticed a small gap between the girl's front teeth.

She reached out and grabbed the girl's hands. They were warm and pulsing with life—solid flesh, with tendons, veins, bones, and capillaries as real as her own.

"You *are* real," Gatsby whispered, as if, for the first time since Sheila had stepped from behind the oak tree, she was finally ready to face the question itself. "How? How can that be true?" She signed again, *You?*

The girl signed emphatically, repeating the six gestures.

Is this her REAL name? Gatsby thought.

A Greek myth—one of the many mythological tales that Thomas Donovan had read to her—stole into her thoughts as she stared at the symbols. The woman in the story could tell the future, but no one ever believed her.

Gatsby's head tipped to one side, her brow furrowed, as she frowned and finally signed the letters—C, S, N, D, R, A—while murmuring the mythological woman's name. "Cassandra?"

The girl signed again and looked expectantly into Gatsby's eyes.

She made the gestures for the symbols again and again—her hands flew. Gatsby watched, transfixed, and then slowly brought her own hands up in front of her and repeated the gestures. Slowly at first, then faster.

Gatsby.

Cassandra.

They stared at each other, breathless from the rapid hand movements, and Gatsby knew that something incredible was taking place at that moment, something wonderful but terrifying. Something that other people would not understand.

She knew what sane was and what crazy was. Crazy was when you saw things that weren't real and you couldn't not see them. Couldn't live in the "real" world anymore. You had to go to a special school, if you were a kid. If you were a grownup, you were taken to the crazy house. Maybe forever.

A memory of a movie she'd seen flashed in her mind; it had been about some people who lived in the crazy house. The crazy people in the movie yelled and screamed and tore their clothes off or tried to hurt themselves, and the awful doctors and nurses had to give them pills to make them settle down.

She moaned, backing away from the images. *No! I can't let that happen!!*

With shaking hands, she signed rapidly, *You/come/from/?*

Cassandra looked at her, her expression almost patronizingly sweet—she raised one hand and pointed at Gatsby.

What does she mean? she thought and signed, *Where/you/house?*

Cassandra pointed at Gatsby's head.

Panic exploded in her chest. *That's not true! I didn't make you! You have parents somewhere and they made you! Not me! You don't live in my head!*

But Cassandra never had seemed to live anywhere or with anyone. Her appearances, always unexpected, were from behind a nearby building or tree, and she never seemed to need to go anywhere. In the instant that Gatsby glanced in another direction or was focused on something else, she'd look up and her friend would be gone.

Like magic.

She felt her eyes burning with tears as fear flooded her. *There IS no magic! You can't think a person and make them real! No one can!* Abruptly, she pushed herself away and started to climb down the tree.

A warm hand caught her by the forearm. Gatsby turned and Cassandra's dark eyes were huge, looking at her, into her. Her other hand rose, signed, *Where?*

"Home," Gatsby blurted, her chin trembling. "I have to go home now." She pulled out of Cassandra's warm grasp and shinnied down the oak tree.

As she ran through the peppermint field toward her house, she thought frantically, *Can I tell anyone about Sheila, Cassandra...Who would believe me? Would they laugh at me? Would they say that I'm making it up, that I just imagined it? Would they...*

Doctors and nurses bringing her pills to make her settle down. To keep her from screaming and yelling and tearing her clothes.

"No," she whispered as she reached the porch and leaned onto it, panting, her heart racing. "I can't. It's a secret."

She leaned her head down to press onto her forearm and closed her eyes. There was nothing in her short decade of life to compare with this experience, no other unordinary events, no other mysteriously appearing and disappearing people or spontaneous acts of magic.

Maybe I'm just dreaming this, she thought, *maybe I'll wake up and find out that I had a bad accident, and I've been...in a coma! And this has all been a long dream...maybe...*

Then she heard her mother and Penelope in the kitchen, laughing. Gatsby swallowed hard and went into the house, acutely aware of how brightly her cheeks were flushed and her eyes wet. She said she had a stomachache and wanted to lie down.

Three days later, Gatsby had settled in her new sixth-grade classroom at Gregg Hill Elementary School. She had a nice, pretty teacher named Miss Connolly, and Lisa and Dana were assigned desks right next to hers. They were going to start the year with some science experiments on different forms of water, a history project on world explorers, and a class reading of a book called *Dinosaur Digger.*

In the excitement of the new school year and reuniting with her friends, Gatsby almost forgot about Cassandra— and, somehow, vaguely imagined that she wouldn't see her again.

But she did.

Her neck muscles lurched, a hunk of thick saliva clogged her throat. She gradually became aware that her eyes were open; she felt cool air wafting across her face.

Breathing came slowly, the muscles that moved her lungs grating like rusty machinery.

It took all her will to turn her eyes downward *(stroke embolism paralysis what if oh jesus what if I can't move)* and orient herself, sitting rod-rigid in her chair. Her desk. Her office. The computer, still humming. The six digitized glyphs shimmering on the blue screen.

The brick walls that had been erected years ago in her subconscious began to shudder. She literally felt rumbling sensations deep inside her core, in a place where her connections to survival were tightly webbed. Her nervous system reacted, pumping out oxygen, adrenaline, and endorphins as body and mind reeled in a maelstrom of reconnected circuits. Behind her eyes, she felt a sensation equivalent to a massive power surge. Vertigo knocked her on the side of the head, forcing her to grab for the armrests— for a moment, she felt her body spinning and flipping, being swept up by a tornado. Her head snapped back, smacking painfully against the metal chair.

C S N D R A...she...

The wall shuddered, groaned hugely, and slow motion spiraling as descent in a dream, toppled.

Using her last ounce of energy, Gatsby held her hands up, hovering them over her lap. She stared at them in frozen desperation. It felt as though she had been born without hands and suddenly, spontaneously, they had sprouted fully formed—like alien creatures—and she had absolutely no idea what they would do.

They began to move. Small but distinct gestures. Repeated once. Cautiously, trembling, then repeated again.

Deep in her black underworld, a hazy web shivered...inside the web there were names...faces...signs...the signs were red, warning...

STOP SIGN

The web began to rend, tearing as streaks of conscious memory split its threads...like waking slowly from the deepest, blackest dream...

her name...

and she *knew*.

C S N D R A
Cassandra.

Her hands made the signs. Again and again. Six gestures, frozen for twenty-six years in an ice cave of memory.

Her body unlocked all at once. Her lungs exploded upward, sucking in oxygen, roaring down her nose and throat and bringing blinding flashes before her eyes, a surge of pain at the back of her head, a spasm in the pit of her stomach.

Then she blew all of it out...back to thirty...all out...back to twenty-five...out...back to twenty...blew it all...back to fifteen...the winds of the future, the present, and the past swirling together in a vortex inside her psyche, blowing away the last shreds of the web of forgetfulness.

To discover her memories. Frozen, lost memories.

"James Whitten."

Though only a hoarse rasp, her voice startled her. It was the name of the child psychologist. The trim beard, glasses, drawstring pants, cologne.

Ritz crackers and peanut butter...Penelope likes Dr. Pepper...

The three blank months, the empty pages in the diary. Mom and Dad...

Pain and fear rose, blurring her vision.

I told them. I told them Cassandra was real! They thought it was beyond childhood daydreaming...psychosis...that I was mentally stunted...'inability to separate from infantile object of cathexion'...

The tearing emotion she had had sitting on her parents' porch—*tell or not tell? real or make-believe?*—and the sessions with the child psychologist during which she had been hypnotized and guided toward forgetfulness, to release her "invisible friend"...

had to let it gohhhh

roared in her mind, and she doubled over in her chair and sobbed.

Twenty-six years ago. An enigmatic girl who had, for a short period in her childhood, been more a twin. An alter ego. The girl had been extinguished by those who could not accept or allow her existence.

had to let her gohhhhh...

Remember everything...

The Peppermint Language.

(Follow me!)

The Forest of Peppermint Trees!

A ghostly voice whispered in her head. She looked down at her hands. Swallowed hard. Flexed her fingers and, very slowly, haltingly, made the six gestures. The right hand in the air, the left pointing downward, toward her lap.

She looked up into her computer screen. C S N D R A...the six phantom symbols floated, whispering, calling for her.

They came back to me...from so far away but right inside of...

Her heart thrummed like machine gun fire in her ears, blocking out all sensory input except for a faint, susurrus sound.

Coming from behind her ear.

Gatsby whirled. A smell assaulted her, and she knew it immediately.

Peppermint.

The light in the office intensified, not from the fluorescent lights overhead but from in front of her. Somewhere just in front of the filing cabinet.

The intensity of the light became a wavering image, something ghostlike and unformed that shimmered and wriggled as it changed shape. Now it was blue, now pink, now green. With glowing radiance, it metamorphosed as Gatsby stared, unable to breathe or speak, watching in dumb terror. The smell became unbearable. Her computer monitor flared brightly and she heard an explosive POP as if a power surge had just fried the hard-drive. The figure began to coalesce into a shape.

It can't...

Gatsby heard a thick moan move at the back of her throat as the room spun. Her eyelids fluttered spasmodically; she knew she was on the verge of blacking out.

The image, now humanoid in form, raised wavering, translucent appendages to eye level and gestured. The six symbols that corresponded to C S N D R A. Then the *slap-thud* gesture that had, decades ago, symbolized Gatsby's name.

Gatsby felt rivers of sweat running down her back, soaking into her T-shirt. Adrenaline flooded the palms of her hands with sweat. She swallowed with great effort, wanting to speak but only managing a grunt. Black dots danced crazily in front of her eyes, and the corners of the world had turned grey and fuzzy. She felt her body loosening, tipping, she was falling and couldn't stop, couldn't fight it anymore. The floor rose up to meet her—

Something warm stopped her, holding her firmly. The girl's hands.

She pushed Gatsby upright and closed in on her. Her fragrant breath, flowing over Gatsby's neck and face, was redolent with the smell of peppermint. At the edge of incomprehensible panic, Gatsby looked into the girl's eyes.

The girl took Gatsby's hands in her own and tried to move them. She pointed to the images shimmering on Gatsby's computer monitor.

Following the direction of her hands, Gatsby stared at the glyphs.

Of its own accord, Gatsby's printer whirred, and a printout of the glyphs pushed itself out of the machine.

The girl reached out and took hold of the printout, and as she did, she began to gesture. Impressions—translations—moved unbidden through Gatsby's consciousness, her subconscious releasing the information it had held there, as if to prove that the well of the mind—recording a thousand bits of new information every second; over a lifetime, a number with twenty-one digits—retains every iota of information that it receives, forever.

Gatsby concentrated everything on the girl's hand signals, breathing slowly to try to keep herself from blacking out. She knew that she was experiencing massive physical, emotional, and mental shock all at once—could she withstand it?

She slowly turned her focus to the fact—fact?—that she was faced with a vivid hallucination, one that was vivid enough to interact with consensus reality. The slip of paper, held tightly in Cassandra's small fist, jittered.

Too...I...can't...

The girl's eyes met hers. The girl pointed down and then sat cross-legged on the floor. She looked up at Gatsby with expectant eyes, pointed again at the floor, and signed here.

Gatsby allowed her body to slide from the chair to the floor with a thud. The room spun again, and she dropped her head into her hands, moaning, terrified.

It isn't! Can't! The voice shrieking inside her head was followed by a barrage of thoughts...*settle down!...infantile object...Ritz...do as are...not real!...coats and walls...no magicians...cathexion...let her gohhhh...*These were followed by the thought that brought tears into her eyes.

Don't let me be crazy, oh please, don't let me...

Something touched her; she jumped with a snort.

Hands touching hers.

Hands!

Gatsby looked up. Cassandra had leaned forward and covered Gatsby's hands with her own. Small but strong, they pulsed. Warmth coursed through visible veins and capillaries beneath the dark skin. Bones and tendons. Muscles, fiber.

They felt so *real*.

Don't let me...

She looked into Cassandra's eyes, lost in their depth. They seemed endless; fathomless, dark oceans that contained every thought, word, and deed of Gatsby's life. Transfixed, Gatsby swallowed and felt a tear well in her right eye. It dropped onto her cheek and, as it fell to her lips and she tasted its saltiness, relief melted over her. Salt was real.

This is real...this is real...I'm real...

Do as are...not real!...let her gohhhh...infantile...

With the slip of paper on the floor near her left hand, and her right hand raised near Gatsby's face, Cassandra slowly began to gesture. Each movement of the right hand corresponded with a symbol pointed out by the left. As

Gatsby watched, swaying, black glaciers of memory, untellably deep, moved millimeter by millimeter.

Translation.

Gesture, pointing—You.

Gesture, pointing—See.

Gesture, pointing—Me.

"I—" Gatsby started.

The girl shook her head vigorously and signed *Here*. She pointed down at the paper.

Hyperventilating, Gatsby shook her head. "I...I don't remember—"

The girl grabbed Gatsby's right hand, pulled the first and second fingers outward, and with her own left hand, pointed to the igloo-shaped symbol on the paper.

Gatsby felt her breath hitch in as the symbol/gesture's corresponding word came to her.

Yes/

Her mind reeled against her systems that categorized reality. The world of this/that, like/different, true/false. Real, unreal. Denial and belief raged inside her.

Cassandra's small hand rose; her fingertip brushed Gatsby's cheek.

Her other hand moved to the printout and she signed (negative)/cry.

The shock of realizing that she had understood the gesture brought a stab of panic in Gatsby's core. She pulled in her breath, staring at Cassandra, shaking her head.

(Negative)/cry Remember/ You/know/me

"No!" Gatsby blurted. She recoiled from the girl's touch.

Remember. The girl's dark eyes swam.

"Stop! You're not...oh my god, I'm talking to my hallucination." She remembered the Stonehenge Convergence and Traussbery's words: Their visualizations will be directed by their desire, and that is a fantastically powerful combination.

Powerful enough to explain this?

I'm seeing what I want to see, that's the only explanation.

She shook her head and dropped her chin to her chest, closing her eyes tight, and counted silently. Then, with a deep breath, she opened her eyes.

The smile playing on Cassandra's lips could only be described as a smirk.

Her reserves were now completely drained. The needle rested on "E." Game over. Gatsby sighed heavily and sat, numb, unable to move or speak. She stared.

As Cassandra's hands moved, words began to filter into Gatsby's mind, quiet as a light mist creeping over a mountain ridge. Gatsby sat quietly breathing, fighting against the denial, and she heard the intonation of a voice speaking melodically inside her head as each gesture was translated.

It/is/hard/to/understand /How/I/am/here/?

Gatsby swallowed, watched.

I/(negative)/know/what/I/am/

Cassandra's hands rested quietly in her lap for a moment. She started again.

Where/I/before/peppermint/trees/?

Cassandra raised her left arm and bent it at the elbow, her hand held straight with the palm facing down. Her right hand moved up and made slow figure eights in the air below her left arm.

*From/down/here...*She made another figure eight in the air...*you/brought/me/here.* She laid her right palm on the upper surface of her left arm.

Gatsby shook her head. The gut-level resignation that she had felt when Traussbery had urged her to go to Peru, and the bafflement she had felt during his speech on quantum physics, now flowed through her. A challenge called her—a conceptual step onto a flight where only the machinery of her mind would take her.

She raised her hands and slowly, groping for the movements that were twenty-six years buried, gestured *I/(negative)/understand.*

I/was/below/

Again, Cassandra made figure eight movements beneath her left arm.

You/brought/me/
She rubbed her right palm against the back of her left arm
again, seemingly searching for a concept for which there was
no gesture. After a moment, she made two signs: *above/top.*
The surface, Gatsby thought. She nodded.
We/lived/in/the/surface/Gatsby   in/peppermint/trees
I/went/below   the/(unfamiliar gesture)   I/(negative)/want
let her gohhhh...
Defiance crept through Gatsby, bringing with it the fear
and frustration she had felt at that young age when she had
first seen Cassandra. Touched her hair, felt her skin, known
that she was real. Real-as-chairs-and-cars-and-houses-and-
firetrucks real. Real as the real glasses on the real Dr.
Whitten's nose, real as pencils and games and Schwinn
bicycles. As real as Thomas, Estre, and Penelope Donovan.
Not a figment, a story, a myth.
Real.
How/? she signed.
You/brought/me/Gatsby   /Above/where/you/live
I/(negative)/want/go/Below   but/I/wanted/to/come/to/you/
you/pushed/me/out/of/your/thoughts   you/forgot
you/(negative)/remember/me   my/name/gone
Her name was gone, Gatsby thought. *May, June, July.*
Three months of blank diary pages. Ritz crackers and peanut
butter.
She took a long breath and pressed her hands against her
cheeks, then against the fibers of the Oriental throw rug
underneath her. The floor, her skin, and the glowing lights
of her office equipment reconnected her tangibly with the
conflict between what she saw and what her mind could
accept. Although still unable to comprehend, she felt herself
breathing more evenly.
You/wanted/come/back, Gatsby signed.
Cassandra nodded, her dark eyes widening. *I/wanted*
I/(negative)/could/until/you /remembered   You/had/to/
remember/me
*But/you...*She reached down and grabbed the printout of
the glyphs that represented C S N D R A.

Flag-Cross, Double-Diamond, Sphere with Wings, Crescent Moon, Igloo, Slanted T.

You/had/to/remember/me, Cassandra signed, *for/me/ to/come/Above   to/come/back/you/had/to/remember Each/came/to/you/help/you/remember/Gatsby   each/ brought/me/closer/Above   C S N D R A   I/(negative) /able/show/you/   completely/until/you/remembered/my/ name   C S N D R A   When/you/remembered I/am/ here/ now/because/you/remembered...*

"These..." Gatsby pointed to the glyphs on the paper, shaking her head. "You caused these images so that I could remember your name? So that you could—" Searching for the word that could somehow approximate the concept, she stared at the floor momentarily and then looked up at Cassandra. "Come back?"

The girl nodded.

"But—" Frustrated, Gatsby tugged her hands through her hair. There were no symbols in the Peppermint Language for the questions, no vocabulary for the questions or the answers.

"It's not possible! You're not possible!!"

Cassandra smiled. *I/am/here/Gatsby,* she signed. *See/Feel?*

She reached out and again took Gatsby's hands in her own. Her fingertips moved to Gatsby's face, gently touching her cheeks, lips, neck, hair.

Gatsby felt the tips of her fingers, felt the softness of her skin, felt her warm breath.

You/brought/me/Gatsby /Above/

A mental flash brought back, in full detail, the conversation with Traussbery at the Punch & Judy:

The world of causal, logical phenomena, the world where the quanta are observed, the world of consensus reality, is termed the surface structure or the unfolded universe. Where the quanta go when not observed, the unknown and imperceptible realm, that is the deep structure. The enfolded universe. And as the bits of the consensus-reality universe shape-shift, we have historically attributed these events to myth, to the supernatural, to the paranormal, to deities, to coincidence, to fate, or simply to unsolved mystery. Yet when we look five thousand years into our past, we see with the eyes of presumed wisdom, assuming that ancient civilizations are our younger siblings. Us at a younger age, less developed. But the opposite may be true! The people who created Stonehenge and other inexplicable ancient accomplishments could well have been more advanced than we are now! What if they had conscious understanding of the cosmology's deeper structures, and a power of consciousness that gave them abilities to shape those structures, to wield them as a painter uses brush and ink to manifest his visualization in tangible form?

Gatsby thought, *This is tangible form? Is it? Until proven otherwise, as tangible as it gets. The truth comes in the proving, not in the trying. But to prove the impossible? Traussbery was right. There is no vocabulary for this. Imagination—creation. To create, to construct a mental image of something never before perceived. A thing imagined in the mind is not, cannot become part of consensus reality until it is assigned a symbol. An identifier. A word for the concept. A name. Only then can abstraction become...*

Gatsby felt her hands move up to alight against Cassandra's warm cheeks.

Consensus reality.

The conflict—real-unreal, denial-acceptance—raged again. Nonbelief crashed against a lifetime of empiricism.

Cassandra signed, *I/want/stay/*

Gatsby shook her head, slapping her hands against her thighs. "Stay? Where?!? In my subconscious or at my flat? Where do...where do you belong? I was a kid, a ten-year-old kid, and I wanted a playmate so I dreamed up...a...well, you...and as much as I couldn't believe that you were real then...I mean, I did, but how could anyone else believe it? How could I tell anyone? I couldn't, it would be madness! No one can accept that, that—"

Her voice trailed off. "God, this is what Traussbery has been saying all along and then he managed to convince me that he'd lost his reason. Bloody god."

Cassandra suddenly grabbed Gatsby's hands and stood, hauling Gatsby with her. *Look/Gatsby   Look/at/me/ I/am/here/*

Flooded with disbelief and bewilderment, it hadn't yet struck Gatsby that perhaps Cassandra understood vocalized English. She hadn't yet considered how she could understand Cassandra's hand gestures without using the printout.

As Gatsby stood on shaking legs, she sighed deeply and looked at the girl standing before her. In every detail, Cassandra was as Gatsby had envisioned her decades ago in Seattle. Exactly as she had appeared in Peru, at Heathrow, and the London streets. The same height, shape, clothing, skin, hair, almond-shaped eyes. If this was an elaborate hoax, it was perfect down to the most minute detail.

"But if I'm an adult now, why aren't you?"

Cassandra smiled and signed, *I/was/born/in/your (unfamiliar   gesture)   but/I/am/more/than/you/now I/have/my/own/thoughts/*

For chrissake then don't think too creatively, Gatsby thought. *God only knows what might happen.*

She looked around her office, still panting, her legs shaking. The blue glow from the monitor bathed Cassandra's face, making her appear ethereal, an azure phantasm. Gatsby took her hands and squeezed them.

"The back way," she whispered.

CHAPTER 29

Gatsby puzzled as she dialed—what was the code?—00, then 1, then 206. There were faraway beeps and then the characteristic ring of her parents' telephone. Three rings and the line connected.

"Hello?"

"Mom, it's me, Gats."

The usual flurry of parental enthusiasm made her smile. Her father picked up on the phone that she knew was in his study and auditorily clapped her on the shoulder, saying, "Daughter, how have you been? When are you coming home to visit your old folks?" His congenial laughter was contagious, and in spite of the churning unease that had prompted the phone call, Gatsby laughed aloud.

Thomas and Estre Donovan chatted amiably while Gatsby reclined on her couch, watching the rolling thunderclouds outside the window and only half-listening to the usual recital of familial news. Cousins' births, an aunt's marriage, a neighbor's prize-winning Borzoi, a planned vacation to Kauai, and Penelope's shocking news that she was moving to British Columbia and oh by the way suspected she might be pregnant. Her sister's eccentric independence made the revelation, to Gatsby, garden variety.

"I don't know what gets into that girl," Thomas sighed, and Gatsby held her tongue to derail a clever but risqué retort.

"How is everything in London?" her mother asked cheerfully.

Gatsby looked down at her hands and took a deep breath. *Now or never, and I gotta know,* she thought. "Busy, as usual—you know me." She chuckled halfheartedly. *God, how to bring this up?...mmmm, this will work...*"It's funny, the other day I was cleaning out one of my closets and came across some old journals from when I was a kid..."

"Oh yes." She could hear both parents nodding, undoubtedly recalling their daughter's adolescent dedication to her diaries.

"You know how it is with old stuff you've hidden away, you just have to dig it out and pore through it again." *Truer words...*

More affirming noises from Seattle.

"I, uh, came across a diary from when I was, oh, ten or so and found something very strange, well, at least it was strange to me, it kind of took me off guard—" She heard herself babbling and elbowed against the panic beneath it. The plastic casing of the phone and the hand wrapping it were both sticky. "A period of, oh, about three months, where there was nothing written, nothing at all and, uh, well, it was so atypical, you know how obsessive I was about writing in those journals every night, that I thought I'd ask you about it. See if you remembered what was going on around that time."

There. She mentally sighed and then did so aloud.

Pan-Atlantic buzz in her ear for a moment. Another moment of silence.

Let's see how they explain Whitten and ninety blank pages in their bibliophilic daughter's diary—and head, Gatsby thought.

"Oh that." Estre's voice was nondescript.

"Yes that," Gatsby replied. More phone buzz.

"That was a very, er, confusing time for all of us, I think," Thomas Donovan said quietly. "We weren't quite sure what to do with...in that situation."

"What do you mean?" Gatsby prodded. *I know exactly what he means: what do to with you. I just want to hear you say it.* A pang rippled through her.

A sprinkling of hushing sounds made its way to Gatsby's ear and she realized it wasn't the phone line, it was her parents conferring with each other in whispers too muffled for her to make out.

Her mother asked cautiously, "What do you remember?"

Oh no, you're not getting off that easy.

"Nothing, Mom. I really don't remember anything about that period. I think it was summer, when I was about ten. It's like there's a blind spot in my memory. And in my diary. And I would just like to know what was happening then. It's...disconcerting." *To say the least.*

"Well." Her father cleared his throat brusquely. "We had some talks with you about...well, we were concerned about you at one point and took you to see a specialist. Do you remember that?"

"What kind of specialist?"

More throat clearing. "A child psychologist. Whitten. We wanted him to talk with you about your persistent belief that you had an imaginary friend, a little girl that you were very fond of and that would keep company with for hours at a time." A forced chuckle. "Time went on, and you were so unwilling to let go of the fantasy that we, well, we were worried. We wanted Dr. Whitten's opinion."

Gatsby nodded, her cheek rubbing against the handset. At least they weren't trying to hide it. From far away outside, she heard Big Ben clamor.

A ghostly memory of the day before—in her office, staring at the six mysterious glyphs on her monitor, then the flash-download of the Peppermint Language and every detail of that summer, and the mind-bending, quantum-bashing, literal reincarnation of a dark-skinned girl with long hair and almond eyes—rose into her mind's eye and blotted out everything else. Gatsby closed her eyes, breathing hard, her muscles replaying the shock and panic.

Finally, she took in a deep breath and said, "An invisible friend, huh? Geez, I just don't," she sighed quickly, "don't remember that at all."

Now who's the liar?

Her mother's voice piped up. "Honey, we weren't sure what to do. All children have a fantasy world and believe the stories of fairies and ghosts and gollums that they are fed, you probably more than other children, with your father reading you mythology all the time." The tone was amused perturbation, a mother's "oh what is your father doing now?" sound. Thomas Donovan's laugh of reply was roguish. "But you wanted to hold onto this friend of yours so badly—what was her name?—and of course, we had no indication that she was anything but imaginary, so we decided to go to a professional. Dr. Whitten was a longtime friend of the Soudens and highly recommended. We thought that, if nothing else, his advice would be helpful."

It was helpful all right. Helped me right into full-blown amnesia that lasted for twenty-six years. The session with Celia popped into her head: the red stop sign, warning her against the dark place, the ultima Thule of imaginary girls who talked with their hands, warning not to reconstruct the peppermint-scented world that highly recommended Dr. Whitten had professionally, clinically removed from her psyche.

While wanting to rail at her parents for the results of their natural concern, Gatsby twisted the phone cord around her index finger and breathed hard, holding the mouthpiece away so that the sound wouldn't carry across the Atlantic. She looked down at her left hand and wondered when it would start fluttering around, uncontrolled, creating signs for words that she had been taken to a child therapist to forget.

"Oh," she said. "And how long did I see this specialist?" *Three months, perhaps?*

Hushed, conferring sounds again, then Thomas Donovan's voice. "Maybe three months or so, is that right, Estre?"

Estre "mmm-hmm"ed assent.

"It's odd that you would bring that up," Thomas continued. "We never discussed it much, did we? And you seemed very happy and well adjusted after the sessions. You never talked about the girl again, and we assumed that as a natural part of growing up, you had moved on and left her behind. Was that the case, Gatsby? Has this been bothering you...or something else?" He sounded worried, even across the phone line.

Infantile object...do as are...cathexion....let her gohhhh...

"No, Dad, not until just the other day when I found that diary with the blank pages. I had some vague feeling about what had happened then but wasn't sure. I just wanted to ask. It's not a big deal." A blatant lie there, but she wasn't prepared to discuss with her parents the implications of theoretical abilities to catapult boulders of saurian proportions or to manifest organic beings.

Something trembled near her chin; she realized it was her lower lip.

"Well, that's good, dear. How's your work going? Still enjoying it?"

She responded with a prepared statement—work was fine, keeping her very busy; she was on sabbatical now but had opted to take on a "project" over the summer. No other details about Traussbery, or Stonehenge, or the incomprehensible fact of the girl who was sitting in her bedroom as she talked on the phone.

They filled her in on more family gossip, and would she be able to make it home for the Christmas holidays? Gatsby said that she would try.

"Do, honey. We'd love to see you. So would your sister."

"I'll do my best, Mom. Give my love to Penelope. I'll call you again soon."

From Atlantic to Pacific, loving goodbyes were said.

Replacing the phone in its cradle, Gatsby stared at it for a moment, then stood and walked to her bedroom.

Cassandra was sitting on the bed, cross-legged, her hands moving. Gatsby realized she was talking to herself using the Peppermint Language. As Gatsby approached, Cassandra looked up and smiled.

For the last twenty-four hours, Cassandra had sat on Gatsby's bed or on the floor in the living room, signing to herself. She hadn't eaten or used the bathroom. The night before, she had slept, or at least lain quietly, on the couch.

Do you need anything? Gatsby signed.

Cassandra smiled, shook her head, and went back into self-absorption, signing fluidly.

As she turned to walk back down the hall, Gatsby sighed under her breath, "I do." In the kitchen, she pulled out a tumbler and some Kahlua and brandy. The White Russian army was on its way and not a minute too soon.

Sipping absentmindedly, she thought, *What the hell am I going to do...with a kid?*

She tipped the glass back and swallowed it all. A part of her wished that none of this had ever happened, another part wondered where it would lead, and something buried in the deep recesses of her mind was running, screaming.

While listening to Traussbery's phone ringing, Gatsby settled on the couch. A few feet away, Cassandra sat quietly on the floor, gazing around the room with an air of serenity.

Watching her, Gatsby found herself biting at her lower lip. Imagining herself afflicted with an elaborate delusion was one thing; watching it fiddle with the knobs on her stereo was another brand of anxiety altogether.

It kept ringing. And ringing.

She glanced at the clock: 4:25. Was he at home, working or writing? Perhaps he was walking the squeak toys.

The line connected. Silence.

"Traussbery, are you there?"

After a long silence and then labored coughing, she heard, "Yes...Ms. Donovan?"

"Are you all right? You sound like you have pneumonia."

He coughed wretchedly and spoke with a rasp. "I...I may be coming down with a chill. What can I do for you, Ms. Donovan?"

"Traussbery," she paused, not quite knowing how to say it. "The glyphs. I know what they mean."

On the other end, Traussbery whooped and then coughed until he could speak again. "Excellent! My god, do tell, do tell!"

Staring at the girl who was now leafing through her books, Gatsby murmured, "It's hard to explain but right up your alley, Traussbery, believe me."

She started with the literal translation of each glyph: C, S, N, D, R, A. Traussbery listened as she went on to recount her childhood fascination with language, her longing for a friend, the "appearance" of Cassandra, and the creation of the Peppermint Language. As she described the evening in her office when her lost memories returned all at once, she watched Cassandra move about the room, carefully touching objects and exploring textures as one suddenly given sight.

"As soon as I remembered everything, as soon as I remembered her name, and how I had imagined her, I—"

"Yes, yes?"

Gatsby took a deep breath and closed her eyes. "I don't know how to describe it—I don't think we have the vocabulary for this. A living being—" She couldn't say it, couldn't give credulity to an illusion being other than illusion, couldn't admit to what she knew, rationally, was impossible.

That impossibility was now curled up in her green love seat.

"Yes?" Traussbery prodded breathlessly. "A living being?"

Exhaling slowly, Gatsby said, "A living being—a person—wasn't there. And then it was. She was. Traussbery, the girl that I imagined, or thought that I imagined, when I was ten years old..." She sighed again, looking to the ceiling. "She became...*real* in my office. A living human. It's Cassandra, Traussbery, and she's sitting six feet away from me, and by christ if this is a hoax or someone's idea of a joke, then it's bloody—"

Desperation cut her off, and she moved the phone away from her mouth, hyperventilating.

"Good lord," Traussbery whispered. "Unbelievable. Unbelievable." He whooped ecstatically. "Fantastic! Good lord! Do you see what's happened? This is—" Traussbery trumpeted laughter until he could hardly speak. "This is beyond even what I had imagined! A bookcase, a teacup, a stone, the possibility of inanimate objects rousing from the enfolded universe, but organic form? A sentient being! Wondrous! How did it happen? What did you do? What," he whispered, his voice trembling, charged with amazement, "what is she like?"

"As I said, when I arranged the glyphs in the proper order, then I knew what they meant. I remembered everything. I had created them, and I had forgotten them or been led to forget them. Cassandra told me that she...she brought the symbols to, well, to me...in order to resurrect my memories. When my memory of her was re-established, she—"

"Re-established as well?" Traussbery finished for her.

Gatsby nodded wordlessly against the mouthpiece.

"Good lord," he murmured. "Ahm, I, I can only imagine what a shock this is for you, Ms. Donovan, quite a shock. Are you at home?"

"Yes." She swallowed.

"And are you all right, my dear?" The gentleness in his voice moved Gatsby. She could tell that he was truly concerned for her.

"Shaken, baffled, unsure of which needs psychiatric help, me or the rest of the known world but, for the moment, fine."

"I would imagine that you want some peace and quiet right now, but as soon as possible, Ms. Donovan, I need to see you and your...the...the young girl. Could you meet with me tomorrow?"

"Not tomorrow," Gatsby sighed, "Friday?"

"Very good. Meet me at the Punch & Judy at one o'clock." A cough rattled through Traussbery's gruff voice, then a breathless chuckle. "Good lord. Good lord. Marvelous."

Not the word I would have chosen, Gatsby thought. She made a brief goodbye.

Cassandra had found an objet d'art on Gatsby's living room bookcase: a crystal geode, flattened on the bottom so that it stood upright on the shelf. Anasazi petroglyphs were painted on one side of the stone. Cassandra returned to Gatsby's love seat with the geode and sat, running her finger across the designs of the petroglyphs, examining them carefully.

What is she thinking? Gatsby wondered. She turned to face the girl, leaning forward with elbows resting on her knees. Cassandra looked up.

Gatsby signed, *Tell me more.*

CHAPTER 30

"Anything else, madam?" Nigel's melodious baritone floated toward her as if from a parallel universe.

Gatsby looked up and shrugged. "No, thank you." With a serviette over his arm, Nigel drifted away, and she drifted back to her glass of Portsmythe and Traussbery's barrage of questions.

This Friday afternoon at the Punch & Judy Pub was quieter than the last time she had lunched at the haut monde restaurant. Lately finding herself without much appetite, Gatsby raised her glass from the linen-covered table and sipped absentmindedly. Traussbery labored eagerly over a shepherd's pie—a cannonball of sourdough bread filled with thick lamb stew—and a pint of ale. Steady rain outside drizzled from an overcast sky. Without the sunshine, Covent Garden lost its shoppers and tourists and took on a deserted and slightly ominous demeanor.

"How have you dealt with new words?" Traussbery asked, popping a chunk of lamb into his mouth and talking while he chewed. "Her vocabulary must necessarily be limited. If you came across, for example, an aardvark, how would you explain it? How would you name or define it? And have you given this new language a name?" He shook his head, beaming ecstatically. "A new language! Marvelous!"

"I've done the best I can," Gatsby replied, lowering her glass to the table, "and been creative. The world that existed when this language was invented contained less technology than we have today. We had no symbols for *computer* or *garbage disposal* or *email*. Those things weren't part of the Forest of Peppermint Trees. Twenty-six years later, they exist. I just," she sipped her ale, "like all language designers, we have to improvise. When a symbol for something doesn't exist," her eyebrows raised, "you create one."

"And what, ahm, what does she do? Does she eat? Sleep? How old do you think she is? Has she ever spoken aloud?"

"She seems content to just be, to watch and listen and learn. She's like a person who has just woken. Everything is new and interesting; she asks over and over, *what is this?* She's like a newborn in a teenager's body. How old? She seems on the cusp of puberty, physically anyway. And no, she doesn't speak out loud, at least not around me." Gatsby stared into her glass. "A name for the language? I just call it the Peppermint Language." She shook her head, smiling ruefully. "Imagine noting that on a resume in the future. Fluent Peppermint. What do you think the World Heritage Foundation would make of that, Traussbery?"

He wiped his lips with his napkin and then stowed it in his lap. "The opinion of the WHF is the last thing we should worry ourselves with, Ms. Donovan. They have plenty to deal with in light of this calamity at Stonehenge."

Gatsby swallowed the last of the ale and waved at Nigel. "Stonehenge." She sighed heavily. "Have you heard anything more? How they're going to find Stone 56?"

"I have heard from colleagues, yes. It seems that English Heritage is calling up specialists in fields from geology to forensic investigation. They want to assemble a task force of sorts to act as detectives and find out what they can about how the stone was moved—a veritably impossible task since the most telling evidence would be found on the stone itself." Finished with his pie, Traussbery dug into his pocket for his pipe and tobacco pouch. He puffed thoughtfully and the air filled with the heady perfume of Borkum Riff.

"Well, what do you speculate?" Gatsby asked. "What moved the rock, and what made it fall over at the moment of the solstice sunrise? Who took it? Was it you? Was it the Druids?"

As a soft cloud of pipe smoke rose and curved, serpentine, around them, Traussbery said quietly, "Frankly, at this point, Ms. Donovan, I am wary of thinking anything about it at all."

Gatsby was silent for a moment, considering Traussbery's story of the bookcase, Travis Norton, the repositioned Stone 56, and the only explanation that had thus far been offered of Cassandra's nativity. She stared at her empty plate.

"Quite," Traussbery murmured. "And yet we must think about it, Ms. Donovan, regardless of the fact that the field into which we have inadvertently wandered is not one susceptible to scrutiny by the common thinker. The greatest minds of our time—Grof, Dunne, Bohm, Pribram, Sheldrake, Lovelock, Einstein himself—have offered theories on the interrelated nature of the cosmos to which the average mind is not willing to listen. Essential human nature, human consciousness, is grounded in understanding by way of opposites: a thing may be A or it may be B, but it cannot be A *and* B. Not in a dualistic universe. However, when there is sufficient evidence—and I believe that we are heading in this direction—that our understandings of consensus reality are due for a restructuring, then we may begin to see glimpses of those events that have heretofore filled the pages of sacred scriptures, mythology texts, or tabloids."

"Or filled the tub in my bathroom," Gatsby muttered.

"Indeed," Traussbery replied, sucking on the pipe.

"But in your experiences...well, for example, the story that you told me of the teacup breaking in the pub, or of a falling bookcase. These are explainable by any number of completely everyday phenomena, but do you really believe that what happened at Stonehenge was caused by mentalism? By psychokinetic power? Or that Cassandra, a figment of a childish imagination, can pop into consensus existence like a special effect in a movie? How, Traussbery? Give me some evidence, some meaningful facts to support this!"

"Ms. Donovan, you must see the impossibility of my doing so." He puffed generously on the pipe. "The meaningful facts that you seek are still illusion, *maya*, still offspring of millennia of dualistic constructs. Our bank of knowledge is based on black-white, yes-no, up-down, true-false. How do we know what we know? This is epistemology. However, what happens when we are asked to consider what we don't know, what we do not understand? Consider the dark matter of the universe. What gravitational force keeps the galaxies from flying apart? The ninety percent of the matter in the universe that cannot be seen and is thus 'missing.' Contemporary scientists argue for the validation of unseen knowledge, the invisible, while at the same time cry for validation of the constant flux of knowledge. Are you familiar, Ms. Donovan, with the anomalon?"

She shook her head, frustrated.

He continued, "It is a subatomic particle, the properties of which change depending on who examines it! The anomalon studied in Moscow is different from one studied in Berkeley. Jahn and Dunne's work suggests that physicists are not discovering particles, they are *creating* them! We are the creators. When our energies resonate with another quantum energy field," he frowned as he waved his pipe, "as the phrase goes, all hell breaks loose. To put it another way, irrational and or inexplicable events may take place. A new resonance, a new set of particles, may burst into being. This being you speak of, Cassandra?"

Gatsby swallowed.

"Perhaps she is your anomalon. Rustled from fluctuation in the implicate fields, rearranged into a form visible to the human eye, in the explicate universe that you and I understand to be our reality."

Stirring the foam in her glass with one finger, Gatsby sighed. She was quiet for a moment before asking, "Traussbery, even if you believe this, who else is going to? The WHF? How will the general masses accept things that they see, or cannot see, but are asked to believe?"

Traussbery waved his pipe at her. "The masses, as you say, have always accepted unexplained phenomena. The medieval inquisitor or the Greek hieratikos didn't have the terms *dynamic energy field* or *holographic connectedness* or *implicate order.* They simply called events miracles, if they were believers, or illusion or trickery, if they were not. We have always been surrounded by mystery, but because something isn't understood does not mean that it will never be understood. In that respect, I must take issue with those who say that not only is the universe queerer than we think, it is queerer than we *can* think. Unadulterated pap!" He banged his fist on the table, causing Gatsby to jump and customers to stare.

Nigel wordlessly coasted by their table and refilled their glasses.

Traussbery continued. "You see, queerness of thought is exactly what happens when one vaults from the trenches of habitual thinking! And that is the birth of genius. Where would Einstein have gotten if he had smothered his genius in the confines of possibility? No, he had to move into the realm of the impossible. To fantasize how it might be to travel faster than light. Is it idiocy to fantasize thus? Many will say it is." He poked his pipe at her across the table for emphasis. "Others, you see, will not. Only by coming to the bosom of science with an open mind, an empty mind, will one ever stumble upon that which has not been conceived."

Good god, Gatsby thought, *every time I have lunch here, I am inundated with his science lessons, and I'm not sure the beer is good enough for that.* She sipped from her fresh pint of ale.

"Obviously, this is difficult for you, Ms. Donovan, but then you are young and only beginning to carve those ruts of thinking. I, on the other hand, am old and balmy enough to not give a blast what others think of me. I am not afraid of tarnishing my reputation." He smiled wryly. "A dangerous position for a respectable scientist, as you will surely agree."

Gatsby pinned him with a look and raised eyebrows. "Dangerous for just about anyone."

Traussbery chuckled, bringing on a wrenching fit of coughing. "Goodness," he finally gasped. "Excuse me."

"Have you been to a doctor, Traussbery? You've been hacking like that for weeks."

"No," he said, wheezing softly. "I know I should, I've just been...putting it off. Ms. Donovan," he took a deep breath, "I wonder if...well, I should like to ask you a favor."

"What?"

"I wonder if you could give me a lift next Monday. To an engagement." He coughed lightly. "I'm not sure that I should drive anymore. My eyesight is terribly poor and worsening. But the event is one I must attend."

"What is it?"

Traussbery sighed heavily. He dug into his coat pocket, pulled out a newspaper clipping, and held it up like a playing card. "This."

Gatsby glanced at the small headline. "A funeral?"

Traussbery's face crumpled with pain. "It's from this morning's World. Eleven years, Ms. Donovan, eleven years Norton lay like, like a rutabaga in a hospital bed, kept alive with pumps and wires. He died the day before yesterday. I'm—" His voice broke and he swallowed back tears. "I am the harbinger of that man's miserable fate. The least I can do is attend his funeral." Traussbery pulled out his hanky and blew his nose with a honk. He sniffed, stuffed the clipping back into his pocket, and stared at the tablecloth. "I must go and pay my respects."

"And ease your conscience, right?" Gatsby asked, leaning back and watching Traussbery. "You still believe that you were responsible for the bookcase that fell on him, don't you?"

His hands grappled in his lap. "Ms. Donovan, it was my doing. I am as certain of it as I have been of anything else in my life." He looked up at her with wide, wet, grey eyes. "Will you drive me?"

Shaking her head, she sighed, "I don't care what you think about homicidal bookcases, but I'll drive you. When is it, next Monday?"

"Yes. Early afternoon." Traussbery sniffed. "Thank you, truly." He wiped his eyes and seemed to have regained his composure. "Shall we? We have an engagement of our own."

They paid the bill; Nigel thanked them warmly and invited them to return soon. Traussbery's Bentley was parked just outside the restaurant; they climbed in and, in a few minutes, were at Gatsby's flat.

"Good lord, this is exciting!" Traussbery murmured as they made their way up the stone steps to the front door of the building. "I'm as nervous as a schoolboy."

"Don't get your drawers in a knot," she muttered, pushing the door open. Once past a tastefully decorated lobby, up a flight of red-carpeted stairs and then down a hallway, they were at Gatsby's flat. She unlocked the door and pushed.

"Come in," she said, motioning for Traussbery to step inside.

While Gatsby took his overcoat and hung it in the hall closet, he wandered into the living room, quickly appraising it. "Quite lovely. Quite a view."

Gatsby nodded. "Thanks. Have a seat, I'll be right back."

Traussbery sat on the couch in the living room. Momentarily he looked up and his eyes widened. "Good lord!"

At the entrance to the living room, Cassandra stood like a glass figurine. In her blue jumpsuit, white blouse, anklets, and flat black canvas shoes, she looked as if she had just left classes at a girl's prep school.

She wandered in and sat in the green love seat, quietly appraising him. Looking up at Gatsby, she signed, *What is this?*

Gatsby's hands flew as she signed back, *A friend. His name—*

Great, we'll have to improvise a name. She quickly conceived of three hand motions that would phonetically approximate the sound of *trauss-ber-ry.* Laying her hands perpendicular, she pressed both palms together and swept the right in one quick movement across the left, making a swishing sound. She then curled her left hand into a fist and brought the right palm down against the tops of the left fingers, just below the knuckles. Last, she smacked her right palm against the flat side of the fist.

Good enough, she thought.

Cassandra nodded and repeated the gesture several times.

"Incredible!" Traussbery whispered. He waved his hands to motion for Gatsby to sit with him and chortled gleefully. "Incredible, most fantastic! Brilliant! I have so many questions to ask! Ms. Donovan, would you mind, er, assisting?"

Settling on the couch, Gatsby replied, "I'll do the best I can."

Traussbery feverishly posed questions and Gatsby translated. Where did Cassandra believe she had come from, and how had she arrived in Gatsby's office? Had she been self-aware before then? Did she have memories and, if so, what were they? How did she know who she was, who Gatsby was? Did she think of herself as a human? As a child? Had she ever been afraid? What did she plan or want for herself? Was she happy? Did she know what thoughts and feelings were? Did she ever feel hungry?

Through Gatsby, Cassandra explained: her self-aware thoughts and memories, before appearing in the office at the British Museum, were those she had shared with Gatsby in the Forest of Peppermint Trees. When she was erased from Gatsby's consciousness, she went "Below," knowing only that she wanted to return to Gatsby's "Above." She knew that she did indeed have a name and that, at some level, it had come from Gatsby's knowledge. She was not ever afraid, or sad, or hungry (she grimaced at the suggestion of putting things into her mouth) and wanted only one thing: to stay in this place, "Above."

In response to Traussbery's question, *Where did you come from,* Cassandra smiled and pointed at Gatsby.

Shaking her head, Gatsby murmured, "Don't ask me to explain that one."

After several more questions, Traussbery pulled his watch from his pocket. "Oh dear lord, I must go." He rose with some effort and gave a curt bow in Cassandra's direction. "Er, please offer my thanks, Ms. Donovan." He paused. "I...well, if it wouldn't be terribly inappropriate, may I touch her hand?"

Gatsby signed; Cassandra grinned and raised her brown hand.

Traussbery reached out and gingerly placed his hand on hers. Eyes bulging, he swallowed, slowly running his fingertips across her dark skin, and then buried his hand in his pocket.

"Fantastic," he whispered.

Gatsby got Traussbery's coat and walked him to the door. "I'll see you Monday morning."

"Yes." He coughed as he pulled on his overcoat. "Eleven o'clock." Turning to look her in the eye, Traussbery gazed at her with gratitude. "Ms. Donovan, I cannot tell you what this experience has meant for me. It is...she is a true wonder. A marvel that we may never completely understand. My thanks, my deepest thanks." He gripped her hand earnestly, then trundled down the hallway to the stairs.

Closing the door, Gatsby went back to the living room where Cassandra was sitting with an open book in her lap.

Gatsby glanced at the title: *Britain's Mysterious Monuments* by Caitlin McNeil.

Cassandra sat deep in concentration, poring over the photographs, running her fingers across the images. She stayed on the couch all evening.

As she brushed her teeth, Gatsby held her hands up in front of her face. Examined them in the mirror. Stared at them. Moved them from side to side, kneaded them, rubbed them, pressed them together.

The convulsive gestures had stopped.

CHAPTER 31

At her breakfast table, Gatsby finished the last drop of her coffee with a satisfied slurp. Only crumbs remained of the pain au chocolate, and only the sound of finches chirping in the maples outside her window broke the morning quiet.

She turned to see Cassandra rising from the cushions of the couch. She had taken to sitting or lying there at night although she never seemed to actually sleep.

How do you feel? Gatsby asked.

Cassandra rose to her feet and signed, *I want to go outside.*

Dandy, Gatsby thought. *Outside is exactly where I'm taking you today.* She went to get her denim jacket and backpack from the hall closet.

A few minutes later, they were strolling down King's Road toward the subway entrance at Sloane and Benedict. Gatsby explained the sights to Cassandra as they walked along. For a few minutes she felt self-conscious about the hand gestures, as if she were a poseur faking deafness. Soon, however, caught up in the environs and conversation, she forgot herself and that they were talking with their hands.

They passed bookstores, boutiques, vegetable stalls, flower carts, panhandlers, street musicians, city parks, dogs on leashes and tattooed gothic urban primitives wearing steel-studded dog collars. Again and again, Cassandra asked, *what is it?* Eventually Gatsby began describing before the question was asked. As if it were something that could be touched, she felt she was watching Cassandra's vocabulary—and understanding—growing by the minute.

They dropped down into the Tube, bought tickets, and headed toward the open train doors. Cassandra hesitated for a moment, then looked at Gatsby and stepped into the compartment. She quietly peered around at the human diversity surrounding her as they found seats.

Gatsby shook her head ruefully, reminded of the day she had arrived in London, six years ago.

Fifteen minutes later, they were at Tower Hill Station. Gatsby said, *This is it, let's go.* As the mechanical PA system voice intoned "Mind the gap," they jumped up and stepped off the train.

Making their way out of the catacombs of the Tube, they crested a flight of stairs to ground level and then walked through a damp tunnel toward the moat of the Tower of London. The July afternoon was hot, the sunshine brilliant; tourists meandered down the sidewalk with them toward the ticket gate. Gatsby flashed her museum ID card. They grey-whiskered gentleman in the ticket booth gave her a once-over look, peered at Cassandra, raised his bushy eyebrows, and waved them through.

They crossed the bridge over the moat—the only pedestrian entrance to the Tower—and stopped for a moment to listen to one of the Yeoman Warders giving a well-rehearsed recital of the Tower's thousand-year history. A crowd stood around him, fixed on his booming, heavily accented voice and brilliant red, black, and gold Beefeater uniform. As the tourists laughed at his jokes, Gatsby and Cassandra moved on.

They strolled past the Royal Chapel of St. Peter ad Vincula, past the ancient armory, and stopped to sit on a sun-warmed bench on the eastside of the White Tower.

Subtly, Gatsby watched Cassandra—every blink, gesture, step, turn; observing what she noted, what caught her interest, how she moved physically, how she made decisions, what prompted her questions.

She's quick and observant, Gatsby thought, *but as far as I can tell, not a mind reader. I still haven't seen her sleep or eat; she seems disgusted by the idea of eating, so she's eating and sleeping surreptitiously or...doesn't need to. I've heard anecdotal cases of people who have gone for years without food or water, but sleep? The human mind breaks down quickly when deprived of sleep. The next question then—is she human?*

With these thoughts churning through her mind, Gatsby pulled a plastic container from her backpack, popped the lid, and took a long sip of apple juice. She lifted the container toward Cassandra with a "want some?" gesture. Cassandra energetically shook her head no.

Gatsby sighed, looked up to watch the ravens that floated by overhead, and turned to face Cassandra. She signed, *In the Forest of Peppermint Trees, we were the same age. Now I am grown. Why aren't you?*

Cassandra sat forward on the edge of the bench and signed fluidly, *I am not adult or child. You must not think of me that way, Gatsby. You know that I am not that. You are not ready to understand what I am, or to admit that you could understand, but you will. Soon.*

Gatsby sat, listening to murmurings and camera-shutter clicks as tourists shuffled by them, taking in the White Tower—the Norman stronghold of Caen stone where kings and queens had dined, fought invaders, tortured prisoners, and passed their deeds into the annals of history.

This isn't a child sitting next to me. I don't know or understand exactly what she is, but apparently understanding will only come with a core paradigm shift. Are the answers to the questions of the last three months sitting right next to me?

She took a deep breath and replied, *Because of you and other recent experiences, I am re-examining many ideas.*

She glanced at Cassandra, who had turned her brown face up into the warmth of the midday sun. Cassandra glanced back, as if aware of Gatsby's thoughts, and closed her eyes again.

She isn't a girl, Gatsby thought, *She never was. Less a tangible, or organic, entity. More a thought, or an abstraction, but something...purer than that? Much simpler and yet much more complex. Paradox in the illusion of human form. Maya.*

Cassandra's hands moved. *Gatsby?*

She turned, almost startled. Cassandra's eyes met hers.

When you look at words, you understand the meaning of many words. But do you understand what words are?

Gatsby frowned, thinking, *What kind of a question is that to ask an epigrapher? I've spent my entire life studying words. She signed back, Of course I know what they are. Symbols.*

glyphs
C S N D R A

Holding her fast in her gaze, Cassandra replied, *Of what? That is the question you want to answer.*

Words are symbols. Symbols of thought, of objects or abstractions. And always open to interpretation. What words are to human civilization, is that what Cassandra is to me? Is that what she's saying?

Again, as if catching her thoughts, Cassandra watched her steadily.

Gatsby shook her head and signed, *I understand that the symbols C S N D R A are the symbols for you. The stone that moved at Stonehenge—I saw a picture of it and one of your symbols was on it. Is there a connection between you and the stone?*

Cassandra smiled. *You will find the connection, Gatsby, but not in the way that you think. You already know the answer.*

The tip of a conceptual iceberg moved in Gatsby's subconscious.

Signing, Gatsby replied, *Where is the connection?*

A soft smile played on Cassandra's lips. *What you want traps you. Words trap. They trap you with meaning, and how you use them keeps the trap hidden. You have forgotten. The connection itself is a trap. Using the word, you allow the belief that there can be disconnection.*

Traussbery's wrinkled face rose onto the canvas of her mind's eye; his gravelly voice sounded in her head...understanding of the cosmology's deeper structures, and a power of consciousness that gave them ability to shape those structures, to wield them as a painter uses brush and ink to...

Cassandra raised her left arm, bent at the elbow, her hand straight with the palm facing down. With her right hand, she made slow figure eights in the air below her left arm. Below.

She then brought her right palm to rest on top of her left forearm. Above.

Above and below, Gatsby. But these are a trap.

Traussbery's words: *Essential human nature, human consciousness, is grounded in understanding by way of opposites: a thing may be A or it may be B, but it cannot be A and B. Not in a dualistic universe...*

A dark shadow crossed the sky overhead—they both looked up. One of the Tower's ravens soared by, its clipped wings forcing it to fly low. Gatsby remembered the centuries-old tale of the Tower's denizens: if the ravens ever left the Tower, it—and the kingdom—would fall. Like many others who had been kept prisoner in the Tower walls, they were themselves imprisoned.

Trapped.

Shiftings—increments of cognition as micro- and macroscopic as anomalons—moved, in flux, shape-shifting as mysteriously as particle becoming wave, wave becoming particle. Gatsby felt the flux inside of her; simultaneously, the concept of "inside" felt fuzzy.

*Inside/outside—what is the difference? Can there be difference? Can a universe have an "in" side and an "out" side? In duality...a linguistic trap...*Gatsby thought and dropped her head into her hands, startled to find herself shaking.

"I...don't...it, but...can't..." She sputtered for a moment and then fell silent. Trapped in the prison of her own words.

Atop a nearby ruin of a Roman wall built in the eleventh century, a raven cawed loudly. Gatsby jumped and Cassandra bubbled soft laughter. She nimbly popped to her feet; the breeze blew her dark hair across her face. She faced Gatsby and signed, *Let's walk.*

Gatsby pulled in a deep breath and slowly pulled herself to her feet. Her body felt ancient and inexplicably expansive. The hardness of the bricks beneath her feet seemed untenable.

She glanced around her, thinking with wonder how the world seemed to have taken on a strange tint, a shade for which there was not yet a linguistic equivalent. She was seized by the compulsion to struggle for it, but it held her fast. In a span of time that could have been seconds or days, and with an almost physical sensation of letting go, she belayed the compulsion to find the equivalent.

Gatsby took Cassandra's warm hand. They walked in silence, passing the Tower Green and the site of the execution block, the Chapel, the Queen's House, and the Jewel House. Then they were at the moat and the entrance gate.

The grey-whiskered ticketer nodded at them and mumbled, "G'day ladies." They slowly walked up the narrow street that led to Tower Hill Station and the Tube.

Back at her flat, Gatsby dropped her backpack in a heap near the front hall closet. Cassandra wandered into the living room and sprawled on the floor, lying on her back and staring up at the ceiling, humming to herself.

Humming?

The thought racing through Gatsby's mind—*She's vocalizing?!—floated* on an undercurrent of fear. Frowning, she tossed her jacket on the couch, got a glass from the kitchen cabinet and a carton of milk from the refrigerator. She filled the glass, returned the carton to the refrigerator, and walked into the living room, glancing at her answering machine on the way. Remembering her promise to drive Traussbery to Norton's funeral on Monday, she wondered if he had called. The red light on the machine glowed steadily: no messages.

She dropped wearily onto the couch. They had only taken a short subway trip to the Tower, but she was dead tired. Head on the armrest, she lay back flat on the couch and closed her eyes, listening with astonishment to Cassandra's throaty humming.

"I still want to understand this," Gatsby said, eyes closed and too weary to sign with her hands. "When you say that words are a trap, I understand the idea that a physical existence cannot be part of consensus consciousness, cannot be integrated into consensus reality, until it has a label. Are you saying that it doesn't have a label? Or that it shouldn't, because the label traps the speaker into a single definition? What about multiple interpretations of the same thing? Why does th—"

She stopped. It was too quiet. Cassandra had stopped humming.

As she sat up, Gatsby opened her eyes. "I mean, wha—"

Her jaw dropped.

Cassandra had been lying face up on the floor. Where she had been, there was now an adult body: face down, rotund, dressed in loose light-colored clothing of an indistinguishable fabric, thin grey hair. The body began to stir.

Sharp pains stabbed Gatsby's heart as her lungs locked. A bile-like taste filled her mouth.

When the body sat upright and turned to face her, she let out a shriek.

It was Traussbery.

She felt her mouth open and close convulsively; a thin trickle of saliva oozed from one corner.

It stared at her with glittering grey eyes and then spoke. "Direct experience is sometimes best."

Cassandra's voice—the voice that had been low humming moments before—merged the intonations of a young girl from the Pacific Northwest with deep subfrequencies that eluded identification of a specific geography or era.

Gatsby shook her head, her heart hammering...*no, no, no, no, no...*

The Traussbery-body-with-Cassandra's-voice moved its hands into its lap, looking down at the body. It was indeed Traussbery's corpus—rounded with fat, weak with age, besieged with a variety of physical ailments. The Traussbery-face grimaced, perhaps to express annoyance or dismay—it was hard to tell which—as it gazed upon its carriage. It spoke.

"They simply called events miracles, if they were believers, or illusion or trickery, if they were not. We have always been surrounded by mystery, but simply because something isn't understood does not mean that it will never be understood." With Cassandra's voice, the Traussbery-body recited the words that Gatsby had heard while sitting in a restaurant having lunch with Martin Baldwin Traussbery, the eccentric professor who taught archeology at the University of Cambridge and owned two sniveling Shih Tzus and claimed to possess telekinetic ability.

Swaying, Gatsby sank back against the couch, hyperventilating.

"I don't want to scare you," the Traussbery-body-with-Cassandra's-voice said, "just to show you."

The image began to blur, the features softening as if Gatsby's eyes had lost focus; they became malleable; the body melted, shortening, collapsing into a smaller body; the features rearranged and redefined; the light clothing became a blue jumpsuit, the hair bloomed long and dark.

Her body was that of a girl. She was Cassandra again—with Gatsby's face.

From where she sat on the couch, Gatsby felt herself spiral into the surrealism of dreams where consensus images meld with the subconscious, where one might fly or breathe underwater, or become an animal, or travel to another world, or explore realms of existence for which there were no linguistic traps.

She looked down at the girl sitting on the floor before her. The face was that of her own as a girl, the ten-year-old Gatsby Donovan.

"Gatsby? Can you hear me?" The voice was still Cassandra's.

At first Gatsby could only gasp, exhaling hard bursts of air. She swallowed hard against unstoppable waves of saliva, grimaced against the iceball of terror in her stomach. Blinking, she sucked in air and wheezed, "Hhhh..." Her mouth overflowed with a stream of sick-tasting saliva; she leaned over her glass of milk and spat.

"This is to help answer your questions. Do you understand?"

Gatsby nodded; a high-pitched tone fired between in her ears. She blinked.

"How? That's what you want to know, isn't it?" The jumpsuited-girl-with-Gatsby's-face tipped her head to one side, subtly smiling.

Gatsby nodded again.

"You want to believe that I am a dream, or illusion, or sickness, but none of these are true. The nature of change—that is your question. You have become familiar with the habits of the world, the world to which you are accustomed. To its consistency. The changes I am showing you now are not your illusion, or dream, or sickness. They are—" She stopped, took a breath. "Gatsby, there are many songs that you don't hear. Songs are what make worlds. Songs are the worlds. You are song. When you breathe, when your heart beats, that is song. When you walk or retrieve a memory, that is song. Everything sings, and songs mix in infinite ways. Sometimes you can hear the song. Sometimes you can't, and it may be because it is a song you have never heard before and did not know what to listen for."

Cassandra turned to look out the window. Minuscule changes had reshaped her face—her eyes, lips, and facial structure. Her hair had grown almost three inches in the span of a minute. Her skin had taken on a darker shade, and the outer edges of her eyes had tilted upward, making them almond shaped.

"All that you have shown me, Gatsby—people, stores, animals, food, buildings, books, streets, houses—everything is song. Resonance. What you want to think of as real is only the song you are used to hearing. I am a different song. One that you are hearing for the first time." She closed her eyes for a moment and hummed.

Gatsby watched, frozen, waiting for a chair to float or the television to transform into a griffin, but nothing happened.

"Song...sound...is something that you know, Gatsby. You are familiar with songs that are not seen or touched."

Sound waves? Gatsby thought. *Vibration? Frequencies? Particle becoming wave, wave to particle?*

"Songs alter. The sound shows the—"

She opened her eyes and looked around. Now with dark skin, almond-shaped eyes, a slightly flattened nose, and black hair flowing around her neck, it was Cassandra. She gazed around the room. Near the entrance to the hallway leading to the bedroom, there was a teak table that held Gatsby's answering machine and phone books. An ornate gold mirror hung on the wall above the table. Cassandra's eyes went to the mirror.

"Like the mirror. The reflection is shown. The shift reveals the event. The event is happening now, when the song is sung. Or it may happen, when the song will be sung. Or it has already happened, because the song was already sung. The word traps are past, present, and future—but song cannot be trapped."

Gatsby closed her eyes for a moment. She thought she would faint but, with all her will, opened her eyes, forcing herself to look, to experience *this*.

"All songs are everywhere. Song is everything. And there are too many songs for you to understand right now. Song is what you use the words to mean *thing* or to mean *event*. It is what you call time and real and illusion. You cannot ever have all the words to define all the songs, because they can't be defined. If they could, they wouldn't be. They would be trapped and so would you. When you experience what you don't understand, what you don't believe is real, or what you cannot trap with words, it is a song—one that you have not heard before."

Cassandra leaned back against Gatsby's love seat, a satisfied look on her face. "This is what you need to know. Now you know it. Take," she giggled softly, "take time to understand. When you want me to sing for you again, just ask."

Sing for me...

In the theater of Gatsby's mind, an image bloomed: a sheer cliff facing another cliff. A deep ravine between them. A rough bridge, manifesting itself out of nothing, appearing to span the chasm.

Her throat muscles moved; a guttural grunt was all she could manage. She swallowed, took a breath, and tried again. "I...I think I..." She leaned forward over her knees, finding her center of gravity. Felt her body weight shift to her feet, transferred weight onto them, then a bit more. Her knees shook but she pressed, grasping the arm of the couch for support. "I think..." She thought of the last time she had felt so utterly drained, almost exsanguinated: a two-week bout of intestinal flu. A final push and she was upright. She began to shuffle toward the hallway, eyes focused on her bed, telling herself over and over that she could make it another fifteen feet and she'd be able to lie down in her warm, soft bed and sleep for an eternity. The journey down the hall took about a year. Grey dots danced in front of her eyes, and she dropped once against the doorjamb of the bathroom but managed to find her balance again, stumble into her bedroom, and crash onto her bed.

She awoke once, sometime in the middle of the night. Glancing through her doorway and down the hall, she saw a small form on the living room couch. It was Cassandra, sitting cross-legged as if in meditation, still as stone, humming softly.

Her body was translucent. Through Cassandra's torso, Gatsby saw the twisting branches of the maple trees outside the window, the entwined patterns in the green fabric covering the couch.

Gatsby groaned and incoherent thoughts flickered like wild, scattered shadows.

Do I do the same in dreams? Do I exist when unconscious? Does the light stay on when the refrigerator door closes? Is the cat dead or alive?

She rolled over into blackness.

CHAPTER 32

Gatsby stuck her head out the window to read the road sign: Bishop's Stratford. Another forty kilometers and they would be in Cambridge.

Nestled in the passenger's seat with her brown legs crossed, Cassandra sat humming to herself, watching as the campestral scenery rolled by. In her conversation with Gatsby that morning, she had signed, using the Peppermint Language rather than speaking aloud. When Gatsby had asked about the switch, Cassandra had said that her "song was quiet now" and given no further explanation, and though unable to grasp the base of the feeling, Gatsby realized that she felt a peculiar sense of safety when communicating in their private language.

Gatsby had explained that they were driving to a city where they would meet Traussbery again. She had also asked that Cassandra stay in the car while she and Traussbery went to a funeral, and with no word to sufficiently explain a "funeral," had settled for the compound "sad-party."

Racing northward on the A53 motorway, Gatsby wondered how Traussbery would react to the funeral. Seeing him so distraught at the Punch & Judy, she wondered if this event, combined with the destruction and then disappearance of Stone 56, might send him over the edge into serious depression. Or psychosis.

While that unsettling thought slithered through her mind—bringing memories of the red stop sign—she put on a cassette of Beatles' songs.

I am the eggman, I am the walrus, I am the matrix of improvable phenomena—koo koo ka choo.

She tapped her fingers on the steering wheel, deep in thought, as the sylvan kilometers rushed by.

A tap on the horn, and Traussbery popped from the door of his brownstone dressed in his familiar black overcoat and black bowler.

"Good day, Ms. Donovan," he said as he pulled open the door on the passenger's side of the Volvo and started to climb in. "Oh! Ahm, hello."

Gatsby asked Cassandra if she would move to the back seat. She nodded, climbed out, and got back in behind Traussbery.

As he settled in the seat, Traussbery coughed lightly and wiped at his lips with his white hanky. "I must thank you again for the lift, Ms. Donovan. My eyesight grows worse almost by the day. I fear that it may one day become so bad that it will cost me my—" He fell silent and stared at the floor mats as he buckled his seat belt.

From his expression, Gatsby read his thoughts: *Cost him his position—the position tragically acquired by way of the late Travis Norton.*

He looked her in the eye. She looked back for a moment, gave a small nod, and pulled the car away from the curb.

"It isn't far and the drive is quite scenic," Traussbery commented as they made their way down the cobbled central avenue of Cambridge. "Whittleham is a beautiful borough of craftspeople and oenophiles. I had a cousin by marriage who lived there. Margaret was her name, I believe."

Curious but somewhat wary of knowing too much about Traussbery's personal life, Gatsby asked, "Is she still there?"

"I really don't know," Traussbery answered absentmindedly, staring out the window as the spires of Cambridge disappeared and open hills, dotted with farms and cottages, unfolded around them. He coughed and wiped at his lips.

Gatsby looked back at the road, wondering at the strange relationship she'd developed with Traussbery. Now that the meaning of the six glyphs was clear, she wasn't sure if reasons to keep in touch remained. Without a doubt, however, Traussbery had claimed a page in her life. While his theories of particle physics or consciousness or telekinetics might amount to nothing, might never capture the attention of the World Heritage Foundation or win academic acclaim, he had been, for her, an enigmatic catalyst.

She glanced at Cassandra, sitting quietly in the back seat, and knew that her life would never be the same. A new and indelible symbol had been drawn on the canvas of her fate.

The road turned and curved as they passed through vineyards and villages and then dove into a region of thick forest. Gatsby nodded and "hmm hmm"-ed as Traussbery chattered about a trip to Tanzania, many years ago, when he'd had the fortuitous opportunity to visit the Olduvai Gorge and literally walk in the footsteps of Richard Leakey.

"Can you imagine how it felt," he murmured, gesturing, "standing in the cradle of mankind, the birthplace of human civilization, walking along the same river beds where the first human beings, our primordial—"

"GOD!!" Gatsby shouted and slammed on the brakes.

Something huge hit the windshield with a sickening WHUMP and a flurry of dark writhing.

Tires squealing as the Volvo skidded, Gatsby maneuvered to a stop at the side of the road. "Are you all right?" she gasped.

From the back seat, tousled but unharmed, Cassandra signed that she was okay.

"No permanent...good lord, what did we hit?" Traussbery said, eyes bulging. He popped his door open. "Better have a look."

"I'm going with you," Gatsby said. She stopped the engine and stepped onto the road. Stay here, she signed to Cassandra. The girl nodded and curled up on the seat.

They circled the car, looking for something that had to have been the size of a large deer and instead found black streaks on the pavement and the windshield. Gatsby ran a fingertip through the dripping fluid on the shield glass and held it up in front of her, frowning furiously.

"Bloody hell," she whispered. "Look at this, Traussbery."

He sidled up next to her and peered at the black goo. "Good lord. It looks like motor oil."

"What kind of animal bleeds motor oil?"

They peered around anxiously, scanning the nearby trees, shadows, rocks, mud, and grass but saw no sign of any animals.

"Was it a deer?" Traussbery asked.

"I don't know, I didn't see anything but a big shadow. But it didn't," she stared at the black residue on her fingertip, "it didn't look like an animal."

Traussbery's face tightened. "You don't think—"

She shook her head, still breathing hard, and glanced toward a rustling sound on her right.

Her eyes bulged.

It was massive, and it was clambering out of the forest.

"Shit!" Gatsby screamed. As he turned to look, Traussbery went dead white and crumbled against the car.

A muscular, ridged neck, long as a giraffe's, snaked from its bulbous body. Its mouth gnashed, chomping pointed translucent teeth. Antennae, two meters long, wriggled over its head as its neck swung back and forth. Its two multi-lensed eyes were the size of footballs, and two appendages, as thick as octopus tentacles, wriggled from its chest. Thick black ooze dripped from its mouth and eyes. Toward its rear, a set of leathery wings, four meters in spread, lifted it as it skittered forward, balanced on bony back legs and its writhing forward appendages.

A heinous, drooling creature; some unearthly, unreal demon; reptilian and insectile, with great gnashing razor-pointed teeth.

It spread its jaws as it lunged toward them and screamed, an eardrum-shattering squeal, the sound of a rod jamming the works of a massive, spinning engine.

It was advancing toward them, howling and dripping black ooze. Gatsby screamed, "Run!"

She grabbed the arm of Traussbery's overcoat and bolted. The fabric jerked out of her hand.

"Do you see? See? It's him!!" Traussbery squeaked, frozen like a statue. "Oh dear god! It's HIM!!!"

"What the f—"

It bore down, snarling, drooling black, oily saliva that rained down on them. Traussbery slumped to the ground and, in a second of terror, Gatsby realized that he wasn't moving. The monstrosity swung its head in his direction, wriggling its leg-things toward Traussbery's limp body, opening its dripping mouth and screaming again.

She grabbed the first rock she saw and hurled it at the thing's head. As the rock sank into its left eye, the creature howled, its neck swinging wildly, spitting long strings of black bile.

"Traussbery! Get the hell out of its way!!" Gatsby shouted. She grabbed another rock and hit the side of the creature's head. It screamed and turned on her.

Cold horror washed through her; hot sharp pain sizzled in her chest. Gatsby turned and darted toward the back of the car. The thing flapped its gigantic bat-like wings, raising itself up into the air as it lumbered toward her.

She screamed over her shoulder, "Forchrissake Traussbery RUN!!"

It had scooped Traussbery up in its meaty tentacles. Traussbery flailed, kicking, as it tore at him with long teeth. He let loose a rattling scream.

"Oh god," she whispered. Any sort of weapon? Even a flare might frighten it—were there flares in the boot of the car?

The passenger door popped open.

Gatsby felt her heart lodge in her throat. Cassandra.

"No!!"

The instant that Cassandra stepped out of the car, the creature dropped Traussbery. He tumbled to the ground with a howl of agony.

Gatsby glanced quickly at its reptilian head and, for half a second, the features looked almost human: two blazing eyes, directed by a malevolent intelligence.

As she began to run, it descended on Cassandra with a shriek. Its pointed, stick-like legs pinned her down; its rubbery appendages slithered like giant anacondas around her head and, with a piercing howl, it tore at her convulsing body with its glistening teeth, gnashing into her like a shark champing into its prey.

"NO!!!" Gatsby bellowed. She scrambled into the scrub, grabbed a thick branch and, raising it high over her head, brought it down with all her strength on the creature's head. The thing faltered sideways and snapped, snarling, spitting. Traussbery had fallen inert and bleeding to the pavement near the rear of the car. Gatsby swung again, and the creature screamed as the branch struck the side of its head. She smashed at it, shouting, raining blows on its head, battering its eyes. One blow knocked one of its long teeth out; resembling an icicle in flight, it flipped end over end, revolving through the air, and landed in the dirt three meters away.

While it spit at Gatsby, its stick-legs pierced Cassandra's body like massive skewers. Cassandra's screams filled the air, and she beat at it with her small fists as it roared and ripped into her body—blood spurted like hot rain, spraying Gatsby in red globs and streaks. Jerking its head backward, like a beast flipping its wriggling prey, it stretched its jaws wide to engulf Cassandra, thrashing, headfirst into its mouth, and her piercing screams dissolved into gurgling.

Gatsby raised the branch once more; it was the last time—her arms were numb.

"Get away, you FUCKER!" she shrieked and smashed the branch to the monster's head. The blow fell on its eye and, like a detonation, the eye exploded, showering out a flood of vomit-green mucus.

The creature screamed, its head writhing in circles on its long neck, and one of Cassandra's shoes rocketed out of its mouth toward Gatsby. Both antennae swiveled downward and poked at the oozing wound as it bellowed. Its black wings shuddered and then unfolded to a width of six meters. Still screaming and spewing black mucus, it hunkered down on its fore-tentacles and then pushed itself upward off the ground. The flapping of its massive wings caused mini-tornadoes of gravel as it rose into the air, crested the tops of the trees, rising higher, and flew off in zigzags over a ridge.

Gripping the branch with white-knuckled hands, sweat streaming down her face, streaked with blood and green and black slime, Gatsby stood frozen, gasping.

A moan came from near the back of the car.

She stumbled toward the sound. Traussbery lay face down near the rear tires, his overcoat shredded and splattered with blood. As Gatsby approached, her knees buckled. She dropped to the pavement next to him and grabbed his shoulders to gently roll him over.

"Traussbery?" she whispered.

He rolled onto his back, eyes closed, breathing shallowly. He pulled in a deep breath, coughed wretchedly, and then was still. His eyes opened blearily. "Ooooooohhhhawful pain," he moaned, wincing. "Ankle...broken."

Her eyes traveled down his body; he was bleeding from several wounds but not severely. The bleeding would stop in a minute. His right foot was turned at an impossible angle.

"Don't move, just lie still." Gatsby ran an arm across her forehead, brushing off the black-gooey strands of hair plastered to her cheeks. She took a shuddering breath and slowly stood. Her knees almost gave out; her entire body shivered violently. She flexed her hands a few times, moaning. She had gripped the branch so hard that the crevasses under her fingernails were jammed with wood shards.

She swallowed with effort. "Don't move," she said again and started toward the spot, a few meters from the front of the car, where the creature had attacked Cassandra.

A glistening swath of blood came into view.

Panting, she spotted something in the dirt, and reached for it. A fragment of Cassandra's jumpsuit, sticky with blood. Gatsby slowly looked around and saw something near the front tires, spider webs of blood splattered across its white surface. One of Cassandra's lace-trimmed anklets.

"No...no," she whispered. She rubbed her face; some of the black substance had trickled into her eyes, stinging horribly.

She knelt slowly; every bruised muscle throbbed, and she felt tears running down her cheeks. Her head spun for a moment and she closed her eyes, sobbing silently. Then, with a shuddering breath, she hobbled toward Traussbery.

"Did you see him?" Traussbery murmured.

"Raise up—I'll support you on your left side. Let's get you into the car." He groaned as she helped him to rise onto one knee and then finally stand shakily on his left leg. Gatsby held his arm tightly as he leaned on her and hobbled to the front passenger's seat where he dropped with a grunt and laid his head back.

"His face...his face...face..." he muttered as Gatsby stumbled around the front of the car to the driver's seat. She climbed in and sat with her eyes closed, panting, her blood-splattered hands splayed against her thighs.

She whispered weakly. "What the hell—"

"The...where is the young girl?" Traussbery said. His eyes darted. "Oh dear lord, is...did...is she..."

"She's...I don't...she's gone," Gatsby whispered.

Traussbery sat stone-still for a moment, then whispered, "H-Horrible. Horrible." He swiped at his nose with the sleeve of his coat and turned to face Gatsby with blazing eyes. "It was him."

Gatsby opened her eyes and stared dully. "Him?"

Traussbery's blanched face, flecked with blood and black ooze, crumbled with terror. "It was him! That...creature! It had a face and I saw, I saw it! His face! His eyes! It was him!!"

"Who?!" she shouted.

"Norton! Norton! It was Norton, it was Norton, *Travis Norton!!* I destroyed him! I ruined his life and now he wants mine!!" His hair spiked and streaked with black ooze, eyes bulging in their sockets, and beads of spittle flying as he babbled, Traussbery had never looked so utterly insane. He fell forward and sobbed.

Gatsby's jaw dropped; then she winced at a biting pang of nausea. A violent recant of Traussbery's sanity gathered on the tip of her tongue, but she didn't have the strength to voice it. Gatsby took a long, deep breath and turned the key in the ignition. The engine roared.

"Whatever it was," she said, measuring the words with deadly precision, "we're going back to Cambridge. You need a doctor, and Travis Norton is dead."

Cassandra...

Traussbery sank in his seat, breathing raggedly and coughing as Gatsby slowly started down the road.

"I saw his face, his eyes—it was him," Traussbery whispered over and over until he passed out.

As Gatsby drove, she stared through the black streaks on the windshield. She rolled down the window when the nausea hit, expecting to vomit at any moment.

Follow me!

had to let her gohhhhh...

Numb with shock, aching with rolling waves of nausea, pain, and tears, she turned the car toward Cambridge.

CHAPTER 33

A feeling—that she was being watched—tickled at the back of her neck. Gatsby looked up from the three-inch-thick file she was absorbed in to see Nelson Clevis standing in the doorway of her office.

"Ms. Donovan. I trust you had a pleasant holiday."

His appearance gave her the disorienting sensation that the last three months had never happened. Stoic and placid in the eternal grey suit, burgundy tie, and Lennonesque glasses, Clevis appeared, down to his last starched thread, exactly as he had at their last conversation.

"Nelson," she replied, taking him in with a long sigh. "It wasn't what I thought it would be."

Eyebrows raised, he pursed his thin lips. "Pity. Well, perhaps the next will be better. But no time to waste. You know that the Nehezra tablets arrive tomorrow?"

She slowly swiveled in her desk chair to face him. "Yes. From Iraq, correct?"

"Indeed. Mr. Kahil Nehezra is the donor. He sold a piece of private property for commercial development, and when groundbreaking began, the tablets were discovered. Nehezra is something of a lay archeologist and aware of the abysmal standards of conservation in his country, so he has donated the pieces to us." Clevis raised his thin, ginger-colored eyebrows. "Laboratory analysis is not yet complete, but I believe they may be second century B.C. They are well preserved, luckily, and covered with cuneiform. The tablets are jumbled, and we look to you to translate the inscriptions so that the pieces may be fitted in the correct arrangement."

The glyphs

CSNDRA

flitted through her mind—the whisper of a ghost—an afterimage of a dark-haired girl, a peppermint eidolon. They sank into the maw of inner darkness.

She forced herself back. Nelson stood rigidly in the doorway with, apparently, no need to come in or sit while they talked.

"I can't wait to get started," she said flatly.

"Right. I will inform you the moment that they arrive in Manuscripts. Well," he stopped, pushed his pink hands into tweed pockets, "good to have you back." He turned on one heel like a dapper soldier and marched away.

Gatsby sat, staring at the empty doorway.

That's it. Sabbatical's over, she thought. She glanced around her office: computer, fax machine, printer, filing cabinet, shelves stuffed with books, folders, organizers, cables, pens, letterhead, paperclips. *All just as it had been when she'd last been there...when...*

The thought would not venture further.

Her desk was already piled with information on the Nehezra tablets, and by the next afternoon, she'd be swamped with memos from the departments that had already analyzed the artifacts. As Clevis had said, no time to waste.

Time.

But she had been floundering in mental quicksand, foggy, losing track of time, forgetting the simplest of tasks, edgy, touchy.

Turning her chair to face the computer, she searched her hard drive and brought up the image file of the six glyphs. They seemed to shimmer in the cyan blue of the computer screen.

C S N D R A

I know. The voice was harsh inside her head. *It's mourning. The question is—what the hell is lost? For something to be gone, it had to once have existed! What was here? How was it here? How do I know that it was here at all?*

Images floated unbidden through her mind—the dark face peering at her through the window at the taverna. Sitting in the branches of the oak tree with pieces of cardboard in their laps, signing. Traussbery's expression of awe as he had timidly touched her hand. The girl standing in the line at Heathrow Airport. The scream of terror and the silence of the absence of breath.

Gatsby looked across the room toward the spot, a few feet away, where Cassandra had stood, her hand outstretched: *I do not know what I am. Remember Gatsby. You know me.*

I do know you, Cassandra, Gatsby thought, but I don't know what you are.

Were.

She closed the file, got her coat, went outside for a walk and, on the campus she had explored assiduously for six years, got lost.

Behind the lectern, Traussbery cleared his throat and faced a fresh crop of twenty youthful faces, tabula rasa ready for enlightenment in the wonders of archeology. They stared back at him, waiting for tutelage. New autumn sunlight filtered into the classroom through large east-facing windows.

He stood favoring the right leg; the left ankle throbbed, just enough to remind him of terrifying anomalies.

"Ahm, good morning, marvelous to see so many new diggers." The class chuckled en masse. Traussbery plunged into a well-rehearsed opening. "Archeology is a fascinating field of study, bridging many branches of science. It has been called the sweet food of antiquity, sometimes referred to as the handmaiden of history. And in that regard, archeology is a complete study, as it encompasses architecture, language, botany, zoology—"

"Sir?" A hand shot up near the back of the room, one belonging to a wiry boy with a high voice and an impish face. "Will we discuss the standing stones at Stonehenge? Though they can't be called standing stones if they won't stand still!"

The class broke into uproarious laughter.

As Traussbery stared, he began to shake. The laughter riddled him like bullets. His knees begin to buckle as the giggles died into awkward silence.

"The...that is, it's...you see..." he stammered, leaning onto the lectern.

The shattered teacup, tea spilled across the floorboards. The look on Travis Norton's face as the bookcase descended on him. The grinding, churning noise in the middle of the night, standing on the side of the motorway near the site, the sound of an avalanche. Stone 56. An unnamable creature, its legs, teeth, wings, the eyes of...

Electricity sizzled through his body; he felt as if on fire, every hair stood erect.

"Professor?" a girl in the front row piped, a puzzled look on her face. "Are you all right?"

Sweat broke on his forehead. "Actually, I don't th...excuse me..."

He clambered down the presentation riser and limped toward the door, followed by the buzz of confusion.

Shaking and queasy, Traussbery limped down the corridor and the length of the building to the private lounge. He found a couch and lay down, closing his eyes and gasping. The last three days had begun exactly the same.

He stayed there for several hours until the department secretary found him.

That night, with a White Russian in hand, Gatsby put on Stravinsky's "Rite of Spring" and collapsed on her couch with the day's newspaper.

The third page of the local section carried the headline MEGALITH STILL MISSING.

She read on. The police were still investigating the disappearance of Stone 56. Substantial clues were yet to be found, but fingers were pointed at groups from the Anarchist Teapot and the Pendragon Fellowship to the Beanfield Battle Federation. Educators, scientists, philosophers, and historians the world over had besieged the media with outraged protests. In conjunction with the British government, English Heritage now offered a "generous reward" for the return of the stone. Several citizens had reported that they had the stone, or knew where it was, or had seen it. Upon inspection, all suspects were found to be fraudulent.

A reward! A buggering reward! Like you could kidnap a forty-five-tonne megalith and hold it for ransom! Bloody buggering...

The stream of curses flowed until it ran dry and she lay back and closed her eyes.

For chrissake, it's not like there is anything I can do about it. And anything that massive won't stay secreted forever. It'll be found, hauled back to Salisbury Plain and re-erected, and this whole insane mess will seem like someone's ergot-induced nightmare.

She raised her glass to her lips and took a long sip. The liqueurs heated the roof of her mouth and the back of her throat, warming and soothing.

I have a full schedule of projects, starting with these tablets tomorrow, and I'm not going to drive myself mad anymore with inexplicable phenomena or appearing glyphs or impossible beings.

She had spoken to Traussbery only once since the day of the funeral, the funeral at which, of course, they had never arrived. A single phone call, two days ago. Traussbery gibbering vehemently, reasserting that "the grotesque creature" that had attacked them was some inexplicable reincarnation of Travis Norton, that it had had Norton's face and eyes, and that he wished it had killed him instead of Cassandra—reiterating that Norton's coma and ultimate demise, the destruction of Stone 56, and now Cassandra's extinction were the results of his vanity and power-lust. Traussbery had wept, coughed until he couldn't speak, and then abruptly hung up.

The CD ended with the boom of kettledrums, and the player clicked off.

She glanced down the hallway to her bedroom where a dark-haired adolescent had once sat on her bed, flipping through books, signing and humming to herself. A girl who didn't eat or sleep, whose existence could not be accepted, could not even rationally be contemplated.

Who had been destroyed by something even less conceivable.

How did it happen? What did it mean?

The thoughts swung in her mind, a psychic pendulum felt viscerally, throbbing in her gut. Just when it seemed as though one question had been at least partially answered, a conceptual Big Bang had created a cosmos of new questions. Questions for which there would be no answer.

Are there questions in my world that ultimately cannot be answered, Gatsby thought, staring out the window, *to which the rules simply don't apply?*

The response seemed to come from beyond her awareness.

If no, then move on and don't look back. If yes, then change the rules.

She walked to the kitchen and dumped the drink down the sink, spontaneously entranced by the sound of ice cubes chiming against steel.

She whispered, "Or change your world."

CHAPTER 34

She arrived at her office at 7:30 the next morning, earlier than most of the staff, and fired up the espresso machine. In a few minutes, armed with a full mug of vanilla Arabica, a twelve-inch stack of books and folders, and a ballpoint pen propped in her mouth, Gatsby made her way down the quiet corridor toward Research 224.

At the end of the hall, she approached a sterile room filled with long, wide tables for examining documents or artifacts. She opened the door, stepped inside, and reached for the light switch. Overhead fluorescents flickered on.

A metal tray, two meters square with six-inch sides, lay on the central table; next to it was a thick blue folder of documents, secured with a locking latch. She peered into the tray. There were the Nehezra tablets: two dozen pieces, all a deep copper color, each about a foot wide and covered with linear cuneiform.

To the right of the central table was a smaller table. Gatsby dumped her heavy armload of folders there and pulled the pen from her mouth.

She unlatched the blue folder and examined the papers inside: reports and documents from Nehezra, the excavators, the museum administrators, and the laboratory. The tablets had been dated at 2800 BC, the late proto-literate period of Mesopotamia.

Quite a find, she thought. *Catherwood in Western Asiatic Antiquities must be doing cartwheels.*

A swing-arm lamp was attached to the tabletop. She turned it on and aimed the bulb toward the tablets. Pushing a wheeled chair up to the table, she sat, pulled a notebook from the stack she'd brought with her and started writing notes: date, the condition of the artifacts as she found them, and the scope of the translation.

C S N D R A...inability to separate from infantile object of cathexion...

Follow me!

had to let her gohhhh

Above and Below, Gatsby. But these are a trap...

Gatsby sighed, shaking her head as though she could rattle the images out of her mind.

From the pocket of her jeans, she dug out a pair of thin cotton gloves. She pulled them on and began gently pulling the pieces out from the jumbled heap in which they had been piled in the tray and laying them flat, in horizontal rows. Each tablet was inscribed on its smooth, lighter side; the backsides were rough, darker, and blank.

As she worked and scribbled notes, she thought, *Okay, what do we have? Twenty-eight pieces, varying from eight to ten inches across and seven- to eight-inches tall. Some of the cuneiform seems to be images of objects...sun, eye, hand, wheat. If I remember correctly, Sumerian contains pictograms, phonograms, and determinatives...top to bottom, in columns...*

She continued separating the tablets and arranging them in rows—seven across, four deep—until all were neatly laid out with their edges touching, cuneiform side up. It was a twenty-eight-piece puzzle, the pieces in random order. Visually scanning the wedge-shaped symbols, she thought that the writing might be a listing of items but, upon sharper scrutiny, she recognized symbols referring to gods and events. It seemed to be a story.

Let's try the Mallery.

She leaned back from the tray and pushed her chair to the smaller table. From the stack of books she had carried in with her she pulled out the linguists' bible: *Writing and Languages* by Sir Jonas Arthur Mallery. The three-inch-thick tome contained descriptions and examples of every written language from cave inscriptions to Esperanto.

She turned to the index and then to the chapter on Sumer.

Something behind her clinked.

Startled, she turned with a gasp. No one had entered the room, nothing had moved...

except...

Her eyes went to the tablets. She had laid them out with the smooth surfaces up, rough sides down. One piece, in the lower right corner, was now rough side up. She stared at it intently. Rather than appearing to be rough clay that had been buried for centuries, the backside of the tablet looked like it had been coated with a pink substance like chewing gum.

"What the—" Gatsby muttered. She set the Mallery down and stood over the tray of tablets. Carefully grasping an adjacent tablet, she turned it over. It too was covered with the viscous, pink substance, and there was something in the substance, below the surface. She poked at it with a fingertip, amazed to find that the pink color didn't transfer to her glove. Something white was under the surface. She tugged on it until almost an inch of it was revealed.

It was fabric. White lace.

Biting her lower lip, Gatsby turned over another tablet. And another. And another, until all twenty-eight lay on their reverse sides.

They were all were covered with the pink goo.

"The lab would have stopped everything if they'd seen this but none of the—" she muttered. She picked up the blue folder again and was flipping through it, searching for notations of unusual pink substances, when the swing-arm lamp flared brightly.

Light bathed the tray, growing intense and hot.

The tablets were melting, as if baking inside an oven. The pink substance began to ooze and bubble like melting cheese.

Gatsby stared, unable to breathe. She looked around frantically—was anyone within calling distance?

The tablets burbled, coalescing into a churning slab of pink lava. Vapor shot into the air like the eruptions of miniature geysers. Like some living organism, the mass began to spread, elongating, growing longer and narrower. The clay split near one end, creating a fissure. At the other end, two more cracks opened. It seemed to be dividing into parts.

"My god," Gatsby whispered.

The bubbling matter slid toward certain areas and away from others, and a shape began to form: below a single solid mass, two outward growths, then two more at the other end.

Like appendages.

The matter slid, moving, running, and more indentations appeared: rudimentary hands and feet. A torso, waist, neck, head. Soft pits fell inward on themselves and became eye sockets and a mouth. A central ridge grew upward; a nose. Fingers and toes appeared.

It was like watching a stop-frame film of a developing embryo.

Sweat trickled down Gatsby's forehead and into her eyes; she brushed her forearm against her face, blinking furiously, unable to look away.

As if drying, the pink coloration deepened to orange-copper and then to light brown. The sockets filled with a brown substance and congealed: eyes, with lids closed. The closed mouth was now edged with reddish-brown lips. The form sprouted fingernails, toenails, genitalia.

Gatsby's knees buckled, and she dropped onto the chair, breathing hard. She brought her hands up, up toward the form, inching closer. As her gloved hand touched the dark hand resting on the mesh steel bottom of the tray, the last features appeared—black hair sprouted from the scalp and flowed to the shoulders.

"Hhh...hhh. . ." Gatsby heard herself panting. "Wha..."

It—*she*—was fully formed. A black-haired girl with dark skin and almond-shaped eyes, naked, formed of earth, given breath, life, anima.

The girl's eyes opened, and they stared into each other's minds.

Cassandra raised her hands and began to speak.

smack-thump

Gatsby...

Gatsby had frozen, breathless. Frozen within the ice cave that kept sanity separate from its horrifying shadow sibling, paralyzed by a terror that no human being could take in. She gasped, drowning in an abyss.

Cassandra stared directly into her eyes—then she smiled.

She sat up slowly. Her hands rose to chest level as she asked, *Did you leave me behind?* She paused and then signed, *Again?*

Gatsby swallowed hard, her mind still locked. Emotions spasmed through her, hammered her—disbelief, terror, amazement—and most incredible of all, elation.

Cassandra's gaze was level and somber. She signed slowly, *It's easier if you*

(Follow me!)

follow me.

The imperative word moved through Gatsby's vocal cords. "How?"

Cassandra's lips curled in a mischievous smile. She raised herself out of the metal tray, moved to the edge of the examining table, and sat with her bare legs swinging over the edge. A peripheral glance reminded Gatsby of her surroundings and the chance that someone might enter the room. A naked ten-year-old girl sitting beside the artifact tray and the Nehezra tablets vanished? The impossible explanation that she would attempt to give Clevis, or anyone else who happened upon the scene, flashed through her head and she brushed it away.

Gatsby thought, *Maybe it is easier if I just follow,* and she signed, *Tell me.*

Cassandra's lips parted and she spoke, as she had once before, her voice deep and resonant. "At first, when you remembered me, that made me," she pointed to her eye, "you could see me and touch me, but you still didn't believe." Cassandra pressed her palms to her head and her heart simultaneously. "And my song was not complete. I was part Above and part Below. When the"—she used the gesture that they had once used to mean Reginald the Blue Dragon—"came out of the trees to hurt me, you tried to save me. You finally believed in me. I needed your belief to be complete, to be completely Above in this song that you understand. Where...what I am now...this is what you call real, Gatsby."

Everyday, garden-variety reality. The kind that is, by many, never called into question. That is, by few, glimpsed. That is, by inhabitants of submerged worlds and enfolded universes, of the deeper structures, understood.

Fleetingly, Gatsby wondered how much time had passed since she had begun to examine the tablets. All sense of time had vanished.

Cassandra's brown eyes sparkled as she spoke. "I let the (dragon-gesture) do what it wanted. At first it wanted the Traussbery, but then it wanted me more. I saw its reflection and saw that it was not complete yet. It was partly here, enough so that you could see it, but it was mostly still Below, the Below where I was before the Forest of Peppermint Trees. So I played a game with it. I let it think it had changed me. I went back to Below, and you thought I was gone, too, but I wasn't. I knew that I would come back Above, and I did."

A stillness had come over Gatsby. She felt as if she were floating in the arms of a naturally occurring tranquilizer. Edges had softened and blurred; the naked girl sitting on the table before her no longer seemed frightening. In fact, the wondrous intentions of the universe had wrapped around her like a warm quilt. Her breathing and heart rate slowed as a surreal peace enveloped her. She closed her eyes, reminded of the stories of persons who had been pronounced dead and then revived. As these survivors always said, there were no words for what they had felt.

Only one person would even begin to understand.

Gatsby opened her eyes. Determination surged through her like lightning and jolted her to her feet.

Cassandra jumped off the table and took Gatsby's hand with the initiative of someone who knows exactly where she is going.

Gatsby quickly gathered up her notebooks and headed for the corridor. Just as she was closing the door behind her, she stopped. "Wait, the tablets—" She turned back and stopped short with a gasp.

The rows—seven across, four deep—were all neatly laid out, their edges touching, their smooth, lighter, cuneiform-inscribed sides facing up within the metal tray. The wedge-shaped story of untenable forces.

She turned back to see Cassandra, in her blue jumpsuit, white blouse, lace anklets and black canvas shoes, a beaded bracelet on one wrist, skipping out the door.

"I need to speak with Traussbery," Gatsby panted, breathless from the jog down the corridor to the archeology department office. She stared into the well-deep glasses perched on the secretary's nose. The woman's green eyes were monstrously magnified.

Her nostrils flared as she replied, "Professor Traussbery has cancelled his classes for the day." The tight bun of grey hair, birdlike voice, and bony facial structure made Gatsby think of iron chastity belts.

"Fine. Marvelous. So where is he?"

The woman leaned in slightly, exposing her utter lack of cleavage. "He's not here."

"Bloody mother of god," Gatsby sputtered. "I have gathered that. Where has he gone?"

The woman looked askance, as if she would deny any knowledge of the conversation. "Home, I believe, but if you w—"

Gatsby leaned over the counter and into the woman's powdered face. "That wasn't so tough, now was it, angel." While the woman's cheeks flushed, Gatsby spun and strode down the corridor.

Outside, Cassandra sat waiting in Gatsby's Volvo. Gatsby crawled in on the driver's side. "Okay, we're off," she said, simultaneously revving the engine and digging through her shoulderbag for the book in which she had written Traussbery's home address.

In less than ten minutes, she pulled up to a two-story brownstone at 50 Adderly Gardens. Gatsby and Cassandra stepped out of the car and walked up the short stairway to stand in front of the entrance door. Gatsby found the intercom button marked with Traussbery's name and pushed it; a short buzz sounded. Momentarily, she pushed it again, and a gruff voice crackled over the intercom.

"For god's sake, who is it?"

"It's Gatsby. Let me—"

"Ms. Donovan? Good lord, what are you doing here?"

She looked at Cassandra. "Traussbery, imperative that we speak immediately."

She heard a congestive sigh and then a dissonant buzz as the door unlocked. "Very well." Taking Cassandra's hand, Gatsby hauled her into the entryway and down a carpeted hall toward flat number five.

The door opened as they approached and Traussbery appeared—glasses in hand, disheveled in ragged grey sweatpants, dog-chewed slippers, and a sweatshirt from the tourist stalls of the Egyptian pyramids. "Ms. Donovan, this is utterly provoking, to be frank, why didn't y—"

He stopped with a snort as Cassandra stepped from behind Gatsby.

"Hello," she said, smiling.

Traussbery jumped. He looked from Cassandra to Gatsby, back to Cassandra, back to Gatsby again, his mouth opening and closing like a netted trout, his eyes bulging. "I...she...wh...wh..."

"Can we come in?" Gatsby asked.

Traussbery stared at Cassandra, gasping.

"Traussbery!"

His eyes rose to hers, and she watched his expressions ripple as decisions were made and his shock abated. He pulled in a deep breath, coughed miserably into his hand, and said, "Yes, of course, please!"

They wandered into Traussbery's flat and Gatsby thought, *I wondered how old Traussbery lives.* She visually scanned the sparsely decorated living room, minuscule dining area and kitchen. A bedroom and bath, she surmised, would be down the hallway. The pervasive doggy smell was accompanied by barking; yapping viciously, Seti and Khufu raced in.

Traussbery gathered the dogs into his arms, trudged down the hallway to the bedroom, and closed the door. He padded back to the living room, pulled a tissue from the tissue box sitting on the table beside the sofa, and coughed into it as he sank into a well-cushioned Morris chair. He motioned toward the worn sofa for them to sit.

Gatsby and Cassandra sat.

"Ms. Donovan," he said, his voice a rasping whisper, "I am certain, as certain as I have been of anything in my addled life, that the explanation you are about to give me will be phenomenally enlightening." A smile struggled about his lips for a moment and then he broke into a grin.

"Not half as enlightening as the story you will give me," Gatsby answered. "I was curious, Traussbery, and looked up Norton's obituary."

"And?" Traussbery sputtered, looking warily from Gatsby to Cassandra.

"Do you still have the obit? The notice that you cut out of the newspaper?"

"I, ahm, well, I do, but Ms. Donovan, I cannot—"

"Let's look at it, shall we?"

Consternation clouded Traussbery's face as he rose, shaking his head and mumbling, "What could this possibly...Norton is dead, and there is no...what is th..." He shuffled back to his bedroom and then returned, a slip of torn newsprint in his hand. "Here. Now what is the point of all this?"

"Look at it very carefully, and tell me the name that you see."

Traussbery patted his pockets. "Glasses, I must find my glasses—"

Cassandra reached toward the table by the arm of the sofa and picked up Traussbery's thick glasses. "These?" she said, smiling. Gatsby had noted that Cassandra was speaking rather than signing more often, though the shifts were unpredictable.

"Good lord! When did she begin to speak aloud?" he blurted.

"In the last week but not consistently. It varies."

"Ahm...well, yes, I see," Traussbery sputtered, "thank you." He took them from her hand, placed them on his nose, and peered down at the clipping. "I don't understand what this is all about, really—"

"Traussbery, look at the *name*."

He stated intently. His eyes widened to bursting, his breath coming in short hitches. He looked up at Gatsby, then at the clipping, and back to Gatsby with terror and confusion.

"But...it can't be..."

"It can," Gatsby replied. She sat back on the sofa and rubbed her eyes. "It does. It says Morton, Traussbery. Travis *Morton*. Morton with an M. You saw exactly what you wanted and what you dared not see. I'm sure I don't need to explain to you how emotions color perception, Traussbery, and that guilt is one of the strongest of all."

Traussbery dropped into the chair with a thump. Elbows perched on his knees, he held the scrap of newsprint as if it were a freshly unearthed archeological treasure. Breathing harshly, he murmured, "I can't believe it...I saw *Norton*. Good lord, I was so certain of it, so certain, so absolutely certain."

Gatsby glanced toward Cassandra and then looked Traussbery in the eye. "Consciousness shaping reality, as the painter uses brush and ink to manifest his imagination."

"But does this mean—good lord!—that Travis Norton may still be alive?" With a lurch, Traussbery hefted his thick body from his chair. "I have to know what has become of the man, if he is alive or dead!" He scurried to his kitchen table where his wallet lay and dug from it a scrap of paper with a phone number penciled on it. Scuttling to the phone that hung on the wall of the kitchen, staring at the paper and the obituary, he dialed.

Gatsby and Cassandra listened as Traussbery muttered, "Please connect me to Room 502, Travis Norton." He was silent for two full minutes as he listened, his lips pursed. "I...I see. Ahm, thank you very much." He hung up, the phone clicking softly in its cradle.

Traussbery ambled back into the living room and propped himself against the arm of the sofa, breathing heavily, staring at the floor and stroking his double chin. Cassandra pulled her legs under her.

All three waited in tense silence.

Gatsby finally said quietly, "He's not there, is he."

Traussbery shook his head. "Eleven years ago, a Travis Norton was admitted comatose to Saint Beatrice Memorial Hospital. He was released in early November of that year and has not been treated since. There's...well, I still—" He turned toward the hallway. "A moment." He walked to his bedroom and closed the door.

Cassandra and Gatsby exchanged puzzled looks; from the bedroom, they could make out the faint sound of dialing and Traussbery's gruff voice. Momentarily, Traussbery emerged and returned to drop into his chair. Within the wrinkles of his fleshy face, his grey eyes sparkled.

"I have spoken with Norton's wife. Unwilling to reveal my identity, I concocted a reason for calling—solicitor—and learned that Mr. Travis Norton, of Croyden, lives with his family in Holland Park. He left academia shortly after his hospitalization and became a successful dealer of antiquities." The white tissue moved to Traussbery's lips; he coughed softly. "Good lord. But then what in the name of the gods did we see on the road? That monstrous apparition that," he looked at Cassandra and shuddered, "that attacked us and devoured you before my eyes?!"

Cassandra gazed at Traussbery, a sly look on her face as she said, "It was from your Below."

His gaze ping-ponged from Gatsby to Cassandra. "My B...you mean that...that it was something of my...my own *creation*?" He leaned forward, ablaze with the internal fire that Gatsby had seen at their first meeting in his Cambridge office, discussing the glyph in Thebes. "My Below? Good lord!" He shook himself, swallowed, and started again. "Ms. Donovan, I cannot help but think of the mystic traditions that speak to physical creation, which have been embraced for millennia—"

"Mystic traditions?" Gatsby asked.

"Yes yes," Traussbery answered breathlessly. "Eastern literature speaks to similar phenomena. The Tibetan gomchen, the shaman, trains himself in the lesson that the world is created by the mind and then, with rigorous discipline, visualization, and meditation, practices the creation of the tulpa, the living being created out of the void.

When he believes himself ready, believes that his internal structures are indestructible, he subjects himself to a ritual called the Dance of Chöd. The disciple must first create a tulpa that is a double of himself, an alter. Then he creates another one, the most horrible tulpa he possibly can, and must allow it to destroy the tulpa that is his double."

"What happens to the gomchen?" Gatsby asked, utterly curious.

"Those who stand firm in their belief that they cannot be harmed survive. But those who waver, die. It's been studied quite scrupulously for many years."

Shaking her head, Gatsby asked, "Now you're saying that you are capable of the same phenomena as these Tibetan shamans, creating physical manifestations from their consciousness?"

"Ms. Donovan, in the course of deciphering ancient texts, you must have absorbed some of their content! Ancient Tibetan scriptures refer to how mental actions produce vibration and that all is tsal. Our collective tsal is our collective reality, our consensus reality. The Sufis called the reality-shaping energy of thought the alam almithal. In Western mythologies, you see, the gods are given the power of creation through their thought or will, but in these Eastern traditions, we are all gods. All living in the aboriginal dream-time, creating what modern science calls reality and physics and particles as we dream our own cosmos, as our consciousness participates in or, for all we know, further creates the deep structure!"

Watching his face and body, Gatsby could see Traussbery gathering steam. At the same time, out of the corner of her eye, she watched Cassandra rise and meander toward Traussbery's living room window, beyond which was a small courtyard and flowered garden.

"Think of the scientists and philosophers who have contributed to our understanding of consensus reality, Ms. Donovan."

"Jung," she heard herself murmur, "The collective unconscious, archetypes. John Lilly. Michael Talbot. Amit Goswami. Carlos Castaneda."

"Yes, Castaneda's nagual, the extension of all possible realities that ultimately negates that consciousness can create matter—because consciousness and matter cannot be separated! And every visionary who has written on creating your reality through visualization, thought forms...the programs fed into the biocomputer of the mind..."

Gesturing wildly and exuberantly, Traussbery leaned forward almost far enough to topple out of his Morris chair and into Gatsby's lap. "You see, Ms. Donovan, our modern Columbuses are just now finding, or creating, the vocabulary to allow us to make sense...no, not to make sense, to conceive how the barriers between mind and matter are self-imposed, linguistic illusions. Maya!"

"Linguistic illusion," Gatsby murmured.

With her back to Gatsby and Traussbery, Cassandra stood staring out the window and began to hum. Noticing, Gatsby thought, *Uh oh*. While keeping a sharp eye on Cassandra, she continued. "Language, in the purest sense, is itself an illusion—the abstraction, the symbol that takes the place of something concrete. The map, not the territory. A ball may be held in your hand but the word or the thought *ball* cannot."

"Exactly!" Traussbery beamed.

"And thoughts arise in the mind—or perhaps thoughts are like the ripples that spread in concentric circles when a pebble is dropped into water—something somewhere ripples and in turn effects other ripples that are the thoughts we attribute to muses or divinities or simply cannot attribute to anything at all." She felt decades of linguistic training swirling inside her. "And thoughts shape and are shaped by words. But words are more than scribbles and phonemes, words are what structure consciousness and consensus reality. Thought, given birth in the mind, creates language—and new reality—and the new reality again restructures the mind."

"And how do we acquire language?" Traussbery asked, wriggling his glasses up his nose by pursing his lips. "Human beings are born with neural wiring for sound, but language is a learned arrangement or composition of sound. As we learn, we create, and as we create, we learn."

"Like the Peppermint Language." Gatsby leaned back into the sky-blue chintz cushions of the sofa. "So what we are hypothesizing—creating!—is the idea that language is the mechanism that shapes our consciousness and our reality. Is that what we are saying?"

At the window, Cassandra hummed softly.

"Well," Traussbery said, "think of medicine and the role that consciousness plays in affecting the very tangible human body. 'Placebo effect' is so well documented that it has become part of the vernacular. Mind has tremendous influence—every psychoneuroimmunologist knows and studies these effects assiduously. A growing portion of the medical community has begun to address the power of the mind to heal and the fallacy of a distinction between mind and body!" He coughed lightly. "Do you remember the case of Bruno Klopfer?"

Gatsby shook her head.

"Klopfer was a psychologist and his patient, Wright, had terminal cancer, his body ravaged with large tumors. Wright entreated Klopfer to allow him to try an unproven cancer treatment drug called Kreboizen. Even though he did not expect the man to live much longer, the doctor relented and injected him. In only days, Wright was examined and his tumors had shrunk to half their size! He was stable and active for two months. Then articles began to appear that asserted that the drug was ineffective. Wright read these, became depressed, and his tumors returned. He was hospitalized. Klopfer decided to conduct a test. He told his patient that the initial compounds of the drug were shown to be weak and that he had a highly concentrated version of Kreboizen. Wright agreed to try the 'powerful' version and, following all the normal procedures, Klopfer injected the man with water. Do you know what happened?"

Gatsby shook her head, eyes wide.

"Wright's tumors melted again and he regained his energy and activity level. Two months later, a new announcement came from the AMA that Kreboizen was undeniably proven to be completely worthless for the treatment of cancer. Wright saw the announcement, his tumors returned, and within two days, he was dead."

Gatsby leaned forward, her mind reeling, associations clicking together, inspiration galvanizing her entire being. "I have read articles where a subject group is told that they will receive a drug that will make them lose their hair, and when administered a placebo, a significant portion still lose their hair! Or where subjects are told that they will be given a soporific but are instead given caffeine and proceed to fall asleep!" She glanced toward Cassandra. "Psychosomatic phenomena are regularly accounted for and documented, but Traussbery, can it possibly be that with consciousness, with language, that we can not only effect the physical world but that we can literally create organic, living, conscious, physical entities?" She pointed toward the figure standing by the window. "Look, Traussbery, you can see her, you can touch her, engage her in lucid conversation. You and I agree that she is real. But where the hell did she come from?"

Ignoring yips from the bedroom, Traussbery replied, "Ova and sperm join and then divide to create new human beings—think how many millennia it took for mankind to understand that process! I believe that we are now faced, Ms. Donovan, with a metaconscious version of the same." He looked toward Cassandra, who still hummed quietly.

As if finally comprehending Cassandra's words, Traussbery gasped, "Good lord, from Below! She's verifying Bohm's surface structure, or the unfolded universe, and the deep structure, the enfolded universe!"

Smiling, he stared into his lap for a long time and then looked up. "We can speculate that—somehow—she emerged from your thoughts, your history, memory, imagination. Some particular set of circumstances allowed for the arrangement of you, me, this time and place in the cosmos, your mental conceptions and, who knows, perhaps an infinite number of other input to produce this effect. Is this a first? Has it ever happened before, in the history of the world? How could we ever know unless the vocabulary used to describe it fell upon ears willing to accept it?"

Gatsby nodded. "Not only the vocabulary itself but its quality. Could the emotional connotation of the word or thought or image be integral? You see," she stared down at her tennis shoes against Traussbery's hardwood floor. "When I was ten years old, I was desperately lonely. For a summer, anyway. I dreamed and wished for someone to keep me company. A friend, an alter idem. I began to fashion that companion in my mind, to know every detail of her until I could really see her—"

"There! An astute young gomchenma you were, Ms. Donovan!" Traussbery chortled with a gleeful smile.

She ran her fingers through her hair. "Whatever I was, I immersed myself in these language patterns, images, and self-talk of want, need, desire. Wish fulfillment vocabulary."

Traussbery nodded, stroking his chin. "Yes yes, I see where you are headed. My own—" He paused, hands folded in his round lap, blinking profusely. He pursed his lips and was silent for a long moment. "My own emotional state has of course colored my thoughts and images." His eyes misted. "Such terrible guilt, Ms. Donovan, such self-deprecation for the vile act that I believed, as completely as Wright believed, destroyed an innocent man. Toward my own gain, no less. Could it have been that the monstrosity on the road, which very tangibly affected our reality, was a transformation of my intellectual and emotional consciousness? Of my malevolent images and self-talk?"

"An ideomorph," Gatsby blurted. "Good god, Traussbery, that's it! An ideomorph, a physical, consensus-reality creation of consciousness."

Barks startled them. The Shih Tzus scampered from the bedroom and jumped up onto the sofa beside Gatsby. Trailing along behind them, smiling, was Cassandra.

Gatsby and Traussbery stared each other in stunned silence.

"We...did she? I didn't—"

Gatsby stammered as Traussbery mumbled, "I didn't...but how did...?"

"Your word traps," Cassandra said, giggling as she plopped down on the sofa and pulled her legs under her, "are much too complicated for what is simple." She closed her eyes, humming, and Gatsby feared for a moment that she might be calling up the black-bile-spitting creature, the hideous winged ideomorph. Instead, she opened her eyes and said, "I have something to tell you, Gatsby. I will stay in this song, in...the...reality...but I cannot stay with you."

Gatsby and Traussbery exchanged surprised looks.

"What do you mean?" Gatsby asked.

"The experiences you will have, you cannot even imagine, at least not yet. But to find them, you must go alone. I can't go with you. It is the song that you will sing, Gatsby."

As Cassandra's words sank in, Gatsby murmured, "But...then...what will happen to you? What is your song?"

Gazing at Traussbery, she said, "It is with you."

Traussbery's newt-like eyes bulged behind his thick lenses. "Me?" An incredulous smile spread over Traussbery's face; Cassandra nodded. "Are you saying that I am...that you wish to live with me?"

"I am not Above all the time. Sometimes I will go Below. But when I return to here, to this song, I will come to the Traussbery. And when you want to see me, Gatsby, find Traussbery. Are you willing?" she said, looking curiously at Traussbery.

Traussbery's gaze moved between Gatsby and Cassandra, and he whispered, "Yes, I am willing. Good lord, yes!"

"Why him?" Gatsby asked.

Cassandra giggled, her vocal cords offering a laugh that was both childlike and timeless. "Because he is easy to find. You won't be."

Shaking her head, Gatsby turned to seek Cassandra's dark eyes. "Then tell me about my, um, song. What will it be?"

"You are going to wonderful places, songs so much more complex than this. You will explore and learn new things, new words for experiences that, now, you can't even wonder of."

"That's it? That's all you can tell me?"

Cassandra laughed. "It's all already inside you."

"Then it's a matter of knowing which questions to ask?"

Cassandra's brown hands moved and she made a series of gestures that Gatsby had never seen. She rose and slowly walked down the hallway toward Traussbery's bedroom. The Shih Tzus scampered along behind her, snuffling at the heels of her canvas flats.

Gatsby stared at the indentation in the sofa where Cassandra had just been. Then she looked out the window at the courtyard that was full of roses, gardenias, and primrose trees. She remembered what Traussbery had said at their first meeting: *These symbols must be investigated, Ms. Donovan—they must. They present an extraordinary scientific challenge—perhaps even a quantum challenge!* Another memory crept in behind it—cold Andean mountain air, sitting on a rock by a campfire, watching Louis eating cuy.

As if catching her thoughts, Traussbery looked at her with eyebrows raised. "Ms. Donovan, the next time we discover a glyph in Thebes, or Mazilaq, or in tea leaves for that matter—"

She nodded, matching his expression. "I know. Proceed with caution." She sighed, exhaling upward and rustling her bangs. "But who can we tell about any of this? Quinn? The World Heritage Foundation? Stephen Hawking? Erich von Daniken?"

Traussbery crossed the room and wandered to the living room window. A narrow antique table below the window held a variety of objets d'art and a porcelain bowl where his favorite pipe was cradled. He picked up the pipe and a pewter lighter and lit the lump of tobacco. As the room filled with the smell of Borkum Riff, Traussbery murmured out of the side of his mouth, "Our revelations, Ms. Donovan, must necessarily be judicious."

Gatsby nodded. She rose from the sofa and walked to Traussbery's bedroom, opened the door, and yelped.

Traussbery scurried to her side and peered into the room. The Shih Tzus sat panting on the bed, and Cassandra was nowhere to be found.

When she had regained her breath, Gatsby turned, gulped, and asked, "Traussbery, do you ever wonder if there are some questions that science cannot answer?"

He smiled. "More things in heaven and Earth than are dreamt of in your philosophy? I am not only certain of it, Ms. Donovan, I *count* on it. At least until we become particle-waveforms, alam almithal, moving freely from explicate to implicate on the wings of thought."

Without another word, Traussbery walked her to the door.

CHAPTER 35

A horse-drawn carriage—complete with utterly British passengers and even more utterly British horses—clopped toward her. Gatsby bit into her tomato-cheese sandwich and chewed thoughtfully. The afternoon was warm for the first of September and provided a perfect excuse to lunch in Hyde Park rather than holed up in the chaos of her office.

She'd had to bite her lip, the day before, when Clevis had come to praise her translations of the Nehezra tablets. They told a story of divine spirits, wreaking havoc in the lives of mortals. "Classic mythology," Clevis had muttered offhand, obviously less interested in the meaning of the cuneiform than in the coup of its acquisition.

She had learned from Traussbery that his ankle was healing and that he had returned to his regimen of classes.

Stone 56 had not been found.

She took another bite, musing over the impossible events of the last four months. While Traussbery had informed her that he had seen Cassandra—spontaneously and unpredictably—Gatsby had not seen her and wondered if she would again.

She sat groping through the morass of her feelings. When she had thought that Cassandra was gone—dead, for lack of a better word—she had been enveloped in sorrow, an oppressive sense of loss. The feeling had now changed. Gazing at the people strolling by, the river that wound quietly through the park, the stately trees and wrought-iron benches around her, she realized that mourning had been replaced with anticipation. She'd see Cassandra again. There was just no knowing when or where.

As if I, or anyone, could have predicted her at all, she thought.

Its buggy holding an elderly couple, the horse-drawn carriage eased by, headed down the walkway, and clip-clopped out of sight.

She finished her sandwich, stuffed her empty Orangina can into her lunch bag, and rose to walk back to the British Museum.

The walkway opened before her but the grass looked more inviting. She stepped off the pavement and wound cross-country through the trees. Squirrels scampered by; fall leaves, now showing hints of Halloween reds and oranges, fluttered through the air and collected in swirling piles on the ground. Suddenly feeling coltish, she kicked through a dry mound, grinning.

Laughter made her look up with a start.

Ten or so yards away, up a slight embankment, she saw a towheaded boy. He shook with laughter but it wasn't directed at her—he pointed at something that was stamping out from behind a thick oak tree.

She stared in the direction of his hand, thinking, *What the hell is that?*

As it stepped forward toward him, she could see that it was squat and covered with a strange grey-brown coat that could have been some sort of fur. Bobbing an amorphous lump that could have been a head, it trotted toward the boy on its three chubby legs, bumped him, and sent him tumbling. The boy burst into delighted giggles, jumped up, and ran to chase it. Making a sound that could only be described as throaty "bubbles," the lumpy creature galloped in circles and they chased each other around the oak with dizzy glee.

"Colin? Colin sweetie?" A voice came from the green building, a public lavatory, to Gatsby's left.

Gatsby turned. A primly dressed woman, her purse swinging from her shoulder, followed by an equally conservatively suited man, ambled toward the boy. "Honestly, David, you were supposed to watch him! What if he had run off?" She scolded as they trudged in tandem toward the embankment.

Drawing in a deep breath, Gatsby looked back toward the boy.

No three-legged ideomorph galloped behind him.

My god, Gatsby thought, amazed not only at the moment of experiencing yet another inexplicable entity but also— even more so—by the wonderful sense of acceptance that moved through her.

A thought flashed through her with heart-stopping intensity. *This is HIS Forest of Peppermint Trees!* She blinked fiercely, focused on the grass beneath her boots, and looked up again.

The vest tails of his blue suit flapping, the boy scampered toward his parents. The couple grabbed his hands and swung him high into the air, laughing as the boy giggled. When he landed, all three meandered away, breaching the top of the embankment and then wandering down its backside and toward the sweep of the river.

The creature was undeniably gone.

"Uh...wh..." A deep breath, held and then slowly blown out, helped to stop the shaking. Finally she started forward, veering to her right across a wide, open lawn.

As she kicked leaves under her feet, she thought, *This sabbatical may have been spent investigating mysterious glyphs and chasing ideomorphs and falling into word traps, but I still have three weeks of accumulated vacation time.*

Impulse drove her, not back to her office, but into the Tube and then to the Hawthorne Holiday Travel Agency at Piccadilly Circus. A tan, the warm beaches of Tenerife, and a course of White Russians served hourly by a muscle-bound chap named Raoul or Jean-Luc were long overdue. Even hourly massages didn't sound decadent enough. Not even close.

EPILOGUE

From Koolagong Ridge, Sara could scan the rocky landscape for signs of predators—jackals or the rarely lucky crocodile. It had been a decent year with relatively few losses, no fires, and unusually plentiful rain. Her herd had grown by almost ten percent and was, while she peered through her binoculars, back at the shearing sheds at Selasara being stripped of their wool.

Shoulda let Day stay and help out. He's old enough, she thought, swiping away the sweat that trickled into her eyes. The cracks in her saddle creaked as her horse, Djinn, shifted and snorted. She patted his hot neck with one hand, holding the binoculars with the other. Sugar gums, bottle brush, mallee, and rock outcrops glittering with fluorspar and hematite, characteristic of the Flinders Range, as far as she could see. Ten miles north was Arkaroola; five to the south, Balcanoona; and a thirty-minute horseback ride to the east, her ranch, Selasara. The locals had helped her name it—sela for *sheila*, woman, and her first name.

Wiping her forehead again, she pulled in a deep breath, muttering, "Damn." October temperatures were normally in the low eighties; this afternoon felt more like high nineties. Her tongue stuck to the roof of her mouth as she swallowed. Water. Mingus, the spring she knew best on her property, was just down the hill. Her son, Davis Murdoch McFleynn, was there now, waiting for her and probably getting into the spiny spinifex.

She reined Djinn around and trotted down toward the watering hole that was encircled by steep, craggy rock walls. Splashing noises told her that Day was staying cool.

He was tromping out of the water, dripping mud and wearing nothing but buckle sandals, as she approached. His deeply tanned face broke into a bright smile.

Sara dropped down off her horse and ambled down to the water's edge. "Staying cool, Day?" she said, grinning.

The smile on his face melted. "Sara, you gotta see it."

"See what?" she said, patting the horse's rump as he plodded past her and into the spring to slake his own thirst.

Day reached for the shirt and shorts he'd tossed over a red boulder and slipped them on, wet mud and all. "I first thought it was a bugger huge termite mound, but it ain't. Come an' look."

Whatever he had discovered, his excitement was contagious. "Let's go," she said, taking his muddy hand.

Walking along the water's edge to where the rock walls ended, Day called, "Through here," and they pushed through a thicket of eucalyptus. Sara stomped along behind her scampering son, thinking that whatever the hell he was so eager to show her, it had better be good. It was too bloody hot to stay in the sun much longer.

They broke through the dark thicket into a clearing. The intense glare of the midday sun forced her to scrunch her eyes tight for a moment. She pulled down on the brim of her worn leather hat, thankful for its shade.

Day moved a few paces forward, then stopped and glanced back over his shoulder at her. "There. That." His gaze turned and his head tipped back as he stared upward.

She took a few steps forward, staring dumbly at it, whispering, "Goddagg—"

The megalith was at least eight meters tall and three meters wide. There was a dome-shaped protrusion, like a baseball cap, at its top. It rose vertical and solitary from the rocky ground, at least five meters from the nearest rock walls, and was a type of grey-blue, mottled stone that she had never seen before at Mingus Spring or anywhere on her property.

Approaching like a wary tribesman before a skyscraper, she slowly moved toward it and reached her hand out to run her fingertips across the rough surface.

"Goddagg," she murmured again.

"Yeah," Day muttered, nodding.

She turned toward him, frowning. "Day, how many times have we stopped here? Dozens, plenty dozen, eh? We've climbed every rock around this spring, we've—" She pointed to a flat boulder near the eucalyptus grove. "We sat one time and ate right there, on that rock, but—"

"I know, Sara," Day swallowed as he stared upward, squinting. "It wont here b'fore."

"But it—" Her eyes widened as she gazed across the breadth of it, shaking her head, unable to comprehend how a stone this massive could suddenly be standing in a clearing that a week ago had held nothing but stick bush and sheep droppings. "It...how...?"

Walking around to the backside, she noticed something just above eye level. Something carved into the stone. A vertical bar and, from the right side of the bar, a short horizontal line that became a crescent shape, like a quarter moon.

As she ran her fingertips over the carving, something fiery and onerous pressed against her lungs, squeezing the air out.

Day ambled up next to her. His muddy hand moved out, reaching up toward the carving, and a flash sizzled through her to stop his hand before he touched it.

As his fingers slid back and forth, caressing the stone, he whispered, "Where did it come from?"

ABOUT THE AUTHOR

Ellery Stone is the pen name of the American author Lori Stephens, pNLP, CCP. Stephens earned a BA in English literature and creative writing at the University of Oregon. Her career in the publishing field began in 1988, and she has edited over 200 books on topics as varied as cancer research, dating for seniors, music therapy, Neurolinguistic Programming, software security, and zombies.

The research for the *Paradigms Lost* series was extensive. In addition to visiting England, France, and Italy, she researched Egypt, India, Peru, Australia, Greece, Crete, and Spain. While writing *Deep Structure*, she spent five years learning about archeology (specifically the history of Stonehenge) and quantum physics. *Alpha Omega* required research into the structure of ancient languages, and she drew on her own experience with NLP and hypnotic language. *Viral Glyph* took her into studies of the Phaistos Disk, theories of its decipherment, and the history of cryptography. Descriptions of the world of stage magic were drawn from her association with a professional magician.

The author at Stonehenge (Wiltshire, England)

ALSO BY ELLERY STONE

ALPHA OMEGA
The Holy Drug
In a London suburb, a cult disciple gasps, dying in a pool of his own blood. The only clue is the holy scripture that he clutches.

Who would kill for the Librah Vaeta? What secrets are hidden within its pages? Do the leaders of the Omega cult know of the terrible violence it can spawn, or was that the intention?

Dr. Gatsby Donovan's abilities to decipher ancient writings pull her into the vortex of a treacherous mystery. Revealing Omega's most powerful secrets will be deadly—the question is not the salvation of her soul but whether she will survive the night.

VIRAL GLYPH
The Rosette Rebellion
When Dr. Gatsby Donovan meets a cocky stage magician, Maceo Affiato, he claims that the most mysterious artifact of all human history—the Phaistos Disk—has been stolen, and he needs her expertise in order to find it.

If the disk on display in the Heraklion Museum isn't genuine, where is the real one? And how is it connected to a terrible massacre? Finding the answers means outwitting the female-only syndicate called The Circle. Its global network of agents will do whatever it takes to protect the disk and conceal its true purpose and power, no matter the price. Can Gatsby connect the dots—and overcome her darkest fears—before time runs out?

www.ellerystone.com

www.ingramcontent.com/pod-product-compliance
Lightning Source LLC
Chambersburg PA
CBHW021419110726
47901CB00008B/2226